Praise for Carol Goodman and *The Night Visitors*

"Carol Goodman is, simply put, a stellar writer."
—Lisa Unger, *New York Times* bestselling
author of *The Red Hunter*

"Brilliantly conceived and executed . . . Goodman provides readers with that delicious frisson that comes from not knowing what will happen next."
—*Publishers Weekly* (starred review)

"You can always call upon Carol Goodman when you need an atmospheric and twisting tale. Full of half-truths and vengeful ghosts of the past, *The Night Visitors* will inspire readers to linger long into the night."
—Lori Rader-Day, Mary Higgins Clark Award–
winning author of *Under a Dark Sky*

"Mary Higgins Clark Award–winner Goodman creeps us out."
—*Library Journal*

"[Goodman] offers puzzles and twists galore but still tells a human story."
—*Boston Globe*

"Well-defined characters, including the marvelous Sister Martine, who runs a sanctuary for women in trouble; slowly building suspense; and an ending that pulls out all the stops make for a really good wintry read that's reminiscent of Mary Stewart and Victoria Holt. Best by firelight."
—*Booklist*

"Goodman specializes in atmospheric literary thrillers."
—*Denver Post*

THE
SEA OF
LOST
GIRLS

THE
SEA OF
LOST
GIRLS

A NOVEL

CAROL
GOODMAN

WM

WILLIAM MORROW

An Imprint of HarperCollinsPublishers

P.S.™ is a trademark of HarperCollins Publishers.

THE SEA OF LOST GIRLS. Copyright © 2020 by Carol Goodman. Excerpt from *The Night Visitors* copyright © 2019 by Carol Goodman. All rights reserved. Printed in the United States of America. No part of this book may be used or reproduced in any manner whatsoever without written permission except in the case of brief quotations embodied in critical articles and reviews. For information, address HarperCollins Publishers, 195 Broadway, New York, NY 10007.

HarperCollins books may be purchased for educational, business, or sales promotional use. For information, please email the Special Markets Department at SPsales@harpercollins.com.

FIRST EDITION

Designed by Diahann Sturge

Title page image © Tracey Jones Photography / Shutterstock, Inc.

Library of Congress Cataloging-in-Publication Data has been applied for.

ISBN 978-0-06-285202-1
ISBN 978-0-06-297963-6 (library edition)

20 21 22 23 24   LSC   10 9 8 7 6 5 4 3 2 1

To my girls,
Nora and Maggie,
and the remarkable women they have become

THE
SEA OF
LOST
GIRLS

CHAPTER ONE

The phone wakes me as if it were sounding an alarm inside my chest. *What now,* it rings, *what now what now what now.*

I know it's Rudy. The phone is set to ring for only two people—Harmon and Rudy (*At least I made the short list,* Harmon once joked)—and Harmon is next to me in bed. Besides, what has Harmon ever brought me but comfort and safety? But Rudy . . .

The phone has stopped ringing by the time I grab it but there is a text on the screen.

Mom?

I'm here, I text back. My thumb hovers over the keypad. If he were here maybe I could slip in *baby,* like I used to call him when he woke up from nightmares, but you can't text that to your seventeen-year-old son. *What's up?* I thumb instead. Casual. As if it isn't—I check the numbers on top of the screen—2:50 in the freaking morning.

I watch the three gray dots in the text bubble on the left side of the screen darken and fade in a sequence meant to represent a pregnant pause. The digital equivalent of a *hm*. *What tech genius thought that up?* my Luddite husband would demand.

I get up, shielding the screen against my chest so the light won't wake Harmon, and go into the bathroom. When I look at the screen the text bubble has vanished.

Damn.

I try calling but am sent immediately to voicemail. I type a question mark, and then stare at its baldness. Will he read it as nagging? If I can hear his eight-year-old voice in a single typed word, he can no doubt see my raised eyebrows and impatient frown in one punctuation mark.

I add a puzzled emoji face and then a chicken and a helicopter. *Mother hen. Helicopter parent.* If I make fun of my own fears maybe he won't get mad. And maybe they won't come true. I am propitiating the jealous gods, spitting over my shoulder, knocking on wood.

I wait, sitting on the toilet seat. Where is he? What's happened? A car accident? A drug overdose? A breakup with his girlfriend? I should be more worried about the first two possibilities but it's the thought that Lila has broken up with him that squeezes my heart. She's been such a good influence this year. Lila Zeller, a sweet vegan, straight-A student from Long Island, who likes to read and cook and hang out on our front porch. Who makes eye contact with Harmon and me, unlike the Goth horrors Rudy dated in tenth and eleventh grades.

Under Lila's influence Rudy has done better in school, quit smoking, joined the track team, taken a lead part in the senior play, got it together to apply to college, and even stopped having the nightmares. Aside from stocking the fridge with almond milk and tofu, I've tried not to let on how much I like her lest Rudy decide she's one of my *enthusiasms* and give her up the way he gave up violin, soccer, judo, and books.

It's too much pressure, he once told me, *when I see how much you care.*

Maybe I've played it too cool. Lila hasn't been around much in the last few weeks. I'd chalked it up to finals week and play rehearsals. Lila is directing *The Crucible* and Rudy is playing John Proctor. Tonight was the premier but I didn't go because Rudy said he'd be too nervous if I were in the audience. I am "allowed" to go to tomorrow's performance. Jean Shire, Haywood's headmistress and a good friend, texted earlier to tell me that the play had gone well and that Rudy had been outstanding. She sent me a picture of Rudy smiling jubilantly. What went wrong between then and—I check the time—3:01 A.M.?

Eleven minutes have gone by since he texted. Where is he? I picture him lying in a burned-out squat in Lisbon Falls or Lewiston, one of those inland towns that run like a dark afterthought to the coastal villages the tourists favor. When we landed here in this pretty harbor town with its sailboats and white clapboard houses I'd thought we'd come to a place where we'd always be safe. But Rudy has always had a nose for the darkness.

I *do* have a way of locating him, I realize. Because we're

4 • CAROL GOODMAN

on the same phone plan I can use the Find My Phone app to track him down. I try not to use it because I know Rudy would consider this *surveillance,* an invasion of his privacy. But this *is* an emergency.

I'm opening it up when the text alert pings.

Can you come get me?

Sure, I text back. I can imagine Harmon saying, *At three in the morning, Tess? You don't even know where he is.* But what does that matter? If he texted me from California I'd get in the car and start driving.

Where are you? I text.

I wait as the three dots pulse at the rate of my heartbeat. The police station? The hospital? A ditch by the side of the road? Where has my wayward son found himself tonight?

SP, he types back.

The safe place.

It was a code we came up with when Rudy was four. *If things are bad, go to the safe place and wait for me there; I'll come get you.* We haven't used the code in years. Haven't had to. What's happened that Rudy has to use it now?

OMW, I type back, which the phone transforms into an overly cheery *On my way!*

WHEN I GET out of the bathroom I notice Harmon isn't in bed. No doubt he's gone to the guest room, where he often goes when I'm restless. Rudy isn't the only one who has nightmares.

I'm glad now that I don't have to answer any questions.

Harmon will be sympathetic but I don't think I can bear the look of disappointment on his face. The what's-Rudy-gotten-himself-into-this-time look.

I dress quickly and warmly: jeans, turtleneck, sweater, wool socks. It's been mild for the last few days but the Maine winter hasn't let go of the nights yet, even in late May. Rudy won't be dressed for it. Downstairs, I grab a folded sweatshirt from the top of the radiator in the mudroom. I left it there for Harmon so it would be warm for his morning run, but he and Rudy wear the same size and I've long since lost track of which XL purple and gold Haywood Academy sweatshirt belongs to whom. I'll replace it when I get back before Harmon wakes up.

The clock above the stove tells me it's 3:06. Almost twenty minutes have gone by since Rudy's first text. Twenty minutes he's spent sitting in the cold.

When I get outside I see that it's not only cold, it's foggy; a thick white blanket obliterates the village and bay. The coast road will be dangerous to drive. But except for a footpath that cuts across campus there's no other way to get to where Rudy is. I feel better when I slide into the Subaru Forester's heated seats, grateful for the warmth and the solid bulk of the car as I navigate down our steep driveway and out onto the coast road.

Although I can't see more than ten feet ahead of me, the reflective markers on the median guide me to the flashing red light before the bridge that connects the village to the school grounds. As with much of coastal Maine the land here is broken up by waterways and pieced together by bridges and causeways like a tattered garment that's been darned. Like me, I sometimes think, like the life I've pieced together for Rudy and me. No wonder Rudy doesn't trust it; no wonder he's prone to outbursts. *When I get really mad,* he told me once, *everything goes black.*

The thought of Rudy lost in that darkness had caught at my heart. We came up with a strategy. We agreed that whenever he felt angry he'd just walk away. Go someplace where he could be alone and cool down. That must be what happened tonight. He'd fought with Lila and then walked away to the safe place and waited for me. Because that's what I'd always told him to do. I made a promise to Rudy once that I'd always come find him in the safe place. I've broken many promises over the years but never that one.

Through the fog I can make out a blaze of light coming from Duke Hall. The percussive boom of rap music and a high-pitched scream make me wonder if I should call Jean Shire and alert her to the after-hours partying, but then I'd have to explain what I'm doing on the coast road at three-fifteen in the morning. Besides, last night was the cast party for *The Crucible.* And it's finals week. They're just letting off steam.

Duke's a horrible party dorm, Lila had complained, *I'm so glad I can hang out here.*

I had been thrilled she wanted to hang out at her boyfriend's parents' house—even though both those parents teach at her school. Two years ago when we agreed to let Rudy live on campus I had promised both him and Harmon that I wouldn't "hover over" Rudy. He could totally ignore us, which is what he did until he met Lila, who, homesick for her close-knit family back on Long Island, was charmed by the idea of having access to an off-campus house. She was the one who had suggested to Rudy they buy food and cook in our kitchen and bring their laundry over.

"I thought we were going to be empty-nesters," Harmon had complained.

"Shut up," I told him. "She's a good influence." And in fact, Harmon had grown fond of her too, even volunteering to help her with her essay for the local historical society scholarship contest.

I park in the lot behind Duke and in front of Warden House, so called because it was the warden's house back in the nineteenth century when the school was the Refuge for Wayward Girls. Rudy and I had lived here when it was faculty housing. Behind the house a peninsula juts into the sea, one of those fingers of land that clutch at the ocean along the Maine coast. This one ends in a promontory called the Point, perhaps because it seems to be pointing directly to Maiden Island, a bare rock separated from the peninsula by a quarter-mile sand and stone causeway that's only passable at low tide. Every year the coast guard holds an assembly about the dangers of crossing the causeway that only seems to increase its appeal.

When I get out of the car I can hear the dense pines that stand sentinel over the peninsula creaking in the salt-laced wind . . . and something else.

A sound like a girl crying.

I freeze and listen. It could just be the wind in the trees or the mournful sigh of the tide retreating over the rocks below the coastal path, but then, peering through the fog, I catch a glimpse of something white that looks like a girl running through the woods.

What if it's Lila? I think.

I walk in between the trees, wending my way slowly through the fog until I come to the clearing with the stone circle where students build bonfires and tell ghost stories about the spirits of the nine Abenaki sisters who drowned on the causeway. Tonight the circle is empty, but as I stand here I remember the ghosts who are said to haunt these woods. I can almost hear them . . . I shake myself and check my phone. It's 3:29. I've wasted ten minutes wandering in the fog while Rudy waits for me.

I look around, remembering that there's a path that cuts straight down the middle of the peninsula to the Point, but the thought of plunging into the fogbound woods unnerves me. There's also a path on the south side of the peninsula but it's rockier and more dangerous. I head to the path that hugs the north side of the peninsula instead, which is fairly level and well cleared. Still, I walk carefully. It's a significant drop to the rocks below.

When I reach the Point, a bank of fog laps up against the rocks like a ghostly sea. But then the mist parts like a curtain being drawn and moonlight silvers the stone and sand causeway that leads to the island.

I turn my back to the sea and climb a narrow path to Rudy's safe place, a shallow cave in a rock ledge above the sea. *You can see for miles but no one can see you,* he'd told me. It is the perfect hiding place. If I didn't know where to look I could easily miss him—but there he is, hunched in a tight ball, his dark purple sweatshirt hood up, head down. He's made himself so small that for a moment I'm sure this can't be my gangly seventeen-year-old son. Instead I see a five-year-old boy, huddled at the prow of a rowboat.

"Rudy?" I whisper.

He doesn't stir. I reach out and touch his arm. His sweatshirt is damp and cold to the touch.

"Rudy!" I grab his arm and shake him. He flinches and flails an arm that catches me on my cheekbone. I step back and nearly topple down to the rocks.

"What the hell, Mom!" Rudy grabs my arm before I fall. "You scared me. I was asleep and you're on my bad side." His voice is aggrieved.

How could I have been so careless? He's deaf in his left ear from an ear infection he got when he was five. I am always explaining to his teachers that they need to remember to be on his good side when talking to him and that he startles easily if approached from his bad side.

"I'm sorry," I say. "I was just surprised by how cold you are. Here, take that off. I brought a dry sweatshirt."

He does as I say for once, peeling off the sodden sweatshirt and tossing it aside. I pick it up. It's not just damp, it's soaked.

"What happened?" I ask.

He shrugs and pulls on the dry sweatshirt. Before he can pull the hood up, I examine his face. The moonlight casts deep shadows beneath his eyes and under his sharp cheekbones. When did he get so thin? A splatter of acne scars his cheek— or is that a scratch?

"Let's get you home and warmed up," I say. "Or do you want to go back to the dorm?"

He shakes his head. "Nah. The drama crowd is having a party."

The drama crowd. As if he's not a part of it. "Jean said you were great tonight," I say. "Didn't you want to go to the cast party?" I hold up his wet sweatshirt and give it a surreptitious sniff to check for alcohol, but it smells merely salty, like ocean and sweat.

He shrugs again and gets to his feet. "For a little while . . . but only because Lila was there. I had a couple of beers . . ." He looks away from me and hunches deeper into his hood. Because he's lying about how many beers he had or because he doesn't remember? A couple of times in the last few years Rudy drank so much he blacked out and couldn't remember later what had happened.

"Did you leave Lila there? What happened? Did you guys have a fight?" I ask.

"She can take care of herself," he says, his voice cold. "Besides, she won't text me back." He holds up his phone. His cracked screen shows a record of text bubbles all on one side. So I wasn't the first one he texted. *And* he must have done something to really piss off Lila if she won't even respond to him.

"Maybe she turned off her phone," I say. "We could stop by the dorm."

"Stop hovering, Mom." He shoulders past me to walk down the path. "I'm not going to stand under her window with a boom box like in some dumbass, lame nineties rom-com."

"Hey," I say as I follow him on the narrow path. "That movie was 1989 and let's not diss John Cusack."

He laughs and I feel a swell of relief. *It will be okay,* I tell myself again. But just in case, I'll call Lila in the morning.

WHEN WE GET home I drop the damp sweatshirt on the radiator and offer to make Rudy something to eat. He declines and slopes off to his room. I listen for the sounds of bedsprings, but instead I hear the ping his laptop makes when he opens it.

I think of going upstairs, but then I hear the door to the guest room open and Harmon's footsteps head down the hall to our room. If I go join him he'll ask me what happened and I don't have it in me to tell him that Lila and Rudy had a fight, to see the look in his eyes that says he didn't expect it to last.

Instead I open my laptop and spend the next few hours grading papers. Twenty-two research papers on *The Scarlet Letter.* Most of them have done a pretty good job. This was a good group. I've gotten through half of them when a ping alerts me to a Twitter notification. I follow so few people on Twitter that I click on it, thinking it might be from Lila and that I'll get some feeling for her state of mind from it, but the tweet's from Jill Frankel, the drama teacher.

> *Congratulations to all the people who made last night's performance of* The Crucible *such a success!!!*

I see she's tagged Lila, so on a whim (and not, I hear myself explaining to an invisible audience, because I'm stalking my son's girlfriend) I click on Lila's Twitter profile. I'm touched to see that one of her most recent tweets is a photograph of her and Rudy in front of the Maiden Stone. Rudy is actually smiling in the picture. *Oh please,* I think, *let this not be a real break-up!*

The tweet has been retweeted and replied to with jokes along the lines of *Nothing to worry about—that rock only disappears virgins* and *Who's holding who back?* I recognize most of the responders as Haywood students. But there's one that I don't recognize—IceVirgin33—who has written, *The daughters of the sun kissed the boy, trying to thaw him and wipe out the kiss given him by the queen—*

"You're up early."

Harmon, dressed in sweatpants and T-shirt, is standing right over me. I guiltily close the laptop. Bad enough that I'm on Facebook; I really don't want him to see me stalking my son's girlfriend's page.

"Did you sleep on the couch down here when you came in?" He kisses me on the forehead and then gives me a closer look. "Or did you not get back to sleep at all?"

I shrug, a motion I've cribbed from Rudy's playbook. "I figured I might as well get some work done." I hold up the folder of essays that I've only gotten half through. "Bet I'm ahead of you."

"Did you have to go out and get him?"

"There was a loud party at Duke. That cast party. He said it was keeping him up. I picked him up in the parking lot." The lie slips easily from my lips.

Harmon looks like he wants to say something else but then thinks better of it—a look that's become familiar over the years. I know that Rudy's behavior has driven a wedge between us. But what can I do? I love Harmon, but he doesn't have kids of his own. He'll never understand that Rudy always has to come first.

I try to make it up by filling his water bottle and getting his sweatshirt for him . . . and realize I never washed the one Rudy was wearing last night, which I'd left on the radiator. I go to fetch it and find a stain on the right cuff, but it's hard to make out against the purple. At least the sweatshirt is dry. I hand it to Harmon and he puts it on. The sweatshirt's too big on him; he's lost weight these last few months from all the running he's been doing.

"Don't work out too hard," I tell Harmon. "I like to have something to hold on to."

He laughs and nuzzles his hips into my ass. When was the last time we had sex? I try to remember. Letting Rudy live in the dorms was supposed to give us more time alone, but having two teenagers hanging around the house hasn't been conducive to our sex life. Maybe, I think, it will be better if Lila and Rudy aren't here all the time.

The thought makes me feel so disloyal to Lila that I decide to text her. Although it's only 6:34, I know that Lila goes jogging early in the morning. I find the last message Lila sent to me, three weeks ago (*Do you have any cumin at the house? I'm making curry for dinner!*), and type: *Hey, just wanted to see if everything's okay . . .* Then I realize this might seem like prying so I erase it and type instead: *I hear the play was a great success! Congratulations!* I add a smiley face and a lilac because it's Lila's favorite flower and hope that if she responds she might volunteer some information about what happened between her and Rudy.

While I'm waiting for a reply, I continue grading papers. I've just come to Lila's paper—"Slut Shaming in Puritan New England and the Age of Social Media"—when my phone rings. It will be her, I think, picking up the phone without checking the screen, and I'll tell her how funny it is that I had just started her paper—

It's not Lila, it's Jean. "Oh, thank God!" she says. "I was hoping you were up."

My heart thuds against my rib cage at the thought that she's calling to tell me something has happened to Rudy before I remember that Rudy is asleep upstairs. "What is it, Jean?" I ask, resentful that she's given me such a scare. I love Jean—I owe her my job here and my life—but sometimes she takes her job as headmistress too seriously. She is probably calling because some parent has complained about the senior class's unorthodox production of *The Crucible* (I've heard it includes references to rape culture) or that Haywood Hull has made some new demand in return for financing this year's historical society scholarship.

But it's not about *The Crucible* or Woody Hull.

"The body of a student was found below the Point this morning," Jean says instead. "I'm afraid it's Lila Zeller."

CHAPTER TWO

I am on the cold tile floor, my back against the wall, without knowing how I got here. I don't remember sitting down. The phone is in my hands and Jean is still talking. What is she saying? Something about Lila? Lila found dead on the rocks below the Point.

"Are they sure it's her?" My voice sounds like someone else's, someone calm, not someone who's had her guts turned inside out.

There's a pause and then Jean says in a choked voice, "They called me down to identify her."

"Oh, Jean," I say. "I'm so sorry you had to do that. Do the police know what happened?" I ask. "Was she . . . attacked?"

"I don't know. I only saw her face. I suppose . . . I know that she went jogging in the morning. That path is narrow and slippery and there was a fog this morning. She could easily have tripped and fallen onto the rocks below."

I'm remembering walking there last night, how easily I could have fallen . . . or how easily Rudy could have. I feel a wave of nausea at the thought it could have been Rudy, followed by the dreadful guilty relief that it's Lila, not him, who's dead. Someone else's child, not mine. Then I think of Rudy being there, so close to where she died, and the nausea sweeps over me again.

"When was she found?" I ask.

"At six-thirty. By an early-morning jogger."

I look at the time on top of my phone screen. It's 8:00. I've been grading for an hour and a half. Where is Harmon? Shouldn't he be back? Suddenly I have a horrible thought. "Was it Harmon?" I ask.

"Was it Harmon what?"

"Who found the body? He went out jogging over an hour ago and he's not back yet." Harmon never carries his phone with him; he's probably at the police station right now. . . .

"No, it was someone from the town," Jean says. "So you know the story will be everywhere by noon. I wanted to give you a heads-up, since you were so close to her. I've also called Woody Hull to see if he can use his influence with the police to get some information. They're not telling me much." Jean's voice betrays her annoyance. She was Haywood Hull's assistant when he was headmaster and he still treats her like a secretary even though she's been headmistress for seventeen years. But Jean is a pragmatist; she uses the resources available to her. Woody Hull is rich—old-money-Boston-blueblood rich—and has endowed many a scholarship for a needy Haywood student. It was Jean who buttonholed him to get me a college scholarship even though it had been six years since I'd graduated from Haywood and I had nothing to show for those years but a five-year-old fatherless boy.

"How did Woody take the news?" I ask

"He was upset, of course, but honestly . . ." Jean lowers her voice even though I'm pretty sure she's calling from home and there's no one else there. "I'm not sure he totally got it. He's been a little . . . *vague* lately. He asked if I'd called the parents—"

"Oh, Jean," I cut in. "Did you? How horrible for you."

Jean doesn't reply for a moment and I know she's holding back tears. "Yes, it was, but when I told Woody he said that he would send his condolences because he knew them."

"The *Zellers*?"

"Of course he doesn't know the Zellers. I think . . . I think he's confused her with a girl who died when he was the headmaster here. I think he's losing it."

"Oh," I say. "Crap."

"Yes. So on top of everything else I'm going to have to keep Woody from making a fool of himself." Jean heaves an exasperated sigh. "I'm convening an emergency faculty meeting at noon and an all-campus assembly at one. I thought you'd want to talk to Rudy before then . . . weren't they . . . ?"

"They were friends," I say. Not *she was his girlfriend*. Shit. If the students know, it will be all over their social media by now. I have to wake him up . . . and tell him that Lila is dead. How in the world will I do that and what will it do to him? I pause another second, then add, "I'm glad he spent the night here. The dorms were too loud after the cast party. Thanks for telling me, Jean. I've got to think about how best to handle this. I'll be in by noon."

I get off the phone before Jean can object or assign me any other duties. I know she's annoyed. She expects me to have her back and I will; I owe her. But I have to think about Rudy first. I go to the refrigerator and open the door, thinking I'll bring him a glass of orange juice to help wake him up, and see the new container of almond milk I'd bought for Lila.

I double over with cramps as if I've been punched in the gut. Lila is dead. Sweet, funny, earnest Lila Zeller from Manhasset, New York, with all her dreams of ending world hunger, bigotry, and war. She's dead, hours after she fought with Rudy, who was at the Point last night.

I grip the refrigerator door and right myself, then pour the orange juice and put on a pot of coffee. I have to stop several times to run calming cold water over my hands. Lila is dead and Rudy was her . . . boyfriend? Do kids even use those terms these days? They don't say *dating*; they say *hooking up*, but that seems crass. In fact, I don't know for certain that they were having sex. I asked Rudy, told him he could talk to me, impressed upon him the importance of consent and the necessity of being *safe* . . . at which point he winced and shut me down. The couple of times Lila slept over here, she slept in the guest room. So maybe they weren't even having sex. They were friends, of course, close friends, but they'd been drifting apart these last few weeks. They had an argument at the party and Rudy left, went for a walk out to the Point and called me to pick him up, which I did at three in the morning—no point fudging on the time; it's in our cell phone records. No need either. That was hours before Lila would have gone jogging . . . *It's a tragedy,* I'll tell the police, *my son is devastated. I'm devastated. But Rudy was here in his own bed since four A.M.*

When I've run through it in my head three times and my

hands are steady enough I pour the coffee and the orange juice. I put them on a tray with a napkin and add a granola bar. Except for the coffee, it looks like the breakfasts I made for Rudy when he was in grade school.

You spoil him, Harmon says.

You don't know what he's been through, I always think, but all I do is shrug. A mother's prerogative. And implicit: *You are not his father to tell me how to raise my son.*

I am on the first step of the stairs when the doorbell rings, nearly causing me to drop the tray. No one uses the bell—or the front door, for that matter. I turn and see a uniformed police officer through the side panel. We make eye contact.

I put the tray down on the side table by the door—the place where we leave the mail, our keys, notes to one another, a potted African violet that Rudy gave me for Mother's Day three years ago—a homely pocket of domestic routine that absurdly makes me want to cry out: *Stop! Please don't take this away from me. I've fought so hard to keep it.*

I open the door and recognize the young police officer. Kevin Bantree, a local boy who came to Haywood on scholarship during my senior year when the school went coed. I remember him as a shy, awkward teenager, miserable at being thrust into a crowd of rich, spoiled girls.

What are you even doing here? Ashley Burton—a mean queen bee from Scarsdale—had asked him one day before class.

Hell if I know, he'd answered, his milky-white Irish skin turning red. *The school made some deal with the town that the kid with the highest GPA would get a scholarship.*

I'd been surprised when I moved back to Rock Harbor to

see that Kevin had become a cop like his father, and his father before him. What had been the point of suffering through a year at Haywood?

Now all I wonder is what he's doing here. "Kevin," I say and then, when he blushes, correct myself. "I mean Officer Bantree. I know why you're here. Jean Shire called me earlier. Come in. You must be on tenterhooks thinking how to break it to me."

I am talking too fast, and he isn't talking at all. I remember that about him, how quiet he was. It would be easy looking at him—the athletic build and wide-open, fresh-skinned face—to think he's a dumb jock, just a small-town policeman, but it would be a mistake.

"I can't believe it," I say, unable to stop. "I'm always telling the girls to be careful of that path, but Lila was very headstrong. Do you know how it happened?"

"I can't say, Ms. Henshaw. I'm here to ask you a few questions about Lila—"

"What about Lila?"

We both look up to see Rudy standing on the stairs. He is rumpled and bleary-eyed, his dark curly hair sticking up—is that a leaf sticking to a lock?—still in his jeans and sweatshirt from last night.

"Has something happened to Lila?" Rudy asks, his voice shaky.

"Honey, I think you'd better sit down." I turn to Kevin. "I was just going upstairs to tell Rudy. Of course he knows Lila from Haywood—"

"What's happened to Lila?" Rudy demands more loudly. I can hear the edge of panic and fury in his voice. I move close to him, on his good side, between him and Kevin Bantree. I don't touch him. He doesn't like to be touched when he's upset.

"Rudy, Officer Bantree is here with some bad news. Lila was found this morning on the rocks beneath the Point, right where the causeway begins. It looks like she might have fallen. I . . . I'm afraid that she's dead."

A muscle on the side of Rudy's face twitches. I can tell that he's clenching his jaw to keep himself from crying but another person, who doesn't know Rudy, would think he looks angry.

"Dead? Lila is dead?"

"Ms. Henshaw . . ." Kevin is behind me. I can smell his peppermint toothpaste and aftershave. "Could you both please sit down and let *me* ask the questions?" There's an irritated note in his voice that makes me remember the time he got annoyed during a class discussion of J.D. Salinger's short story "A Perfect Day for Bananafish." *Why can't it just be about a day on the beach?* he had demanded.

"Of course," I say, not taking my eyes off Rudy. "We want to help. Don't we, Rudy? Why don't we all sit down . . ." I place my hand gingerly on Rudy's arm and guide him toward the couch. His face is closed, impassive to an outsider. Only I know that he is shutting down, going inside himself.

Kevin Bantree pulls out a side chair and sits. Rudy and I sit facing him, only Rudy turns his head slightly. It makes it look as if he's turning away, but he's only trying to favor his good ear.

"Can you both tell me where you were last night?" Kevin asks.

"I was here," Rudy says. "I came back here because the dorm was too loud."

"You live at the dorm?" Kevin asks.

Rudy nods and Kevin makes a note. I know what he's thinking: Why would we pay for room and board when we live ten minutes from campus? It must seem like a ridiculous waste of money. Kevin will be thinking that Rudy is a spoiled rich kid.

"We wanted Rudy to have the full Haywood experience," I say, then shut my mouth when I realize that I've made it sound as if Kevin, who had been a day student, did not get the full Haywood experience.

"Sure," Kevin says, "but last night you came back here?"

"Yeah, there was a loud party after the play. I texted Mom and asked her to pick me up. I needed to get some sleep."

"And what time would that have been?"

Rudy shrugs. "Around two-thirty?" He looks at me.

"Three," I say, and then get out my phone. "Here . . ." I hand the phone to Kevin. *Look at how helpful I'm being! We have nothing to hide!* "There's Rudy's text to me at 3:01 A.M." I make a face. "It woke me up but you know what it's like with kids. Do you have kids?"

"What's *SP* stand for?" Kevin asks, ignoring my question.

"Student parking," Rudy says. "It's the lot behind Duke."

I'm startled by the lie—and by how quickly Rudy came up with it—but I immediately, unthinkingly, back him up. "That's right. I picked him up around three-fifteen, and yeah, it was loud. I considered calling Jean. Maybe I should have . . ."

"And where was Mr. Henshaw when you were driving to campus?" Kevin asks.

"Mr. Henshaw?" I stupidly parrot. Why is he asking about Harmon? "You mean my husband? Harmon?"

"Yes. Was he at home when you left?"

"Of course. He was in bed."

"And when you got back?"

"Yes, but why . . ." I'm about to add that I didn't actually go upstairs when I got home, but I remember that I'd heard Harmon moving from the guest room back to our room, so really, there's no point. It's none of Kevin's business.

"And where is he now?"

"He went out for a jog early this morning," I say. "At around six-thirty. Harmon goes every morning—" As if summoned by his name I hear the latch of the back door. "In fact, that must be him now."

I stand up, absurdly happy to see Harmon coming into the room. Harmon will make this all right. He makes everything all right. His face is glowing with the cold air, moisture clinging to his graying but still full hair, sweatshirt damp and smelling of the sea air even from where I am. He's smiling when he enters the room, but quickly frowns when he sees Kevin. "What's happened?" he asks, looking directly at Rudy. His expression's clear for anyone to read. *What has this boy, who I took into my home and heart, done now to break them both apart?*

"What's happened?" he asks again, turning from Rudy to me.

I can't blame him for assuming this is about Rudy; it wouldn't be the first time. Rudy was caught shoplifting when he was ten, smoking pot when he was thirteen, and spray-painting the town water tower when he was fifteen. Still, the ease of that assumption makes me angry and I answer more sharply than I might have otherwise.

"It's Lila," I say. "She's been found dead on the rocks under the Point."

"No," he says, shaking his head. I've seen him at faculty meetings give the same curt dismissal when someone says something he disagrees with. But now I see something else in his eyes, something I'm not accustomed to seeing there: fear that he might be wrong. He turns to Kevin Bantree. "Are we sure about this, Kevin?"

"I'm afraid so. In fact, I need you to come down to the station . . ."

"Of course," Harmon says. "You'll want me to identify her . . . call her parents . . . ?"

For a moment I'd forgotten that Harmon is the dean of Lila's class year, as well as her advisor. *That's* why Kevin is here, not because he suspects that Rudy had anything to do with Lila's death. I'm so relieved that when Harmon turns to me I have to reassemble my face to match the shock and grief that are now etched on his. "Does Jean know?"

"Yes," I say, "she called me earlier. Do you want me to go with you?"

"No," he says, "you stay here." He looks at Rudy, who has remained quiet throughout, huddled in his sweatshirt. "I'm so sorry, son. I know you and Lila were good friends."

Tears prick my eyes; I'm grateful that Harmon has thought of Rudy's feelings and that he's not fooled by Rudy's impassive affect. He even puts his hand on Rudy's shoulder—which makes Rudy flinch. It must look to Kevin like a shrug.

"Why'd she have to go out jogging every goddamn morning

at the crack of dawn?" Rudy says angrily. "Why couldn't she sleep in like a normal person?"

"It's natural to be angry," I say, glancing at Kevin. He's not looking at me or Rudy, though. He's looking at Harmon. Harmon commands that kind of respect. People turn to him in times of need. I know I did.

"We should get going," Kevin says.

"Of course, Kevin, I'll just go change out of these jogging clothes—"

"No need for that." Kevin glances down at his watch. "You can come as you are."

Two lines appear between Harmon's eyebrows, a sign he isn't happy being told what to do, but then he quickly smiles. "Of course, what does my appearance matter? I'll come as I am, sweat and all." He leans over to kiss me on the cheek and whispers in my ear, "Call Morris."

I start to ask a question but Kevin Bantree is standing at the door, watching with the same quiet, slightly disdainful attention he used to train on the Haywood girls. Like he's trying to figure us out . . . or he's waiting for us to mess up. I'm relieved when he follows Harmon out of the house, but I'm still left wondering why Harmon wants me to call his personal lawyer instead of the school's lawyer.

CHAPTER THREE

After they leave I hear a choking sound behind me. I turn and find Rudy gasping like someone drowning. I run to the kitchen and come back with his inhaler, but he bats it out of my hand. His face is red, but not blue or purple, so I crouch beside him, close enough so he can feel my body warmth. But not touching him or looking at him. I make my own breaths long and steady to guide his, just as I would when he was a baby and I'd lay him on my chest so he could feel my heartbeat. Back when he still let me touch him. Back when I thought the rhythm of my heartbeat could keep his heart beating.

When his sobs subside and his breathing evens I inch a centimeter closer to him. "We'll get through this," I tell him. "Together. The way we always do. I know how bad you must feel, especially since you argued—"

"That wasn't my fault," he blurts out. "She's the one who broke it off with me."

"Oh," I say, stung for him. "That must have hurt."

"I didn't fuck up, Mom. That's what you're thinking, isn't it?

That I did something stupid. But I didn't. I knew how lucky I was to have a girl like Lila want to be with me—"

His voice cracks and I reach out for him, breaking the rules. For once he doesn't flinch or move away. "Oh, sweetheart, I know. You've been doing so well this year. Your grades, the track and field team, the play, getting into college . . ."

"But none of it was enough," he says, his shoulders tightening beneath my arms. "I was never going to be good enough for her once we graduated. With her at Brown and me at some state school, I'd be her yokel boyfriend. That's why she broke up with me."

"Did she say that was the reason she broke up with you?" I ask. I know it had been a sore point. There was never any question that they'd end up at different schools. Rudy was lucky to have gotten into the University of Maine at Orono while Lila, a straight-A student with perfect SATs and summers spent working for Habitat for Humanity, had her pick of top schools. She'd told me she was considering going to Bowdoin, close enough to Orono for her and Rudy to spend weekends together. But then she'd gotten into Brown and the lure of an Ivy was too much to resist. Harmon had taken her aside and had a long talk with her one night and she'd come out of his study with red-rimmed eyes and told Rudy she was going to say yes to Brown, but they would still be able to see each other on weekends because it wasn't really that far away at all.

"No," Rudy admits. "But I could tell there was something she wasn't telling me."

"So you don't really know that's why she broke up with you. Did she tell you last night? At the party?"

He shakes his head. "She wouldn't have done it in public like that. We met down by the Point."

"The Point? Did you walk back with her to the dorm?"

"Of course, Mom. I'm not a jerk. I walked her back, but then when I saw the dorm—with everyone there—I just couldn't face it. I couldn't watch her with everyone else and pretend. The worst thing is we'd always kept it quiet we were . . . you know . . . in a relationship. So people wouldn't even know anything was different."

"Huh," I say, secretly glad people might not know Rudy was Lila's boyfriend, "whose idea was that?"

Rudy shrugs. "I dunno. I mean, she knew I'm not into the whole PDA thing, and she wasn't into the whole cis-normative coupling routine, so we just kind of let people think what they thought. Harmon was helping her with that big essay for the historical society contest so we let people think that was why she spent so much time over here."

"Well, maybe that's for the best, sweetie. Now you don't have to explain to everyone what happened."

"Yeah . . . only it makes me wonder if she ever really cared for me at all, you know? And whether I ever really *knew* her."

I pat his arm, not knowing what to say. *People are mysteries,* I could say. *Sometimes the people we thought we were closest to are the biggest mysteries of all.* But he doesn't really need me to tell him that.

THE FIRST THING I do when Rudy goes upstairs is to call our lawyer, Morris Alcott. I get his voicemail and leave a message that Harmon is at the police station talking to the police about the death of one of our students. Although I'm still puzzled as to why Harmon asked for his personal lawyer, I simply ask Morris to check in with Harmon.

After I hang up, I open my laptop to check emails. There are a slew of Reply All's from fellow faculty members with the subject line *Tragic News*. I scroll down to find the original email from Jean, sent out to faculty, students, and parents at 8:13 A.M.

It is with a heavy heart that I share this tragic news with our community. Lila Zeller, an accomplished and remarkable Haywood senior, was found dead this morning off campus...

That's an interesting choice of words, I think. It's true that the Point and the woods around it are technically state land but most people consider them part of the campus. As I scroll down I see that Jean never mentions where Lila was found or anything else specific about her death. Perhaps the police told her not to. Or maybe it would alarm parents to learn there's a lethal cliff within walking distance of the campus.

Jean ends with: *Our hearts go out to Lila's family. In times like these we must look to each other for support and condolence. Haywood prides itself on its strong community, and each of us will feel the loss of Lila deeply. My hope is that we will come together in this time of grief. There will be an assembly at one pm, followed by a nondenominational service in the chapel. Attendance is mandatory for all students, faculty, and staff.*

I look at the time and see it's already past ten. The pipes

have stopped clanging so Rudy is out of the shower. I should head up, shower, get ready for the noon faculty meeting, but the thought of facing my colleagues does not engender a warm feeling of community support. It's not that I don't have friends on campus, but taken together, the Haywood faculty are an exhausting bunch. I already know who will be hysterical (Jill Frankel, of course, the drama teacher), who will be accusatory (Brad Sorensen in math has long campaigned to make the woods off-limits), and who will pat my hand with commiseration and ask, *Wasn't Rudy close to the girl?* (Martha James in English). How will I answer that?

Instead of going upstairs, I open my laptop again and go to Instagram. Lila's face fills the screen. It's a picture taken at a track meet early in the year. She's tanned, in T-shirt and shorts, nose sunburned, grinning into the camera. My heart flip-flops at the thought of those strong, young limbs broken on the rocks below the Point. The photo's been posted by Jill Frankel. *Our hearts bleed,* she's written, *Lila Zeller 1999–2017.* One hundred and seventy-three people have responded to the post. I'm not surprised that gregarious, outgoing Jill has so many followers. In addition to teaching at Haywood, she does community theater in Rock Harbor and is active in independent theater in Portland.

I scroll down and find other pictures of Lila posted by students and teachers. *Lila was the best!* Taylor MacIntosh, a junior on the hockey team, has posted. *Haywood won't be the same without her,* Doug Weiss, a science nerd from New York City, has replied with a weeping emoji. *People living deeply have no fear of death—Anais Nin,* Rachel Lazar, a theater kid from a suburb of Boston, has written. Does she mean that Lila didn't fear death because she lived life deeply? As is the case with many of Rachel's quotes (and as I've pointed out on many of her papers), her point is unclear.

There's another literary quote below Rachel's post. *And the daughters of the sun kissed the girl, trying to thaw her and wipe out the kiss given her by the queen of the glaciers . . .* It's the same quote that was tweeted in response to Lila's photo of her and Rudy and the Maiden Stone except that the "boy" has been changed to a "girl," and it's been posted by the same person—IceVirgin33. I click on the name, hoping to find out who IceVirgin33 is, but I get an ambiguous photo of a glacier on his profile page and an even more enigmatic bio: Historian, Seeker of Truth, Explorer of Depths Unknown.

Certainly pretentious enough to be a student. Maybe I can ask Jill Frankel later who IceVirgin33 is.

When I look up from the screen I'm shocked to see it's already eleven-fifteen. I've somehow lost a whole hour and fifteen minutes to mindless scrolling. *It's just a big time waster,* Harmon always says about the Internet, *no wonder our students never have time to finish their homework or read a book.* Now I barely have time to shower and dress for the faculty meeting.

I run upstairs but stop outside Rudy's door. I pause, listening . . . for what? Sobs? What I hear instead is the ping of a message alert. Whom is he texting? I knock on the door and hear a grunt I choose to take as permission to enter. His room is dark, blinds drawn against the day, the only light the glow of his laptop perched on his chest as he lies in his rumpled, unmade bed. He may have showered but he's still wearing the sweatshirt I gave him last night.

"Hey," I say, "I noticed that people are already posting about Lila. It must be hard to see—"

He makes a face. "They're a bunch of fakes and hypocrites. Half of the people posting didn't even know Lila."

"Everyone feels vulnerable when something like this happens," I say, sitting down at the foot of his bed.

"Dakota Wyatt tweeted"—he changes his voice to a Valley-speak falsetto—"'Heaven has a new star.' This after she called Lila a dyke bitch at the Spring Fling."

"Dakota Wyatt is an idiot," I say. "She probably can't even spell *dyke*."

This earns me a smile. I know I shouldn't discuss other students with Rudy—I certainly shouldn't make fun of them—but sometimes it's the only way to get his attention.

"Anyway," I say, "I have to be at a faculty meeting at twelve so I'm getting in the shower. If you want to drive in with me we'll need to leave in thirty minutes."

"I can walk," he says.

"Okay, but make sure you get there. It—" I'm about to say, *It won't look good if you're not,* but say instead, "It's to honor Lila, after all." To which he makes a grunt I choose to take as assent.

As soon as I'm in the shower I wonder why I waited so long; the hot water feels so good. It releases the tension that has built up in my back and shoulders these past few hours . . . and the hold I've put on my grief, which comes spilling out of me now in long choking sobs that sweep over me like waves, relentless as the tide that would have washed over Lila's body. It's a relief to cry for her even if I know that she's not the only one I'm crying for.

CHAPTER FOUR

B uilt in 1811 by hardy Congregationalists, the Haywood chapel is a plain white clapboard meetinghouse. Entering it, I always feel like I'm about to be tried for witchcraft. I bring my students here when we read *The Crucible* and *The Scarlet Letter* and ask them to sit in silence for a few minutes, to imagine that there is nothing outside the little circle of houses but wilderness and the sea. If you're cast out of here, there is no place for you to go.

During that session this year Paola Fernandez started crying. I took her aside and brought her into the back room, where she told me, over hot chocolate and cookies provided by our pastor, Celia Barnstable, that she was afraid that if she didn't get her grades up she would lose her scholarship. "My parents will be so mad. This is supposed to be my big opportunity to make something of myself, but it's so hard. All the other kids, they just know stuff I don't. My teachers in Yonkers hardly even showed up. How am I supposed to catch up?"

Although her writing was full of grammatical and spelling

errors, she was a smart girl and if she worked hard with me she would be all right. I told her that I would tutor her after class and talk to her other teachers, feeling guilty about the lesson that had caused such stress.

"I terrorized the poor girl," I told Harmon that night, "all in the name of historical context."

"If you hadn't she might not have talked to you. She's doing poorly in my class too. I don't think that school she went to taught the most basic U.S. history. I'll be happy to work with her too."

I'd talked to Jean and got all Paola's teachers on board. I suggested she be paired with a high-achieving student as a mentor. Jean had suggested Lila, who had taken on the role so enthusiastically that when Paola's roommate dropped out, Lila offered to room with her. I was gratified to see that with the extra attention Paola's grades improved. She'd written an excellent essay on *The Scarlet Letter* and Harmon said she'd done well in his class. She was due to graduate in two weeks and had gotten a generous scholarship to Mount Holyoke. A success story.

I suppose I'm one of Haywood's success stories too. I don't know what would have happened to Rudy and me if I hadn't had this place to come back to. I don't know what will happen to us if we have to leave. The thought makes me feel suddenly breathless, reminding me of a story about the chapel, that on lonely nights here a voice can be heard sobbing and crying out, "I'm drowning, I'm drowning."

And why would anyone have drowned on high ground a quarter mile from the water? Mr. Gunn, my English teacher, had asked us when he brought my Senior Seminar to the chapel.

When no one had an answer, he told us that in 1918 so many of the girls at the Refuge had gotten sick with the Spanish flu that the church had been used as an infirmary. The afflicted had lain in long rows in the sanctuary. *Do you know how you die of the flu?* he had asked us. *Your lungs fill up with fluid and you drown.*

I hear a sob now, as if one of those suffering girls were here. The sound is coming from the first row, where there's a woman whose head is bowed so low I didn't see her at first.

I consider backing up and leaving her to her grief, but I've hesitated too long to retreat. I can tell by a shift in the woman's back that she knows I'm here. And besides, I recognize the well-cut silvery hair and cobalt-blue suit jacket. It's Jean. I walk forward and sit down beside her, put my arm around her, and give her a moment to collect herself. Then I say, "I'm sorry, Jean. I know how hard this must be for you."

Jean's own daughter died five years ago of a drug overdose. She had struggled for years with depression and addiction and Jean had struggled with her—fighting to get her into one rehab center after another, dealing with her outbursts and stealing, the fear and uncertainty when she disappeared for months at a time. It was always a marvel to me how Jean managed to keep herself together and still run the school so well. *I have to keep working,* she told me once, *or I'd go insane.*

"I was doing all right until I got here," she says now, blowing her nose, "and then I remembered Tracy's funeral . . ." She takes a sharp intake of breath and waves a shaking hand in front of her face, as if to fan away the waves of grief rising in her. I sit with her quietly, knowing there's nothing to say. "It's selfish, really," Jean says after a moment, "to feel every grief through the prism of my own. Lila deserves her own mourning. She was a lovely girl."

"She was," I say, the past tense reverberating in the empty chapel. When I heard that story about the flu victims drowning here in the chapel I pictured the waves off the Point crashing over the church, sweeping the dead out to sea. *You are never safe,* Mr. Gunn's story seemed to say. The sea could reach out and take you even on dry land. "Have the police told you anything more?"

"No," Jean says. "Do you know they put Kevin Bantree on the case? He's turned out quite good-looking. I always thought it was a shame he didn't go to college, but his mother got sick his freshman year and he came back to take care of her."

"I didn't know that," I say, regretting my earlier thought that he'd wasted his time at Haywood. "Poor guy. He looked miserable having to ask Harmon down to the station."

Jean looks surprised. "He asked Harmon down to the station?"

"Yes," I say, sorry now I've brought it up. I had assumed she knew. "I imagine because he's dean of Lila's form. I'm sure he'll be back by the faculty meeting." I look at my watch. It's almost noon.

Jean sighs. "I suppose we'd better go. How much do you want to bet that Brad Sorensen brings up cordoning off the woods again?"

"That would be a sucker's bet," I say, getting up and offering Jean my arm. She leans on it heavily and I notice how frail she's grown this winter. She's so sharp, so energetic, that I never think of her as old, but she must be getting close to seventy. Harmon, whose mother was on the board and still hears gossip from its members, says that there's talk about her retiring, but it's hard to imagine what she would do without the school. Since Tracy's death she's poured her whole life into it. Without the school, she would be like those Puritans I teach my students about: cast out into the wilderness.

As we're entering the corridor that leads to the back room behind the stage, I hear the front door to the chapel open behind us, followed almost immediately by a long keening cry. Jean and I turn around.

The slight figure in the central aisle looks too small to have made that sound. Long black hair and layers of black cloth drip from her like seaweed. She could be Lila's ghost risen from the sea to demand vengeance, but it's only Rachel Lazar come early to the chapel to vent her grief. I feel Jean's arm stiffen. She's had a number of conflicts with Rachel the last three years over issues ranging from demands for trigger warnings on all reading assignments to complaints about "creative differences" with Lila's direction of *The Crucible*.

"Let me handle her," I whisper.

Jean gives me a grateful look and squeezes my hand. "If you're not back in ten minutes I'll send Martha to check up on you."

I smile. As I walk toward Rachel, I can feel the waves of emotion radiating off her like blast waves from an explosion. I am trying to recall if she was particularly close to Lila but what I remember is them always arguing in class. They were two alpha girls—both smart, pretty, and vocal—who clashed on everything from literary interpretation to social activism. Rachel once accused Lila of playing a "social justice warrior"; Lila told Rachel she was "sexualizing" the role of Abigail Williams in *The Crucible*. But, I remind myself as I arrange my face into an expression of compassionate sympathy, their past conflict might make Lila's death particularly hard on Rachel.

I raise my arms, meaning to take her hands, and am taken by surprise when Rachel suddenly rushes toward me. She slams into my chest with such force that I stumble back a step and have to wrap my arms around her to keep my balance. She's hot and damp and shaking.

I pat Rachel's back and actually say, "There, there," but I doubt she hears me over her cries. I stand as straight as I can, trying to keep us both upright. Having a son who doesn't like to be touched, I'm unaccustomed to this kind of physical display. Even Harmon, while generous in bed, isn't physically demonstrative out of it. *I'm a WASP,* he's fond of saying.

After a minute I shift one arm around Rachel's shoulder and maneuver us both to a pew. I dig in my purse and hand her a tissue. Her face is streaked with kohl and so, I realize, is the white silk blouse I'm wearing.

"We're all grief-stricken over Lila—" I begin.

Rachel shakes her head. "No, no, you don't understand—" A fresh volley of sobs ripples through her body. It's like there's something in her chest trying to come out, like her body is at the mercy of some uncontrollable force. It reminds me of the convulsions that beset the girls in Salem—

In fact, it reminds me that Rachel has been playing one of

those girls. I scoot a few inches away on the pew and examine her more closely. How much of this show of grief, I find myself wondering, is a performance?

"What don't I understand?" I ask.

Rachel sniffles and wipes her nose. "This is all my fault."

"What do you mean?" I ask. "It was an accident."

"It was not," Rachel says, her voice an octave lower and steady as the pew we're sitting on. "Lila was murdered." Her well-trained voice reverberates in the hollow shell of the meetinghouse. I can feel its echo in my gut.

"We don't know that," I insist.

"I know that Lila was scared," she said. "Someone was hurting her."

"She told you that?" I ask skeptically. Why would Lila confide in Rachel?

"She didn't have to. I could tell. We had an argument about the play last week. She said she didn't like how the play depicted the girls as false accusers. She thought it reinforced a stereotype of the hysterical female accusing a man. I told her that was exactly the point. Abigail Williams was a victim of sexual abuse but because the patriarchal system she was in didn't allow her to express that, she was forced to co-opt a different language to confront the inequalities of her world. She had to become a witch—a symbol of feminine power."

There is so much shaky about this theory that I wouldn't know where to begin to correct it, but this isn't a term paper—this is an accusation of murder. Although it's unclear whom she's accusing. "What does that have to do—"

"Don't you see? Lila must have been the victim of sexual

abuse but she hadn't found the courage to confront her abuser. When I explained how Abigail did it, Lila must have decided to confront *her* abuser. And he killed her."

"Did Lila tell you she was being sexually abused?" I ask. It's hard to keep the skepticism out of my voice.

"She had all the signs. She was secretive, she'd lost weight, she cut herself—"

"She did not," I interject, my voice coming out harsher than I'd intended. "I would have seen."

"She always wore long sleeves." Rachel holds up her own hands. The tattered cuffs of her black turtleneck are pulled down to her knuckles. She's cut out holes for her thumbs. I try to remember if Lila wore her sleeves like that. Maybe . . . but then, everyone bundles up during a Maine winter. And spring.

"None of that is proof that she was being sexually abused," I say, and then, more kindly, "At times like this it's natural to feel guilty. It's survivor's remorse, and it's a very normal way of processing your grief. If you know something concrete about Lila's death you should share it with the police. Otherwise . . . well, it won't help Lila or anyone else here at Haywood to spread rumors."

Rachel gives me the same disappointed look that my students give me when I make them put away their cell phones. "Why don't you ask Rudy what he thinks?"

"Rudy?" I say, startled.

"Your son." She narrows her kohl-rimmed eyes. "I saw him arguing with Lila at the party last night. Did Lila tell *him* what was bothering her? They were . . . *close,* weren't they?"

"They were friends," I say. "He would have said if Lila told him anything . . . and she would have told me. We were close. She spent a lot of time in my home."

"That's right," Rachel says. "She was doing some project with your husband, right?"

"Yes," I say, eager to move Rachel's attention from Rudy to Harmon. "He was helping her with her essay on the history of the school. Harmon thought it would win the historical society essay contest. I imagine it still will."

Rachel blanches. This is a direct hit. Rachel has also entered the contest. But Harmon, who's read Rachel's essay, says it's not half as good as Lila's. "That wouldn't be fair," Rachel says petulantly, all pretense of mourning for Lila gone.

"Well," I say gravely, "it's not fair what's happened to Lila either."

Rachel rolls her eyes. "No, I mean the prize for the contest is a college scholarship. What's Lila going to do with that now?"

CHAPTER FIVE

'm so relieved to be away from Rachel's insinuations and pettiness that I don't even mind walking into the faculty meeting late. No one notices my entrance, at any rate, so engrossed are they all in the argument being waged between Jean and Jill Frankel.

"Our students need a conduit for their emotions," Jill is declaring in her loud, stage-trained voice. "What better vehicle than the play?"

"You don't mean to go on with the performance?" I ask.

"If you had been here on time," Jill says, "you'd have heard my suggestion that the cast perform a memorial tribute to Lila *tomorrow* night. After all, she was the director. It's really her production. It's exactly the right vehicle for processing the complicated emotions surrounding Lila's death."

There's so much here to unpack—the accusation of lateness, the idea that the students would be up for performing tomorrow night, the substitution of *processing* for *grieving*—but what I come out with is "Complicated? A beautiful, vibrant young woman is dead. What's complicated about that? Shouldn't we let our students grieve rather than trying to process their emotions like canned meat?"

Noor Saberian, the school counselor, raises an elegant, well-manicured hand. "I agree with Tess. We need to let our students express their grief without judgment, but we also have to be careful not to allow their grieving to become a cult of mourning."

"So we have a memorial service and get on with finals," Bill Lyman, the physics teacher, says. "I feel horrible about what's happened to Lila—I have a daughter her age, for Chrissakes—but I've also got a passel of students taking the SATs next weekend. They need to focus on their work or their own futures will be compromised."

"We'll certainly have a memorial service," Jean says. She looks older and more tired than she did when she walked in here ten minutes ago. "Celia"—she nods at the Unitarian minister who is our campus director of religion—"will be working with me and Noor on the details of that."

Planning a teenage girl's memorial service will be hard on Jean. I raise my hand. "I'll be happy to help too," I say.

"Thanks, Tess," Jean says. "Which brings me to the last bit of business. The police have asked to speak to each of Lila's teachers after the assembly, as well as a few students whose names they've given me." She holds up a piece of paper. "I suggested, and Celia agreed, that they use this room for their interviews. I ask that you all stay in the chapel after the assembly until you're called by the police."

"I have a meeting with the cast to discuss tomorrow's performance," Jill says, "and this is our dressing room. We'll need it."

"I haven't decided yet about the play," Jean says sharply. "Our most pressing responsibility now is to honor Lila and tend to the emotional well-being of our students. Let's put everything else aside for now, shall we?" She gets to her feet, signaling the end of the meeting—and an end to discussion. I admire her resolve and her strategy. Keeping us in the chapel, with its repressive atmosphere, should at least limit histrionics. I wonder if the police suggested it. And I wonder which students are on that list.

I LOOK FOR Harmon as soon as I enter the chapel and am relieved to see him sitting a few rows back talking quietly to Paola Fernandez. He's bending toward her, one hand on her shoulder, talking softly to her. Paola nods and wipes her hand across her red-streaked face and Harmon hands her a tissue. It occurs to me that with all the drama online I didn't see one post from Paola. And unlike the drama girls, she isn't wearing black. She's wearing the same outfit of crisply ironed button-down shirt, wool cardigan, and jeans that she always wears, her only jewelry a gold cross at her throat that she's touching now with a trembling hand. I rebuke myself for not thinking about Paola earlier. Lila wasn't just her roommate, she was her mentor and friend. I'm grateful that Harmon has stepped forward to talk to her.

When I approach, Paola looks up and seems startled to see me. She gets to her feet, hugging a chemistry textbook to her chest.

"Paola," I say, "this must be so horrible for you. If there's anything Harmon or I can do for you—"

Paola turns her stricken face to me. "It's just . . . if I had gone to the police . . ."

"Paola feels bad that she didn't notice that Lila didn't come back to her room last night," Harmon explains. "And I was saying that I felt guilty too for not going with you when you picked up Rudy last night. Maybe I'd have seen something . . ."

"You wouldn't have," I say quickly, wishing Harmon hadn't used this particular strategy to comfort Paola. "I picked Rudy up in the parking lot and drove straight home." I notice that Harmon's neck is red and raw from a hurried shave; his navy tie is knotted crookedly and it clashes with the black jacket he's wearing. He's not thinking about placing Rudy so close to where Lila was last night; he's rattled and upset. I remember when I first laid eyes on him, at the university in Orono where I was taking classes and he was teaching part-time, I'd loved the neatly pressed Oxford shirts he wore, the way he was always clean-shaven and smelled like aftershave. I still associate that smell with order and calm.

"Exactly," Harmon says, turning to Paola. "When my wife and son came home I was just relieved they were home safe, which of course makes me feel selfish now. But we can't blame ourselves for what we didn't see, for being at home in our own beds when this terrible thing happened." Harmon gives me a pointed look.

"No, of course not," I say, wishing I could feel so blameless.

Paola darts a quick glance at me and bites her lip. Her head jerks up and down in a tight nod. "I just want to go back to my room but the police are searching it."

Harmon looks up at me. "Tess, do you think you could ask Jean to have another room made available for Paola?"

"Of course," I say, giving Paola a quick squeeze on the arm. I turn and see that Jean is standing at the front of the chapel talking to Celia a few feet away from a young female police officer who is watching the students and teachers warily.

As I make my way down the aisle, I scan the rows for Rudy, but he isn't here. I wish now I'd insisted he drive in with me. It will look bad if he misses this.

I explain to Jean what I need and she quickly finds Ruth Harley, the dean of housing, and asks the young female officer to escort Paola back to the dorm. When I go back up the aisle with Ruth and the police officer, I'm aware that people are watching me. "Where's Rudy?" I hear someone ask, and "Weren't he and Lila . . . ?" I'd like to stop and explain to the whole chapel that my being with a police officer has *nothing* to do with Rudy, but of course that would look even worse. So I deliver the officer to Paola and Harmon.

"Thanks, Tess," Harmon says, leaning in to kiss my cheek and to whisper in my ear, "I'm going to go with them to make sure Paola's all right." To the crowd it must look like he's comforting me for Rudy not being here.

"Get some rest and take care of yourself," I tell Paola, patting her on the arm. "There will be plenty of time to grieve for Lila."

She nods and gives me a grateful smile before leaving with Harmon, Ruth, and the young policewoman. Watching them go I think about how this will stay with Paola for the rest of her life. People are always saying things like the young are resilient, but the truth is that wounds at a young age can be like a canker on a tree. Bark may grow over it but the tree will always be a little off-kilter.

I make my way back to the front of the chapel, where Jean has saved me a seat—unfortunately right next to Haywood Hull. It's been a few months since I saw our former headmaster and I'm startled by the deterioration he's undergone. Although he's dressed in his usual uniform of khaki slacks and Brooks Brothers navy blue blazer, he looks somehow . . . *seedy*. His blazer is missing one of its buttons, his slacks look unpressed, and there's a piece of tissue clinging to his badly shaven chin. His hands are resting on the brass knob of his cane, his eyes closed as if he's praying. Or sleeping. I think of Jean's confession this morning that she is worried he might be losing his faculties, and though I suppose I should feel sorry for him I don't; I had an unpleasant run-in with him when he was my headmaster. I owe him my college education, but I can't quite bring myself to feel personally sympathetic.

I look over his head to scan the crowd for Rudy, and see instead Rachel surrounded by a gaggle of girls in similar dark mourning weeds. Sitting next to her is Dakota Wyatt, daughter of a Silicon Valley billionaire and the girl who called Lila a dyke bitch. She's wearing a pillbox hat and veil like the one Jackie wore at JFK's funeral. Samantha Grimes has draped her head and shoulders in a lacy purple shawl. Sophie Watanabe is wearing dark glasses and dark red lipstick. The four of them are perched on their pew like crows on a wire, alert and tense, and Samantha Grimes is glaring so hard at me I begin racking my brain for what I did to offend her. Did I take her cell phone away in class? Scoff at her request for a trigger warning? And then I realize all four of those girls are in *The Crucible*. They play the girls who accuse their neighbors of witchcraft; they must have practiced those steely glares in drama class.

Nevertheless, I'm rattled. When someone touches me on the arm I flinch as if the magistrates have come to haul me away to prison on charges of witchcraft, but it's only Haywood Hull, awake from his nap. "What's going on?" he demands, scowling at me as if I've done something wrong.

"One of our students has died," I explain. "She was found on the rocks below the Point—"

"Damn fool girls," he sputters. "They go out there and get themselves drowned."

I'm about to explain that Lila Zeller didn't drown, but Jean leans across me and hisses at Haywood, "Be quiet now, Woody. The sermon is beginning."

Woody looks at Jean like a boy who's been caught stealing candy, but he only grumbles and shifts restlessly in the pew. I squeeze against Jean.

Celia steps up to the lectern, clasps her long, elegant hands together, and looks out at us, her turquoise eyes gleaming in the pale, clean light of the chapel as the murmurs and rustlings settle down. I know from Jean that Celia used to be a bond trader at Cantor Fitzgerald, but after losing many of her colleagues on 9/11, she quit and went to divinity school. She worked in El Salvador for ten years, ministering to women in a rape crisis center. When the funding ran out she moved back to New England and wound up here at Haywood, her alma mater, one of the lost chicks Jean has gathered back in the fold. Like me.

When the room has grown quiet, Celia speaks into the silence. "Let us pray," she says, closing those laser-blue eyes. She bows her head, her curly white hair catching the light and glowing like a halo.

I close my eyes and bow my head. I try to picture Lila's face but instead I see Rudy: Rudy at age five in the prow of a rowboat, huddled in a soaking-wet sweatshirt, his body rounded into a hard, compact knot. I want to go to him, to wrap my arms around him and chafe warmth into his frozen body, but I have to row the boat. We are moving fast across the water, as fast as I can move us, but no matter how hard I row, and how fast I go, I cannot bridge the three feet between me and my son. I think sometimes that those three feet still lie between us, that I'll never bridge that gap.

Although Celia hasn't given the sign to end our moment of silence I can't help but open my eyes and turn around to scan the bowed heads for Rudy. I'm relieved to find him at the very back of the chapel, leaning against the wall, hands stuffed in his pockets, sweatshirt hood up. I want to go to him but I can no more squeeze through the crowded chapel than I could bridge those three feet in the rowboat when he was five. It makes me ache to see him so alone. He's gone to Haywood since he started middle school but he's never made real friends—not until Lila. Lila was the first one to thaw the ice wall my son has built up around his heart. What, I wonder now, did she find behind it?

Rudy lifts his head and my heart squeezes at the thought that he has felt me looking at him, but he's looking at someone to my right. I turn my head and see Dakota Wyatt lean toward

Rachel and whisper something in her ear. They're both looking toward Rudy, an identical look of malice on their faces.

I turn back toward Rudy—but he's gone. The chapel door swings shut behind him, making a bang that startles the praying congregants. It is quickly swallowed up in a deep, sonorous chord. Someone—Jean, I'm guessing—has signaled the organist to play to cover up that jarring sound. I look back to the front where Jean is now standing beside Celia and give her a grateful smile, but she is looking over my head—over all of our heads—to where my son has fled the church, a worried look on her face. Which means I am not the only one to have witnessed the scene between Rudy and the two girls and wonder what it was about.

I CONFESS I don't pay attention to Celia's no doubt excellent sermon. I am too busy worrying about Rudy—where he's gone, what silent message Rachel and Dakota have sent to banish him from the chapel, what malicious gossip those two are spreading about my son. The bowed heads of my students don't fool me. They aren't praying; they're texting.

Rudy's been the victim of cyberbullying before. In fifth grade a girl started a rumor that Rudy was autistic and that he'd been raised by wolves in the woods. The girl was good enough at Photoshop to have made pictures of Rudy in the company of wolves. Kids started calling him "Wolf Boy." Rudy had obliged by howling and snapping at his classmates.

I'm tempted to pull out my phone to check for any new tweets or Instagram posts. But of course I can't do that, here in the first row sitting next to Jean. I have to get out of here and check on Rudy to make sure he's okay, to make sure his grief and anger haven't made him do anything . . . *rash*. I find an excuse, finally, when one of the girls in the back row lets out a keening sob and runs out the front door.

I'll check on her, I mouth to Jean, getting to my feet. I stride down the aisle, my lace-up oxfords making a terrible clatter on the wide plank floors. A susurration of murmurs grows as I near the door. Muttering—that's what the witches were accused of. The Puritans hated and mistrusted the sound, sure it hid multitudes of curses and demonic rituals, and though I can't make out any one voice, I believe I know what the voices are saying: *Wasn't he going out with her? Didn't they have a fight last night after the play? Wasn't he the one who got into a fight freshman year with a kid in town? Didn't he punch a hole in the wall of the dorm? Wasn't he picked up for smoking pot? And spray-painting obscenities on the town water tower? Does anyone even know who his father is? Didn't she just show up here twelve years ago with a five-year-old boy—a wild child who didn't talk and didn't know how to use an indoor toilet? I heard his third-grade teacher found him squatting on top of a toilet like he was used to crapping in the woods. I heard she was raped during her senior year and went away to have him—*

And threaded through all of it that ghostly voice—*I'm drowning, I'm drowning*—only that last voice belongs to me. I'm the one who's drowning.

I crash through the double doors and land gasping in the bright sunshine like a beached fish. The girl who ran out is sitting on the chapel steps scrolling through her phone. Beyond her, in the graveyard, Rudy is sitting on a gravestone smoking a cigarette and talking to Kevin Bantree. *Shit*. What is Kevin asking him? What is Rudy answering?

I start toward them but the girl sees me and stands up, blocking my way. She's holding up her phone. "Ms. Henshaw," she says as I struggle to remember her name, "is it true?"

"Is what true . . . ?" Michaela? Miquel? Michelle? Whatever her name, she looks visibly shaken by my sharp tone.

"Th-they're s-saying," she stammers, "they're saying that Lila's death wasn't an accident. They're saying she was murdered."

CHAPTER SIX

W ho is *they?*"

The schoolmarmish question just pops out of my mouth. It's what I ask my students when they use the vague *they* in class. *Do you mean the author? The narrator? A critic? Be specific. Cite your sources.*

Michaela—that's it, Michaela Palmer, a junior from Westfield, Connecticut, who was in my women's lit seminar and cried when we read *The Handmaid's Tale*—turns red and looks down at her phone.

"People online. Someone said . . . here it is . . . on Twitter . . . 'The police are treating Lila Zeller's death as suspicious because she had defensive wounds on her arms.'"

"How would anyone know that?" I ask. "Can I see who's saying it?" I reach for her phone but Michaela holds it against her chest as if I'm trying to confiscate it.

"I don't want to get anyone in trouble. And besides, my feed has private stuff on it."

I am tempted to explain to Michaela the contradiction between *feed* and *private* but looking past her I see that Kevin Bantree and Rudy are walking toward a police car. I don't have time to give a lecture on rumormongering on social media.

"Put your phone away and go back inside the chapel," I snap, already walking away. I hear her calling behind me, something about needing to phone her parents, but I am already entering the graveyard. I want to stride purposely toward Kevin Bantree, making it clear he can't just take my son away, but the soft, spongy ground sucks at my heels, causing me to wobble uncertainly like a drunk or a madwoman. Ahead of me, Rudy is loping alongside Bantree, shoulders rounded, hands in pockets.

"Hey!" I call, my voice shrill and desperate sounding. "Wait up!"

Kevin and Rudy turn and watch my lurching progress across the boggy graveyard. I'm panting and sweating by the time I reach them, and when I wipe my hand across my brow I see I've got some kind of black sludge on it. *Grave dirt,* I think, before remembering Rachel's kohl. It's on my shirt and hands. I must look like a crazy woman.

"Where are you taking my son?" I demand.

Kevin straightens his back while Rudy shrinks further into himself. "Rudy's volunteered to come down to the station to answer some questions."

"Not without a lawyer," I say.

"It's all right, Mom," Rudy says. "I want to help. It's for Lila."

His voice is so tender when he says Lila's name that I find I can't argue with him. "I'm going with you," I say.

"It would be better if you stay here," Kevin says.

Better for whom? I want to ask but before I can Rudy says, "Please, Mom, I have to do this myself." He might be five, asking to tie his own shoe, or ten, begging me not to yell at the boys who call him Wolf Boy. *Let me fight my own battles,* he is asking me, *or don't you think I can?*

But Rudy doesn't understand how the police will bully him into saying things he doesn't mean. "Okay," I say, "but I'm calling our lawyer and asking him to meet you at the station. Don't answer any questions until he gets there, okay?"

Rudy nods and gets into the police car. I turn to Kevin. "There's a rumor going around the Internet that Lila's death has been ruled suspicious because there were defensive wounds on her arms. Is that true?"

"I can't say anything about that." Kevin's face is carefully blank, as if he's trying not to give anything away, but his lack of denial gives *everything* away. It must be true that Lila was murdered.

I nod. His expression has told me all I need to know. "I'm holding you responsible if anything happens to my son in your custody, Kevin Moore Bantree. You understand?"

His poker face falters; he's surprised that I remember his middle name. I am too. A teacher must have used it in class; for a moment I see not Officer Kevin Bantree standing in front of me but his younger, teenage self.

Kevin is looking at me as if he's seeing my teenage past too. "Your son is safe with me, Teresa," he says gently.

Before he can see how it unnerves me to be called by *my* full name—no one calls me that anymore—I turn around and make my way back across the treacherous, boggy ground, fear-ing at each step that some hand from beneath the soil is about to reach up and grab me.

It starts to rain as I return to the chapel. Students are coming out of the assembly now, veering away, some toward the dorms, others in the direction of town. They look like rats fleeing a burning building, desperate to get far away from the repressive atmosphere of the chapel. As soon as they're outside its orbit their voices get louder. The word *murder* rises off the damp graveyard earth like a miasma. *Murder, murder, murder.* A muttering of witches.

I don't blame them. I don't want to go back inside the chapel either. But where else can I go? Home? Back to the polished hardwood floors and ticking silence of our solid, safe Colonial? Without Rudy there, what does safety matter? What I *want* to do is drive to the police station, grab Rudy, toss him in the car, and head north. *Disappear.*

But Rudy's not five. I can't *toss* him in a car. And the last time I fled north I found out that disappearing wasn't the same as being *free*.

I stop outside the chapel to call Morris Alcott, but find that my phone is dead. I never recharged it after picking Rudy up last night. I need to find Harmon—surely he's back from escorting Paola to the dorm—and ask him to call Morris. At the thought of Harmon I feel better. Harmon will know how to handle this. Despite all the friction and tension over the years, Harmon has always stood behind me whenever there was trouble with Rudy. He told Rudy's third-grade teacher that she didn't have the credentials to diagnose Rudy with ADHD.

He spoke to the school about the cyberbullying Rudy was subjected to. He'll have my back now.

Inside the chapel I see that the teachers have spread out into the empty pews. Only about a dozen students remain, including Rachel Lazar, Dakota Wyatt, Samantha Grimes, and Sophie Watanabe, all of whom are in the play. Of course, I realize, they're the group from the cast party last night, the ones who would have seen Lila last.

I find Harmon near the front talking to Bill Lyman. He moves away when he sees me. "I need to talk to you," I say. "Kevin Bantree has taken Rudy in to the station to question him. Will you call Morris? My phone is dead."

"Why has he taken Rudy?" Harmon asks.

"Well, he and Lila *were* close. But, Harmon . . ." I lower my voice. "There's a rumor on social media that the police are treating her death as a murder. I don't want Rudy to answer any questions without Morris. Will you call him, please?"

"Of course I will." He hesitates a moment as if he's reluctant to tell me something, then decides he has to. "I think you should know that the police did ask me a number of questions about Rudy."

"What kind of questions?" I ask, my mouth going dry.

"About his past record—the pot, the fights."

"What did you say?" I demand, trying to keep my voice down despite my rising fear.

"I told them the truth, Tess," he says. "That Rudy's had some rough patches but we've both been working on his anger management—"

"That makes him sound like a nutcase!" I cry, much too shrilly for the quiet chapel.

"I only told them the truth," Harmon says reprovingly. "Did you want me to lie?"

"Harmon," I say, appalled. "You don't actually think Rudy could have hurt Lila, do you?"

"He's lashed out before," Harmon says. "That incident in seventh grade, that time last year at the track meet . . . that time he hit you in the eye."

"That was an *accident*," I snap, recalling the incident. I'd gone into Rudy's room and caught him standing at the mirror. Embarrassed, he'd pushed me out and the corner of the door caught me on the cheekbone. "You're not suggesting Rudy had anything to do with what happened to Lila?"

Harmon puts his hand on my arm and pulls me down into a pew while shushing me. Harmon hates it when I raise my voice; I've never heard him raise his. He's certainly right that now is not the time to be seen squabbling over Rudy.

"I'm not suggesting he would *deliberately* hurt Lila," he says in a controlled whisper. "But if they were arguing out on the Point and she said something to make him angry, he might lash out."

"That's not what happened. They argued at the party and then Rudy left." It's a lie. Rudy told me they argued at the Point, but if I tell Harmon that Rudy was on the Point he'll know that Rudy lied to the police.

"So you picked him up at the dorm."

"In the parking lot." It's better, I think, that I tell Harmon what we told Kevin. It would be unfair to ask him to lie to the police. "By Warden House. You know we used to live there. Rudy goes back there when he's upset."

"Because living with me in our house is such a burden," Harmon says in a wounded voice. It's an old sore point. After Harmon proposed to me he asked Rudy how he'd like to come and live with him in his house in town (his big, beautiful, tastefully preserved Colonial) and Rudy had replied that he'd rather live in Warden House because it was closer to the woods.

He doesn't like change, I'd explained to Harmon. *It's not personal.* But the truth is that Rudy never really adjusted to living in *Harmon's house,* as he still calls it. And Harmon had never gotten over the hurt at having his generosity rebuked.

I take a breath to tell Harmon how much that generosity—his constant generosity, to me and Rudy both—means to me but before I can he says, "He'll always come first, won't he?"

"You're the adult," I snap, forgetting to keep my voice low. "Why should I have to protect you?"

A sudden silence in the chapel tells me that everyone has heard this last salvo. Harmon's lips have gone white, his jaw clenched. "Your son is an adult now too," he says with icy dignity as he gets to his feet. "What exactly are you protecting him from?"

CHAPTER SEVEN

As I watch Harmon walk out of the chapel I see that everyone else is watching him too. Jill Frankel leans toward Martha James and whispers something that makes Martha turn red and shake her head. Samantha Grimes texts something that is clearly meant for her group because they all look down at the same time and smirk. Brad Sorensen shakes his head and goes back to grading a stack of papers. I hear Dorothy Shoemaker, the gym teacher, say, "Why does *he* get to leave?" followed by Janelle Williams, the French teacher, answering, "He's already talked to the police."

So have I, I think. Why shouldn't I just get up and go? But the thought of marching down that aisle under the scrutiny of all my colleagues and students is paralyzing. I'll wait long enough for everyone to go back to whatever they're doing—grading papers, playing Candy Crush, or reading *The Scarlet Letter*, which, I notice with some gratification, many of my students are doing. They're cramming for my final, which is scheduled for two days from now. But will we even be holding finals?

I left the house without my usual massive book bag; I've got nothing to read, grade, or write in. I can't even resort to my phone for entertainment—or to call Morris Alcott. But Harmon will do that. Even after our fight he won't let Rudy face the police himself. I clasp my hands and close my eyes, and try to do what the chapel was meant for: quiet contemplation. Surely I can spend half an hour with my own thoughts. Surely I can give that to Lila.

But when I picture Lila's face I see her standing on the Point with Rudy. I see her trying earnestly to draw Rudy out. I see her telling him she can't stay with him if he isn't willing to share himself. And I see Rudy withdrawing deeper and deeper into himself, as he does when any deep emotion threatens to breach the ice walls he's built around his heart. Then I see Lila reaching out to him and Rudy flailing out—and Lila losing her balance, falling to the rocks below—

I snap open my eyes to banish the picture—and find Martha James staring at me. She's just come out of the back room from her interview and her face is white and drawn. She's looking at me as if she has just noticed for the first time that I have two heads. Martha James has always been friendly with me. In fact, I've often suspected she wanted more of a friendship. She invited me to join her book club, go to readings in Portland and on hikes with the outing group. But now when I smile at her she looks away and hurries up the aisle. She stops to pick up her heavy book bag and to whisper something to Jill Frankel, who immediately looks at me. As Martha leaves, dragging the bulky wheeled bag she uses to tote the enormous load of papers and thick Norton anthologies she assigns in her classes,

Jill gets up and makes her way up the aisle. I think she's going to stop and say something to me but she keeps on going, studiously avoiding eye contact, and goes into the back room.

That's all Martha had been saying: *They want to speak to you next.*

But then, why that look at me?

I sit now with my eyes trained on the door to the back room. Ten, fifteen minutes pass and Jill comes out. She doesn't look at me, but it seems to me she's trying very hard *not* to look at me. She taps Rachel Lazar on the shoulder and whispers to her.

It takes some time for Rachel to collect herself. Scarves have to be redraped, her shoes found, an ornate tooled-leather journal carefully stowed away in a velvet carpetbag. All the while, Jill stands by her side, softly whispering. What is she saying to her? Surely this is not what Jean—or the police—intended by sequestering the students and teachers in the chapel. Isn't this *coaching the witness* or something? And is it my imagination or is Rachel cutting her eyes in my direction each time Jill tells her something?

Finally Rachel traipses toward the back door with Jill watching her like a proud mother sending her child out onto the stage to perform her first piano solo. I can't stand it a moment longer. I get up and walk toward Jill.

"Can I speak with you a moment?" I ask.

Jill purses her lips disapprovingly. "We're not supposed to—"

"That didn't stop you from having a rather long conversation with Rachel. I just want a minute. We can step outside."

"You're not supposed to leave until you've spoken with the police."

"I *have* spoken to the police, this morning. I'd just like to know what you were telling Rachel. We're not supposed to coach our students before their interviews."

"I wasn't *coaching* her," Jill replies in a loud, offended voice. "I was giving her emotional support. I was urging her to tell the truth no matter how intimidated she might feel by conflicting loyalties."

"Toward whom?" I ask incredulously. "Who is Rachel Lazar loyal to except herself?"

Jill looks at me aghast, as well she ought; that isn't what I meant to say at all. But before I can backtrack her shock is replaced by something even worse—pity. "I can see how this will be hard for you," she says, laying her hand on my shoulder. "It's never easy to have our eyes opened to unpleasant truths about the people we love. But maybe it's for the best. It might be just the wake-up call you need."

Before I can respond—and *really*, what possible response is there?—Jill turns away and walks out of the chapel, head high, spine ramrod straight, turning briefly to look back at me with the smug, self-satisfied look of an actress who has just delivered an Oscar acceptance speech that managed to thank all the little people while denouncing social injustice and climate change.

I sit back down and face the altar, trying to keep my face calm while I sort out what Jill said. A wave of nausea floods over me as I realize that Jill, who shared faculty housing with us at Warden House, knows an awful lot about Rudy's history— his tantrums and screams in the night when he woke up from nightmares, or worse, the nights he wouldn't wake up from those night terrors and I'd have to run his hands under cold water until he calmed down.

Shouldn't he be in therapy? Jill would ask.

Of course he should be! I'd wanted to shout. But I couldn't take him to a therapist. A therapist would dig to find the trauma at the root of Rudy's nightmares and then they would take him away. So I told her that yes, of course we were seeing someone—a very good children's psychologist in Boston. I started leaving the campus with Rudy every Saturday. We did take the train to Boston, but instead of going to a psychologist we went to the Harvard Museum of Natural History. Rudy loved the glass cases full of dinosaur bones and animals and sea creatures and could spend hours staring at them. He liked the underwater ones the best, the beautiful glass models of sea creatures that had been made in the nineteenth century by German glass artisans. He liked it when I stood beside him as he looked at them. I thought at first it was because he was afraid of getting lost in the museum. Then one day I noticed that he was looking from his reflection to mine in the glass, and I realized he was imagining us both underwater. Afterward we would go to the gift shop and I'd buy him one of the plastic animal figures as a treat. On the train ride home he would sit the new toy on the tray table while he drew pictures of the two of us underwater with the seals and polar bears. He'd be calm for days afterward. I told myself that these outings were as good as therapy. He was working out his trauma by making up stories.

Even Jill had said how much better he seemed. But then one day I came home and found her playing with Rudy. They had all the little plastic figures that I'd bought for him in the museum gift shop—the dinosaurs and polar bears, the Arctic wolves and seals, the great blue whales and giant squids—spread out on the floor. Rudy was pushing the wooden cigar box that served as sled, boat, dirigible, spaceship—whatever mode of transportation his story required—across the blue bath mat that served as lake, ocean, or faraway galaxy. Two polar bears—a big one and a small one—were riding in it.

"The mama bear and baby bear are escaping from the Bombable Snowman," Rudy was narrating.

"*Abominable,*" Jill prissily informed him. Then she held up the T. rex that was apparently playing the part of the Abominable Snowman. "Where's Papa Bear? Can't he protect Mama Bear and Baby Bear?"

Rudy had stared very hard at the T. rex for several seconds and then swatted it out of Jill's hand. "Ow!" she had screeched dramatically. It couldn't have hurt *that* much. "That wasn't very nice, Rudy."

"*You're* not very nice," Rudy had retorted, picking up a triceratops and lobbing it at Jill's head. The prickly ridges on the dinosaur's back struck Jill in the forehead and drew blood. Jill squawked as if she'd been clubbed by a baseball bat. I'd stepped in then, but Rudy was already on his feet, kicking at the plastic figures, scattering them across the room, screaming, "There's no Papa Bear in this story, dumbass!"

Then he ran out. I'd run after him. Later, after Rudy had gone to bed, Jill had confronted me in the shared kitchen. "You'd better open your eyes to what's going on with that boy or one of these days you're going to get an unpleasant wake-up call."

How satisfying it must have been to tell the police that story. *He was always violent, he threw things at me, something was really off about him but Tess just wouldn't see it . . . If you ask me, there's some bad history there that she's hiding. And if she'd hide that, well, how can you believe a thing she says?*

A door slamming makes me look up. Rachel Lazar storms into the chapel trailing black streamers. One scarf slithers to the floor like a snake. Her eyes dart to me and then she covers her mouth with her hand and scurries over to her friends, who swarm around her and shoot obviously "covert" glances in my direction. Then Dakota lifts her chin defiantly and marches into the back room.

Enough. I get to my feet. I can't sit here another minute. I'll go to the police station. Demand to talk to Kevin Bantree. I will tell them that yes, Rudy called me from the Point last night. I went to meet him there. And when I got there Lila was with him. She was breaking up with him. She was breaking his heart. I couldn't stand to see my son hurt like that—everyone would vouch for my obsessive protectiveness—so I pushed her off the Point. I killed her. *It's all my fault.*

And since that last part is true I will make them believe the rest of it.

I've made it to the end of the pew but Dakota Wyatt is blocking my way, her face veiled, as if she's a ghost in a nineteenth-century horror story. "Dakota," I say, trying to swerve around her. "I don't have time. I have to go."

"But I'm supposed to tell you that it's your turn. The police want to speak with you."

"Good," I say, "I'm heading to the station now. I'll talk to them there." I bump past Dakota but encounter another obstacle. Haywood Hull is stalled in the middle of the aisle like a foundering trawler.

"Miss Levine," he says.

The sound of my maiden name in Haywood Hull's Blueblood Boston accent sends a shiver down my spine. I'm instantly transported back to my schooldays. And from what Jean told me this morning, my old headmaster might very well think I'm one of his adolescent charges. "Mr. Hull," I say, careful not to call him *headmaster,* "such a terrible day. I'm afraid I have to be going—"

"I need to have a word with you," he says, reaching a trembling hand toward my arm.

I do not want him to touch me but neither do I want to be seen batting an old man's arm away. I step back and motion for him to sit down in the pew. Dakota is still hovering in the aisle.

"Tell the police I'll be there in five minutes," I tell her. She leaves, as loathe to be near the old man as I am. For one thing, I realize as I sit down beside him, he *smells.* "I imagine this is terrible for you, Mr. Hull," I say carefully.

"Not as bad for me as it will be for you," he says.

"What?" Is this senile blathering? But Woody Hull's eyes don't look *vague* right now; they look keen as a hawk's. They're fixed on me with all the sharp attention I recall from the last time he called me into his office.

"I've had a word with the police," he says, "and I see where their questioning is going. I think you'd better prepare yourself."

My mouth turns dry. Have the police actually told him they suspect Rudy? "I don't know what you're talking about."

He grabs my arm with a claw-like grip and all the breath goes out of my lungs. "I understand the instinct to deny the truth. Heaven knows I've been guilty of that myself. Do you remember Luther Gunn?"

"What?" The name shocks me into speech. *Of course* I remember him. Luther Gunn taught Senior Seminar—the class I teach now. Every senior took that class. I no longer think Haywood Hull is senile; he knows *exactly* what he's doing.

"He was a fine teacher. A fine young man. I knew his parents, and hired him myself to teach English." Woody goes on, "All the girls loved him. But then that girl accused him of making unwelcome advances toward her."

"Ashley Burton," I say, the name rising up in my throat on a surge of bile.

"Yes, Ashley Burton," Woody repeats with a look of distaste on his face. "The little slut."

I look around to see if anyone is close enough to have heard those words come out of our former headmaster's mouth, but no one in the chapel is recoiling with shock and horror. Did I *imagine* he just called one of his former students a slut?

"But of course I did have to do *something*. I felt terrible about letting Luther go, but what choice did I have? It had become a *witch hunt*! A thing like that ruins a man's reputation. Apparently he just vanished afterward, went off backpacking through Nepal and was never heard from again." He looks at me as if I might tell him what became of Luther Gunn. He looks at me as if he *knows* I know. "It can be so hard," he says with a horrible gentleness, "to face the truth about the people we believed in."

"Yes," I say, getting to my feet. I have to get away from him, *now*. I push past him in the pew, my skin crawling as my legs brush his knobby knees. I have to get to Rudy. Hull might be calling my name as I run down the aisle but I don't hear him. All I hear is a voice in my head crying, *I'm drowning I'm drowning I'm drowning.*

CHAPTER EIGHT

get in the car to drive to the station but my hands are shaking so much I drop the keys twice. It finally gets through to me that if I can't hold the keys, maybe I shouldn't be driving.

I can still feel Woody Hull's bony hand on my arm. The place he touched me burns. The name Luther Gunn is drumming through my head like a jackhammer. Why did Woody Hull bring him up? As an object lesson of how we never know people and therefore I can't even really know my own son?

Or because he knows?

I grip the steering wheel and look through the windshield. I'd parked at the back of the lot, facing Warden House. It looks in even worse shape than when it was faculty housing. The paint has been stripped off the clapboard, and tarps cover the slanting gabled roof. The cupola on top is encaged in metal scaffolding to stabilize the structure while it's being renovated. Jean has done an amazing job raising funds for the building's renovation but part of me wishes she'd let it collapse and rot. Not all relics of the past should be preserved.

Luther Gunn lived here when I was a student at Haywood and he held his senior English seminar in the faded grandeur of the east parlor. *Why not take advantage of this historic landmark to teach the landmarks of English literature?* he would say. It was the kind of unconventional idea he liked to put into motion, like taking the Senior Seminar on field trips, not just to the usual Salem and Boston, but on camping trips in the local woods so that we would "experience the wilderness" and know what the Puritans feared in the dark. He would tell us the local legends and ghost stories. *Listen to legends,* he would say, *the truth often lies beneath them.*

It was those unconventional habits that made him so vulnerable to Ashley Burton's accusations. *He came into my tent on the camping trips,* she claimed. *He said it was because he saw that I'd been scared by the ghost stories he told. He told me that I was unusually sensitive. I was special. On those first nights he only lay beside me stroking my hair, telling me how beautiful I was. Later, when we were back at school, he asked me to stay after class. He'd say he wanted to show me a book he had up in his room. That's when he started touching me . . . that's when we started having sex.*

Luther Gunn denied Ashley's allegations but he couldn't provide an alibi for any of the times when Ashley said she was with him. And it came out that there had been accusations against him at the last school he'd taught in . . . and at the one before that.

Teenage girls have big imaginations, he said. *I ask them to use them and sometimes as a consequence I become the focus of their fantasies. They get carried away, become hysterical, like the girls in* The Crucible. *It's a witch hunt.*

He didn't ever say directly that he was a likely candidate for the fancies of a teenage girl because he was so handsome. He didn't have to. He had curling black locks, golden skin, wide-set amber eyes. He looked like Lord Byron and played up the resemblance by keeping a bust of the poet in the east parlor, in front of which he would often pose during his free-ranging lectures. All the girls—and some of the boys when the school went coed—had crushes on him. It wasn't hard to believe that some of these girls would fantasize an affair and then, rebuffed, accuse him of one.

But he didn't have an alibi for those times with Ashley and so Headmaster Hull had to let him go. *Sanctimonious hypocrite,* Luther had railed, *like he isn't leering at all of you all the time. I bet he's screwed half a dozen Haywood girls over the years. He's definitely fucking that mealymouthed secretary of his, Jean.*

Perhaps the only one who knew he was innocent was me. I knew Ashley was lying because all those times she said she was with Luther Gunn, he was with me.

MY HANDS ARE steady enough to drive now but I don't go to the station. There's something I need to do at the house first.

It's possible Woody Hull knows about me and Luther—I tried to tell him once—or maybe he's just senile and the tragedy of Lila's death has brought up the accusation against Luther and its aftermath. Either way, he's given me an idea. After all the years of keeping what happened between me and Luther Gunn a secret, coming clean now might actually help Rudy.

The false story Ashley told (and which Luther conveyed to me) was eerily like the real story of what happened between me and Luther. It did start on the camping trip in the woods. And yes, Luther had been telling us scary stories each night.

On the first night he told the story of ten Abenaki sisters who went night clamming in the sand flats bared by the ebb tide. The eldest sister went first, carrying a lantern to light the way and to watch for the returning tide. The girls sang as they dug. Just as the eldest sister saw the tide was returning, she heard her youngest sister cry out that she was caught in the sand. The next-youngest sister went to her aid but she too was caught in the quicksand. The sisters formed a chain across the sand between the mainland and the island, but each in turn was pulled into the sand and drowned. Only the eldest sister, standing on a rock near the island, survived. Stranded by the incoming tide, surrounded by water, holding a lantern to light the way, she wept for her sisters until she was turned into stone. When the tide retreated there were nine large stones leading from the peninsula to the island—a causeway that hadn't been there before that the Abenaki named the Sisters. The standing stone they named the Maiden. When the tide comes in, they said, the Sister Stones shift and the drowned girls pull the lost girls down into the sand where they either drown or, if they follow the ghostly light to the Maiden Stone, vanish. Luther had told us that the legend persisted into the early eighteenth century.

Fourteen-year-old Abigail Sumner crossed the causeway to the island to collect plover eggs and vanished. The settlers combed the island for her but she was never found—but a red ribbon from her hair was discovered caught on the Maiden Stone.

Some people believed that Abigail had run away to Boston and become a prostitute. After all, look at that red ribbon. What self-respecting Puritan girl wore a red ribbon? But then Martha Hubbard, a fifty-three-year-old spinster, crossed the causeway to dig for clams and she too disappeared, leaving behind a scrap of red cloth torn from her flannel petticoat on the Maiden Stone. "Serves her right," the settlers muttered, "drawing attention to herself by wearing a red petticoat!"

When the minister's niece, an eleven-year-old girl of unquestionable virtue, vanished, though, the settlers began whispering that the Maiden Stone demanded a virgin sacrifice. At night they thought they heard the cries of voices in the wind crying, I'm lost, I'm lost, *or sometimes,* Come find me.

When you go to sleep tonight, Luther had slyly concluded, *listen for them.*

I hadn't been scared that night. I wasn't a virgin. I'd lost my virginity to Jeff Schlotnick six months before on his parents' living room couch. I had proceeded to sleep with three more boys in quick succession, and when my parents found out they sent me to Haywood. I had nothing to fear from the Maiden Stone.

Nor was I afraid on the second night when Luther told the story about the girls who went missing from the Refuge in the 1890s. They, like me, had been sent north for crimes of sexual misconduct. These were girls from Boston or Lowell or Providence—or one of the many mill towns in New

England—picked up by the police for prostitution and sent to the Haywood Refuge for Wayward Girls. Three of them went missing in the 1950s, but there was no hue and cry, no public demand to solve the mystery of their disappearances. They were wayward girls, after all. Hadn't they already gone astray?

On the third night Luther told the story of Noreen Bagley, the sixteen-year-old Haywood junior who vanished in 1963. Noreen was not a prostitute or a wayward girl but she *was* very alone. Her mother had been killed in a hunting accident and when her father, a well-to-do Boston doctor, had remarried, Noreen was sent away to boarding school. Awkward and unpopular, she'd made few friends at Haywood, so no one noticed at first when she vanished after a holiday break. Even when school resumed her teachers assumed she'd gone home to Boston and simply stayed over. She'd been missing three days before the headmistress realized her mistake and reported Noreen's absence to the police. A search was mounted, but the only traces of Noreen Bagley ever found were her coat, a glove, and a red knit cap perched on top of the Maiden Stone, which was largely suspected of being a student prank.

That story scared me. Not because of the cap on the Maiden Stone or any of the ghostly pretensions. What I understood from the story was that Noreen Bagley just stepped out of her life one day and no one cared enough to find her. When Luther Gunn came to my tent that night (Ashley Burton was *supposed* to be my tentmate but she'd squeezed in with two girls who were more fun and popular than me) he found me sobbing in my down sleeping bag.

I knew that one got to you, he'd said. Then he'd crawled into my sleeping bag and held me. That's all he did that night—he didn't even stroke my hair like in Ashley's story. But he did listen to me talk about how, when my mother was diagnosed with cancer the year before, instead of dutifully sitting with her through chemo and radiation and surgery and chemo again, I'd started drinking and smoking pot and sleeping with boys until my parents had no choice but to send me away to a girls school—and not just *any* girls school but one that started out as a home for prostitutes! I wasn't even home when my mother died the month after school started.

Well, Luther had said, *if that was really intentional you have to give them points for dramatic irony.* He stayed with me that night until I fell asleep and maybe he *did* stroke my hair or maybe I dreamed it. I dreamed about him a lot after that, waking and sleeping. I still dream about him but the dreams aren't very nice anymore.

When Ashley told her story (*She's jealous,* Luther told me, *she wanted me to pick her*) I said I would go Headmaster Hull and tell him that I was with him those times Ashley claimed to be with him.

What good will it do, Luther had asked, *to ruin your reputation along with mine?*

But he didn't try to stop me, so I went.

Headmaster Hull's office was in Main Hall, in a room that had once been the warden's office when the school was a refuge for wayward girls. There were old photographs on the walls of girls in high-necked long dresses standing awkwardly in front of the gates, or sitting in circles with their heads bowed over their sewing, or working in the refuge's laundry, stirring enormous steaming vats like the witches in *Macbeth*. It occurred to me as I took a seat in the hard straight-back chair in front of the headmaster's massive mahogany desk that I was sitting where those girls had sat in more ways than one.

"I have to tell you something about Luther Gunn," I began, but he cut me off.

"*Et tu,* Miss Levine?" He shook his head heavily. "Let me guess, you've come to say that you too were molested by Mr. Gunn. I would think very carefully, Miss *Levine*"—he pronounced my name like it was a curse word—"before you say anything else. Do you really want to drag your poor father— who just lost his wife and moved to Florida to start a new life— into a lawsuit? Do you want him to find out how you've been using his hard-earned money here at Haywood?" He flipped open a folder that lay on his desk. "What *have* you been doing, Miss Levine? Certainly not schoolwork. You're getting C's in everything but Mr. Gunn's class. Are you saying that your grade there has been influenced by some special relationship with Mr. Gunn? Do you expect, Miss Levine, that you could sleep around like a little slut and get by on your"—he slid a look down at my chest that I could feel through my sweater— "*charms?*"

I was stunned. When he asked me if I had anything to say I looked at the mute girls on the walls. *At least you can leave,* they seemed to be saying to me. I looked back at Headmaster Hull and shook my head. He smiled, his eyes still on my chest. "I thought not."

Then I went back to Luther and told him I wanted to go away with him, that I was ready to step out of my old life.

He'd looked at me a long time, measuring my conviction, I thought, although later I surmised that he'd been deciding if I was worth the trouble. But I didn't know that then. I didn't really know *him*. I knew an idealized version of Luther Gunn that he'd invented: a brilliant, misunderstood writer who'd dropped out of his PhD program at Princeton because it was too sterile. Who'd moved from school to school because he was a nonconformist, an iconoclast. I didn't know about those other girls—and if I had I'm not sure I would have cared. Hadn't we both been accused of sexual misconduct? Neither of us belonged at Haywood.

Let's do it, he'd said at last. *I know a cabin north of here. We can live there together. I can write my book and you can write too. I know you've got it in you. What do you need college for? I'll be your college.*

I still wonder if I would have said yes if I wasn't already pregnant with Rudy.

WHEN I REACH the house, Harmon's car isn't here. Maybe he went to the station to make sure Morris was there to represent Rudy. Maybe he's already figuring out some way to help Rudy.

The thought gives me pause. Despite the fights we've had over the years about him, Harmon has always done his best to help Rudy. He's tutored him and taken him to Red Sox games and bought him a drum set when Rudy said he wanted to learn. He's offered countless times to pay for therapy.

We tried therapy for years in Boston, I'd lied, *and it only made things worse.*

What will Harmon think if I reveal now the real reason I

could never take Rudy to therapy? What will he think when he finds out how much I've been lying to him all these years?

I can't think about that now. If Rudy is accused of killing Lila, if they have evidence that he was there on the Point with her, if Rudy *did* push Lila off that cliff, his only hope will be if I can convince the police he acted out of temporary insanity as a result of past trauma. For all Harmon called him an adult, he's seventeen so legally still a minor. If he's declared mentally incompetent he'll be sent to a juvenile detention center or maybe a mental hospital, but not a prison. But to convince them I'll need proof of a past trauma.

I go into the house and straight up the stairs. On the second-floor landing there's a string hanging from a trapdoor in the ceiling. I pull it down and slide out the stairs for the attic. When Rudy and I first moved in with Harmon six years ago I'd gotten the movers to carry the small trunk straight up to the attic. *Baby clothes,* I'd told Harmon, *mementoes from high school.*

It was the trunk my parents had bought when they sent me to Haywood: purple with brass hinges and a padlock, imprinted with my initials and the Haywood seal. *It's called a tuck box,* my mother had told me, *it's what all the kids take to boarding school.* As if I were going to Hogwarts and not being sent away in shame.

Luther had laughed at it when I made him carry it down to his car in the predawn dark. *It's like something out of* Tom Brown's School Days, he'd said, which he'd had to explain was some British book about a boys' boarding school.

Later it had come in handy to have a place that locked.

I almost left it behind in the cabin because I knew it would weigh down the rowboat, but I brought it because Rudy's *trea-sures* were in it. The key is hidden in a tea tin buried in another box. For a moment I'm afraid I can't find it. Harmon moved some boxes around last summer when he brought up the drum set, which was gathering dust in the garage. I finally locate the box under the drum set and find the key inside the tea tin. When I open it, it smells like pot.

No wonder you keep this stuff up here, Harmon had said when he'd caught a whiff from one of the boxes. I'd told Harmon that after I left Haywood I'd gone to Portland, gotten a waitressing job, and smoked a lot of pot while grieving for my mother. I told him Rudy's father was a seasonal fisherman who'd moved on by the time I found out I was pregnant.

When I open the trunk it doesn't smell like pot; it smells like woodsmoke. A wood-burning stove was our only source of heat at the cabin. Our clothes and blankets—even our hair and skin—always smelled like woodsmoke. When we moved in with Harmon the only change I asked him to make was to convert the fireplace into gas. The smoke would bother Rudy's asthma, I told him.

I unfold the knitted blanket folded on top, forest green with a pattern of owls, that had taken me nearly a year to knit, and find a small array of wooden animals nestled inside. These are Rudy's *treasures,* the animals that Luther carved for him. A deer, a bear, an owl, and a mountain lion. There once was an otter too, but Luther threw it in the fire when Rudy disobeyed him. Rudy asked me to hide the other animals then, in *my treasure box,* but after we left the cabin Rudy didn't want to play with them anymore. He preferred the brightly painted plastic toys, which Luther would have despised, that I bought for him at the Natural History Museum.

Beneath the blanket is a pile of composition books. Each one feels swollen and spongy from the time Luther tossed them into the lake. I wonder if the writing is legible, but I don't check. Maybe the journals I kept during the five years I lived with Luther will be of interest to the lawyer who takes Rudy's case or the doctors who examine him, but I don't have the time—or heart—to read them right now.

Beneath the journals is a flat tin that once held colored pencils. When I open it now I can still smell graphite. Inside are three sheets of paper and two photographs. One is Rudy's birth certificate—his original one from the hospital in Skowhegan, not the one I had forged five years later in Portland. On the forged one the name of the father is entered as "unknown" instead of Luther Gunn. The birth date is also three months later than the date on the original. I've always known that eventually I might have to use the original again if my forgery were ever detected, but I never thought it would be to convince a court that Rudy suffers from post-traumatic stress from living in an abusive household.

The next sheet of paper is an incident report from the Moose River Police Department describing a domestic violence call made by a kayaker who heard screaming and loud crashes coming from a cabin on a remote island on Moosehead Lake. When the police investigated, the woman at the cabin, one Teresa Levine, refused to press charges against her domestic partner even though she clearly had burn marks on her arm. "I was clumsy," the report quoted her as saying.

The last piece of paper is a copy of a patient's record from the Skowhegan hospital for one Rudy Gunn, who visited the emergency room at age four for a broken arm. A picture accompanies the report of four-year-old Rudy proudly displaying his cast. The eyes that look out of the faded Polaroid are trusting. He still believed that I would protect him. *When your father's mad, run to the safe place. I'll come find you.* And then on the last day, *Wait in the safe place and then we'll leave.*

The second photograph is of Luther holding Rudy when he was a baby. I don't look at it now. I leave it in the trunk.

Will these be enough to make a case that Rudy's behavior is a result of past trauma? Will I have to tell them what happened on the last day? I've kept it a secret so long that to reveal it now feels like the ultimate betrayal, but it might be just what saves Rudy. Never mind what it will mean for me.

I take the papers and the photographs downstairs and slip them into my school book bag. I look around the house for a moment—at the pretty antique furniture, the muted rugs, the tasteful framed prints. All the peace and order of Harmon's world that's about to be shattered. Then I turn my back on it all and walk out. Part of me never believed I would be allowed to stay here anyway. But then, part of me never thought I'd make it off that island.

CHAPTER NINE

As I drive to the police station I think about the island. I've spent twelve years trying to banish the memory from my mind but I have to let it play in my head now, seeing it as a policeman would (I picture Kevin Bantree watching with me) so I'll know how much of the story I can tell. It's been so long since I've allowed myself to think about that time, at first I'm not sure I *can* think about it, but once I open the trunk I've stored it in (something much rustier and less quaint than the tuck box my mother bought for me) the memories surge up as relentless as the tide, as indelible as the smell of woodsmoke.

The cabin Luther took me to was only a three-hour drive from the school but it might as well have been in another world and time. As we drove, the towns and buildings grew sparser, the trees taller and closer together. Perhaps this is what happened when those girls Luther told us about touched the Maiden Stone. They didn't vanish; the woods swallowed them up.

It certainly seemed as if Luther was trying to bury us. He drove down a long winding dirt road that opened up at the end to a general store, a trailer home, a dock, and a wide expanse of water. While I sat on the dock drinking a warm Coke to settle my stomach, Luther traded his car for a rowboat and a year's worth of grocery credit. That's when I realized he meant for us to stay. We rowed—or Luther rowed; I didn't know how—to an island on the north half of the lake while Luther recited verses from "Hiawatha." The water was so bright in the June sunshine that I could barely keep my eyes open.

When I think back to that first summer on the lake, that's what I see—a dazzling brightness that encroaches on the bare outline of the pointed tops of fir and pine, the rock hump of the island rising from the water like a turtle's back, the wood frame of the lone cabin on the island. They were all like stage props in this fantasy-scape Luther had invented for us. Luther himself was a cutout figure in a shadow puppet show—the dashing iconoclast, the transcendentalist woodsman, the Romantic poet reciting love poetry and telling stories, only now the stories weren't about vanished girls, they were about us. We were soul mates in our refusal to conform to the world. We couldn't be constrained by binary categories like teacher/student, adult/minor, husband/wife, father/mother. We would create our stories and poems and novels just as we created the flesh growing inside of me. I was so dazzled that I half thought Luther was carrying the baby with me and would do his share in birthing it.

Here is what Luther's stories didn't tell me, and I didn't think to ask: what we'd do when it got cold and the lake froze. How we'd get to the store for food or to the hospital when my time came. What we'd do for money when the credit at the store ran out. If I had asked, I imagine Luther would have told me we'd walk across the ice; we'd deliver the baby in the cabin; we'd sell our books at the end of the year and be rich enough to live on the island forever.

And that summer was dazzling. My morning sickness was soon over and the hormones from my pregnancy seemed to tranquilize me into a complacent stupor. We swam, sunned, and feasted on fresh fish and blueberries as if we were the only two people on earth. Adam and Eve in the Garden of Eden before the fall.

Only as summer drew to an end and the bright dazzle of the lake faded to a mist-drenched autumn landscape did I begin to notice some flaws in the picture Luther had painted. The first was that Luther wasn't writing. While I was filling up the composition books he'd brought with stories and poems, he barely touched his. He spent most of the day swimming and sunning on the dock or, as the weather grew cooler, chopping wood with maniacal intensity. Maybe, I figured, he would turn to writing when winter came and we were stuck inside.

The thought of being stuck inside brought up another concern: we didn't have enough wood. Our island was mostly rock. Even if we cut down all the trees we wouldn't have enough wood to make it through the winter. When I mentioned this to Luther one day in early October we had our first fight.

"How do you know how much wood it takes to make it through the winter?" he demanded. "From your Girl Scout troop on Long Giland?" *Long Giland* was the way the Haywood kids from Westchester and New England said it to make fun of me. Luther, who had grown up in the suburbs of Boston and gone to Choate before Princeton, apparently shared many of the same prejudices.

"We had a fireplace," I told him. "My mom liked making fires. My dad used to make me s'mores."

He laughed. "Did you think that's what this was? A camping trip with Mummy and Daddy with wieners and s'mores?"

"N-no," I replied, "but I remember we'd go through six or seven logs just in one night and it wasn't like we were trying to heat the whole house."

"If you wanted central heating maybe you should have gone home to Long Giland . . . oh, wait, Daddy S'mores sold the ancestral manse and debunked to Boca. Maybe you thought we'd be joining them for the winter in an adjoining condo? Maybe it's not too late for you to go."

I didn't understand why he was being so mean, but then the next thing he said gave me a clue.

"Or maybe we can burn the notebooks you're going through so fast. Unless you think there's something worthwhile in them."

"Are you jealous that I'm writing and you're not?" The question popped out before I knew I even thought such an absurd thing. I thought he would laugh it off. Luther Gunn jealous of me? Luther had gone to Princeton, backpacked through Nepal, hung out with famous writers in New York City, gotten his first story published in *The New Yorker*. The only reason he'd taken a job someplace as provincial as Haywood was because he was doing research for the novel he was writing about his boarding school days.

But the expression on his face stopped me in my tracks: a look of shame followed by mortification. He turned his back on me and walked out the door. A few minutes later I heard in the stillness the scrape of the canoe against the dock and I panicked. By the time I got out to the dock the rowboat was thirty feet away and Luther was only a dark silhouette against the setting sun.

That's the first time it really sunk in how precarious my situation was. We only had the one boat. What was I doing living on a barren rock in the middle of a lake with a man I barely knew? And then it struck me that this might be my best opportunity to learn something about Luther. I went back inside the cabin and straight to the duffel bag he had brought with him, which he kept under our bed. I was remembering how heavy it had been when he put it in the back of the rowboat. But it wasn't weighed down with clothes; Luther wore the same three flannel shirts—sometimes layered over each other—and two pairs of jeans day after day. What else had he brought with him?

I expected to find books inside his duffel, but there were only two: a children's collection of Hans Christian Andersen stories and a clearly unread copy of *Gravity's Rainbow*. The rest of the duffel was full of notebooks and eight-by-ten manila envelopes. I slid out the contents of one manila envelope: twenty typed pages paper-clipped together. *The Ice Virgin* was typed on the center of the first page, *a story by Luther Gunn*.

Wasn't there a Hans Christian Andersen story of the same name? I scanned the first page. It was a story about a boy named Rudy who fell into an icy lake and was seized by a creature called the Ice Virgin, whose kiss froze Rudy's heart. The story seemed familiar. I turned to the next page, loosening a paper clip, which left a rust-colored shadow behind, and read to the end. The story was a fairy tale of sorts, about a boy who is unable to feel any of the normal emotions because he has been cursed by the Ice Virgin, a demonic hag that hungers for his death after his near-escape from her. The boy grows up and learns to pretend to be like other boys, but he always knows he's different, and so do the girls he pursues. Whenever he kisses a girl she turns into the dreaded ice hag. Only a perfect love will set him free from his curse. At last he finds a girl who is so pure, who loves him so unselfishly, that he is cured. When he kisses her his heart melts. They travel to a sacred island to be married but on the journey the Ice Virgin rises up on a tidal wave, seizes the boy, and drags him down to her ice cave to live with her forever. The girl is washed up ashore on the island. Without a boat she cannot ever get to the mainland. She lives out the rest of her life alone, mourning for her dead lover.

When I got to the end of the story I felt like my heart had frozen. I was the girl in the story: stranded on an island in the middle of a lake, trapped in Luther's fantasy.

I opened another envelope, hoping for another story with a happier ending, but I found the same story in the next envelope and in the next and the next. Eighty-six envelopes (I counted) contained a typescript of the same story. Some of them had notes attached to the paper clip, many bearing the masthead of a literary magazine—some famous like *The New Yorker* or *Ploughshares*; some obscure like the *Kalamazoo Gazette, Fernspores, Dragonsprite*—with a few words scribbled below: *Sorry. Not for us. Try us again.* One had a longer note attached. *Dear Mr. Gunn, your story is not without merit. There is some fine writing here but the story, besides its obvious reliance on the*

Hans Christian Andersen story of the same name, feels stilted and a bit self-serving, as if its author is trying too hard to justify his own limitations. One might say it suffers the same malady as its hero—a heart of ice.

Luther had scribbled in the margin, *Pretentious prick!*

There was one envelope left. I opened it, assuming it would be more of the same, but instead I found a sheaf of letters. The first one was from the headmaster of a boarding school in Massachusetts. *We regret that we must terminate your appointment with Mt. Greylock Academy for behavior incongruent with the values of our institution. We wish you luck in your future endeavors.* The next three letters said much the same. But Luther had only mentioned working at two previous schools. How had he even had time to work at so many when he was only twenty-six?

But then, at the bottom of the pile of termination letters, I found a copy of his birth certificate. He wasn't twenty-six. He was thirty-six.

I had to stop reading then to go outside and throw up. While I was leaning over the dock, clutching my full, seven-months-pregnant belly, I measured the distance to the shore. I could swim it. And then walk the five miles to the store. I'd call my father in Florida, tell him what an idiot I'd been, and ask him to wire me the money to buy a plane ticket. I'd tell him about the baby when I got there. I had two months before the baby came. There was still time to get away.

I went back inside to get my shoes. I would tie them around my neck while I swam to shore. When I saw all the papers scattered across the cabin I thought, *Leave them, let him see what I know.* But then I couldn't resist looking at what was left in the last envelope. Like Bluebeard's wife with that bloody key.

They were letters—not from the headmasters but from the girls, the ones he'd had affairs with.

Dear Luther, one named Heather scrawled in a childish hand, *please don't go! I'm sorry that I said anything! I didn't know the nurse would tell!*

Dear Lukey, another named Haley wrote, *I'm not sorry for the things we did. Please write to me at camp—*

At camp?

Lukey?

My stomach cramped at the realization of how young these girls were. These were children. One named Shannon dotted her *i*'s with tiny hearts. Another wrote on Little Mermaid stationery. I would have thrown up again if there'd been anything left in my stomach.

Once when I was twelve or thirteen I'd gone to the movies with my mother. She sat on my left side and a man I didn't know was on my right. Midway through the movie I realized that the man's hand was on my leg. I picked it up and removed it, glimpsing as I did so a satisfied smile on the man's profile. I didn't get up, didn't tell my mother. I sat through the rest of the movie feeling nauseous, not so much because of what the man had done, but because I hadn't *known*. How long had I sat with his hand on my leg? How had I not known it was there? What did that say about me?

That's how I felt after reading those letters. As if I had awoken in the middle of an act of violation. Only I hadn't exactly been asleep. I wasn't really sure where I had been. But I suddenly saw clearly where I was and knew I had to get out.

I got up, not bothering to take my shoes, leaving everything behind—the notebooks I'd filled with sentimental poems and lovesick journal entries no better than the dribble written by Shannon and Heather and Haley, the tuck box my mother had optimistically purchased for my school days, the prissy baby-doll tops Luther liked me in (of course, I saw then, he was looking for the perfect love that would thaw his frozen heart). I walked to the dock and straight off it, stepping into the ice cold water like stepping onto a train.

CHAPTER TEN

It was the baby who saved me. Jolted by that cold water, he kicked—a drumbeat to my spine that woke me up and got me kicking too, propelling myself up into the air, where I took a moment to get my bearings before striking out for shore.

I'd swum this far before with Luther to gather berries and sun on the flat rocks, but not with an eight-pound weight dragging me down. My legs and arms felt heavy, like I was swimming through molasses. By the time I got to shore and climbed up onto the rocks I was exhausted and I still had to walk five miles to the store.

I was soon sorry I hadn't brought my shoes. The forest floor, which had been invitingly carpeted with moss and ferns in the summer, was now prickly with pine needles and dead leaves. And I was cold. My wet clothes clung to me like winding shrouds. What had I been thinking? I considered swimming back to the island, but I couldn't bear the thought of going back into that ice cold water. So I walked, or crawled, mostly, clinging to the rocky shore so I wouldn't lose my way in the woods.

Sometimes I stopped and leaned my cheek against the rough bark of a tree and cried. In one of the fairy tales Luther had read to us in class a tree grows up from a dead mother's bones and watches over her daughter. But my mother was buried far from here. No one was watching over me.

By the time I got to the general store it was, of course, closed. But there was a light on in the trailer next door. I knocked on the door, my hand so numb I couldn't feel the aluminum door under my knuckles. I wasn't fully convinced that I was really there. If the old man who opened the door—grizzled, wearing two flannel shirts and a Red Sox cap—had looked right through me I wouldn't have been surprised. Instead the shock on his old creased face told me how bad I must have looked.

"Sweet Jesus!" he said, pulling me into the cramped, smoky trailer. He sat me down by a kerosene heater and put a blanket around me, muttering, *I knew that city fella was up to no good, gone off and left you, has he? Well, don't you worry, Samuel'll have you all fixed up in a trice.*

Samuel fed me hot coffee and gave me warm clothes and the privacy to change into them. It was when I was changing that I saw the blood.

"Could you take me to the hospital?" I asked him. "I think my baby is coming."

It was a forty-minute drive down unlit backcountry roads to the hospital in Skowhegan. The contractions started halfway and I wondered if I'd have to ask Samuel to pull over and deliver the baby on the side of the road. But we made it, Samuel pulling his truck into the emergency bay at an angle and hollering for help as he carried me through the sliding glass doors.

Luther had told me that Western medicine imposed the notion of birth pains on women but Luther was clearly full of shit. The pain wrapped around me like a riptide and carried everything with it—me, the white walls, the glistening, distended IV sacs, the masked faces of doctors and nurses that bobbed over me like channel buoys on a rough sea. We were all underwater, riding the surf that poured out of me. The final push delivered us all to shore: me and the beaming nurse and the wet, blood-soaked creature screaming in her arms. In the bright lights he shone like a pearly mollusk. A bit of flesh that clung stubbornly to life.

And then he was gone. The doctor was telling me that since he was early he had to be taken to the NICU. I needed stitches and rest and something for the pain. My grandfather would be in to see me soon—

I drifted off then. Luther told me later that I lost so much blood I nearly died. I was unconscious for sixteen hours. When I came to, Luther was sitting in a chair beside the bed, holding the baby.

"He has red hair like you" were the first words he said to me, "so I named him Rudy."

Why did you go back to him? I hear a voice that sounds like Kevin Bantree's ask me. I've reached the police station. I'm in the parking lot, sitting in my Subaru with its Bluetooth and seat warmers. What will I tell him? How will I explain?

I felt worthless, I'll say. *I felt overwhelmed. What was I going to do with a new baby on my own?* And Luther seemed genuinely devoted to our son. He took care of him in those first months like he was the most precious thing in the world. When we went back to the cabin there were stacks of firewood surrounding the cabin. *I went to get firewood,* he told me, *that's why I left that day.*

I thought having a son had changed him. He gave him the name from the Hans Christian Andersen story, the name of the boy who escaped from the Ice Virgin. I thought that Rudy was *his* escape, I imagine telling Kevin Bantree.

But?

But. Just as all those girls failed to save Luther, Rudy eventually disappointed him too. Or rather, I disappointed him because I wasn't raising Rudy right. When I didn't make enough milk and had to buy formula Luther blamed my "Western neurosis." He hated going to the store because even though he'd made me tell Samuel his disappearance had been a misunderstanding, Samuel always looked at him with suspicion. When Rudy awoke crying at night Luther said it was because he sensed my fear of the dark. When I objected to leaving Rudy unsupervised on the splintery cabin floor he said I was "enabling his helplessness." After all, the Yanomami let their toddlers handle knives. I was crippling our son with my overprotectiveness.

I thought he might be right. I *was* afraid all the time. I had thought motherhood would transform me into someone calm and wise, like my own mother, but instead it had heightened every fear receptor in my body. I worried constantly about all the possible threats to Rudy: What if a bear snatched him? What if he ate a poisonous berry? Or a snake slipped into his cot? Or he was stung by a bee and turned out to be allergic?

I tried to silence my fears and let Luther have his way. I held my tongue when he tossed Rudy into the air and bit my lip when he let him crawl over the forest floor straight into a patch of poison ivy. This was normal, I told myself, mothers were protectors and fathers were challengers. Rudy needed both. I could tell that Luther loved him; surely he wouldn't let any harm come to him.

Until Luther dropped Rudy into the lake. *Babies know how to swim naturally,* he said.

But thirteen-month-old Rudy didn't swim. He sank like a stone.

I leapt in after him. The water was so cold it froze my limbs and so dark it blinded me. I couldn't move. I couldn't think. I couldn't, for a moment, even remember why I was there.

Then a stir in the water beneath me shattered my paralysis and I plunged down and grabbed Rudy. I pushed us both up to the light, shattering the surface as if it were ice, into air that seared my lungs, Rudy crying out as if he'd just been born. Luther was sitting on the dock, cross-legged, staring down at us, his face as frozen as if he were the one who'd just been baptized in ice water.

"Congratulations," he said. "You just made him scared of the water for the rest of his life."

And he was right. Rudy was terrified of the lake after that. He would scream if I tried wading in while holding him. He'd refuse to get in the rowboat and at night he'd wake up gasping for breath as if he were drowning. All of which made Luther more determined to break him of his fear.

"I'll do it when you're not around since you're not able to

control yourself," he said, which of course made me determined never to leave him alone with Rudy. When I tried to reason with him he flew into a rage and threatened to throw Rudy into the water then and there even though it was winter and he would have frozen to death. When Rudy was two I told Luther I wanted to leave. He said that I was free to go but that I couldn't take Rudy. He told me that if I tried to take Rudy he would kill me.

When Rudy was three he got sick from some berries Luther fed him. I begged Luther to take us to the emergency room but he refused. *He has to build up a tolerance to natural foods. If you take him to a hospital for every little thing he'll always be dependent on Western food and medicine.*

When Rudy was four Luther drew the poker out of the fire and brandished it in the air as if to strike me. Rudy screamed and threw himself at his father's legs. I reached out my arm to shield Rudy and the poker seared my arm.

"Look what you made me do," Luther said. "Look what comes of being so afraid all the time."

Not long after that Rudy fell from a tree that Luther had insisted he climb and broke his arm. I convinced him to take us to the emergency room then. I thought that this was my chance. I could tell the doctors what was going on and ask to stay, but when I walked out into the hall after Rudy's arm had been set I overheard Luther talking to a young nurse.

My wife was supposed to be watching him, he was explaining, *but she gets distracted. I'll keep a more careful eye on both of them from now on.*

When we got back to the island I took Rudy on a walk in

the woods. We found a hollowed-out log in a shaded cove. I told him that when his father started shouting he should come here and hide until I came to find him. I promised him I would always come. We called it "the safe place."

One day when Rudy was five we had gone out berry picking. Luther had learned how to make wine and he wanted us to get more berries. We left him in the cabin, drinking the home-made wine *to get it right,* he said. When we came back he was standing on the path by the water waiting for us, clearly drunk.

"I've got a surprise for you," he said, lunging awkwardly for Rudy. I shoved myself in between them, sure that Luther was about to throw Rudy in the water. Luther stumbled back unsteadily, surprise and then rage on his face, and then he drew back his arm and drove his fist into my face. The blow knocked me off my feet. Rudy crouched behind me, covering his head with his hands, screaming *stop stop stop* as Luther loomed above us.

"I was only going to give you *this*!" Luther shouted, thrusting a wooden figure of a deer into my face. "Why do you always always always get in the way!" He threw the wooden deer in the lake.

"Run," I whispered to Rudy. "Run to the safe place."

Luther went back to the cabin and I stayed on the shore, listening to him stomping and yelling and breaking things. *I knew that I had to get out of there,* I would explain to Kevin; *now that he'd started hitting me he wouldn't stop. He'd always find a reason it was my fault. How long would it be before he found a reason to hit Rudy?*

I waited until he was quiet and then I snuck back in the

cabin. Luther was passed out on the bed, snoring. I grabbed the tuck box—only because I thought Rudy might want those wooden animals one day—and ran back down to the dock and put it into the rowboat. I rowed to where Rudy was hiding and told him to get in. Then I started rowing across the lake.

But Luther wasn't as passed out as I thought he was. When we were about forty feet from the dock Luther came out of the cabin and ran down to the dock. He leapt into the icy water and swam toward us and grabbed the prow of the boat.

He grabbed Rudy by the hair and dragged him into the water, I would tell Kevin. *I was afraid he was going to drown him.*

His own son? Kevin would ask. *I thought you said he loved him.*

He didn't love Rudy for who Rudy was, I would explain. *He only loved him as an extension of himself. If he couldn't have him, he wouldn't let me have him. I knew he was going to kill him. I stood up, with one oar in my hand, and I drove the blunt end of it into Luther's skull as hard as I could.*

You only meant to make him let go of your son, Kevin might suggest.

No. I meant to kill him—and I did. He fell backward into the water. I saw the blood spreading on the surface. I reached down and grabbed Rudy by the collar and he came up as blood-soaked as on the day he was born. I hauled him onto the boat—

You're pretty strong.

It was my son. I did what I had to do. If I was really strong I would have left long before. I would never have let Rudy see his father try to kill him or see his father sink to the bottom of the lake. But he did, he saw all of it. He watched the water as we

*rowed away, and then he turned and watched me. I wanted to
hug him but I was afraid to stop rowing.*

*Rudy didn't cry, he didn't ask questions, he didn't complain even
though by the time we got to the store he was frozen stiff. He was
shivering and his lips were blue. Samuel gave him dry clothes and
hot cocoa. He drove us as far as Lewiston, where I told him my
mother was coming to meet us and he reluctantly left. I didn't want
there to be anything tying me to the island. After he left I realized
that Rudy was burning up so I took him to the hospital. He had
pneumonia. He nearly died. He lost the hearing in his left ear
and by the time he came to he wasn't the same little boy anymore.*

*Imagine knowing your father tried to kill you. Imagine watch-
ing your mother kill your father. Rudy was—is—traumatized.
Whenever anyone tries to grab him he strikes out. It's a reflex, part
of his PTSD. But I couldn't take him to a psychiatrist because I
was afraid of going to jail for killing Luther—not for my own sake
but for Rudy. How could I let him lose his mother too?*

You know that's what will happen now, Kevin will say. *If we
go to that lake and find a body—*

I'll take you to it, I'll tell him. *I don't care what happens to me.
As long as the court knows that Rudy couldn't help it. Whatever
he did to Lila—it's not his fault; it's mine.*

Kevin Bantree will understand. He knew me when I was a
girl. He knew Luther Gunn. He'll believe me and he'll make
others believe me. He's my best chance to save Rudy.

I get out of the car, clutching my book bag. The day has gotten cold and overcast, the sky spitting icy rain. I see Harmon's
car—a matching forest-green Subaru—parked crookedly in a

handicapped spot. How upset he must have been to park il-legally! How horrified he'll be to learn his wife's a murderer!

When I come inside the station the woman at the reception desk looks up. I recognize her as one of the mothers at the soc-cer games I used to take Rudy to before he was kicked off the team for hitting another kid. She frowns at the sight of me.

"I need to speak to Kevin Bantree," I say.

"He's in an interview—" she begins.

"It's about the case he's working on," I cut in. "I have impor-tant information. He'll want to see me."

She purses her mouth disapprovingly but punches a button on her phone. "Sergeant Bantree, Mrs. Henshaw is here to see you. She says she has *important* information regarding the case you're working." She manages to inject a load of skepticism into the word *important* but her self-satisfied smirk fades at what-ever Kevin's response is, and she says to me grudgingly, "Offi-cer Bantree will be down to see you as soon as he can get away. You can have a seat in the waiting area."

I am too hyped up to sit. I pace the short stretch of muddy linoleum in front of a bulletin board full of notices for Pancake Sundays at the local church and Chili Night at the firehouse. What a nice town. When Jean, whom I called from the Lew-iston Hospital because I couldn't think of anyone else, offered me a secretarial job and free housing at the school, I thought that Rudy and I would be safe here.

But just because the monsters are dead doesn't mean they're all gone.

Rudy's had to carry his monster inside of him all these years.

Maybe now, once I've come clean, he can get the help he needs to rid himself of that.

I hear footsteps behind me and whirl around, expecting Kevin Bantree, but it's Morris Alcott. His face is an unhealthy florid pink, his Harvard tie askew. He looks flustered. Morris is used to handling tax evasion and DUIs, not murders. I feel sorry for him, but not so sorry that I don't grab him roughly by the arm.

"Where's Rudy?" I demand.

"Rudy? They let him go after questioning him half an hour ago. Now they want to question you. Hopefully you can put this ridiculous affair to rest. They're hinting they've recovered DNA evidence but that might be a bluff. But if you can confirm Harmon's alibi—"

"*Harmon's* alibi?" I repeat, not sure I've heard right. "Why does Harmon need an alibi?"

Morris looks at me as if I've lost my mind. "Because they think Harmon killed Lila," he says, as if explaining to a child. "They're insinuating he was sleeping with the girl and claiming that they've recovered DNA evidence from the sweatshirt he was wearing when they brought him in."

CHAPTER ELEVEN

That's impossible," I say, shaking my head. It feels like my ears are clogged with water. Maybe I misheard Morris. "Harmon wouldn't . . . he *couldn't* hurt Lila."

"Of course not," Morris tuts as if I had just suggested that his grandfather voted for a Democrat, "but this Bantree fellow has fixated on Harmon. Apparently he suspected him right away because of some rumor he'd heard in town about Harmon being 'especially solicitous' of his students. Just the kind of small-minded gossip our local townspeople favor. Do Harmon and Kevin have a history? If I could show prejudice—"

"Kevin Bantree is the one who thinks Harmon killed Lila?" I think back to Kevin's visit this morning, his asking when I left the house, when I came home. I'd thought he was after Rudy, but he'd been establishing how long *Harmon* had been alone. And when he asked Harmon to come to the station it hadn't been because Harmon was the dean of Lila's class; it was because Harmon was a suspect. That was why he told Harmon not to change out of his sweatshirt—

The sweatshirt. It was the one Rudy was wearing last night.

". . . if you can give him an alibi he should be all right."

I've missed some of what Morris has been saying but I come to attention on this. "You mean you want me to talk to them *now?*"

"The sooner they rule Harmon out the better. Otherwise they'll be collecting evidence that might seem . . . *untoward*."

Untoward? I stare at Morris as if he had suddenly started speaking another language.

"Do you mean they think Harmon was . . . that he made . . ." All the euphemisms for *sexual advances* scroll through my head. *Call it what it is,* Noor says when she talks to classes, *rape*. But I can't say that word in connection with Harmon. ". . . that there was something *sexual* in his relationship with Lila?"

"It's absurd, but yes. Now they'll demonize every innocent gesture Harmon made toward that girl. That's the climate we live in today. A man makes an innocent joke or accidentally brushes against his secretary, God forbid he compliments a woman, and the next thing he knows some hysterical girl is crying sexual harassment. It's a witch hunt, I tell you!"

I stare at Morris's suddenly red face, hearing Luther's voice in my head. *Teenage girls have big imaginations . . . they get carried away, become hysterical, like the girls in* The Crucible. *It's a witch hunt*. But Harmon isn't Luther.

"There was nothing *untoward* in Harmon's relationship with Lila. I was there—" Except when they went into Harmon's study to work on Lila's essay or when they went to Portland or Augusta to visit some archive or library. "I'll make that clear to the police. And Harmon was at the house all night . . . It is the night they're talking about, right? Not the morning when he went jogging."

Morris leans close to me. "The body was found at six-thirty A.M. so as long as you can tell them that Harmon didn't leave the house until six-thirty—preferably a little later—and that he didn't have time to leave the house when you went to pick up Rudy—that should suffice." He lifts his head at the sound of footsteps; Kevin Bantree is coming down the hallway toward us. He adds in a barely audible whisper, his lips hardly moving at all, "And see if you can suggest that someone *else* might have worn that sweatshirt. Perhaps Lila herself. Perhaps she wore it while cutting carrots and nicked herself."

Then Morris composes his face into a mask of benign supportive faith and gives me an avuncular squeeze of both shoulders, which no one would *ever* misinterpret as sexual harassment. "I can't be present at your interview because I'm representing Harmon," he says. "Just stick to the plan and all will be well." And with that he leaves me to greet Kevin Bantree.

KEVIN'S FACE IS carefully neutral as he asks me to come with him to the interview room. As I follow him down the long hallway I scramble through my options. I could still follow through with my plan. I can tell them the sweatshirt is Rudy's and that he was wearing it when I picked him up last night. That will divert the investigation from Harmon to Rudy.

But I can't do it. I can't offer Rudy up to save Harmon.

And *besides,* I don't have to. I can save Harmon by giving him an alibi—*of course* he was upstairs when I came home—and paint a heartwarming picture of Lila cutting carrots in that

sweatshirt. Harmon deserves that much, surely, after everything he's given me.

I've never really belonged in Harmon's world. A single mother
from Long Island. *Jewish* (even though it was my father who
was Jewish, which meant I wasn't technically Jewish). Belatedly getting her degree from a *state college*, not one of the Ivies
or Seven Sisters, where Harmon's crowd had gone. I was always
suspect. An outsider. *Why me?* I asked him once, meaning,
Why not one of those girls from Smith or Vassar? And he had told
me he had fallen in love with me the first day of class when I'd
taken out my worn copy of *The Scarlet Letter* and, when asked
by the student next to me if I'd read it, replied, *Five times. I
keep hoping for a better ending.*

It made me want to find that better ending with you, he told me.

I never told him that the reason I'd read *The Scarlet Letter*
five times was that it was the only novel I'd brought with me
to the island.

Kevin opens a door at the end of the hallway and waves me
inside and toward a chair on the near side of a table. He sits
on the other side, next to a young female officer, the one whom
Harmon asked earlier to go back to the dorm with Paola Fernandez. I wish I remembered her name. Although she doesn't
smile she does make eye contact with me and I think I detect
a hint of sympathy there.

Kevin doesn't look at me. He's too busy lining up the tape
recorder, notepad, and pencils in front of him. I recall this
punctiliousness from class. He always had the day's reading as-
signment, notebook, and pencils lined up on the desk in front
of him. *OCD much?* some girl had teased.

I like to be prepared, he'd replied.

He reels off his name, his partner's—Katherine Gough—the date, my name, and then finally looks at me. "Thank you for coming in, Ms. Henshaw."

"Anything to help find who hurt Lila," I say.

"You were close to her?" Kevin asks.

"Yes. She was my student. A lovely girl."

"She was at your house a lot, wasn't she?"

"Yes," I say, torn between saying she was my son's friend, and that Harmon was helping her with her essay. "I think she was homesick. She liked being with a family. She liked to cook . . . and she hated the cafeteria food . . ." I laugh and it turns into a sob.

"Do you invite all your students over for family dinner?" Officer Gough asks.

"Not all," I say, considering, "but a few. Paola Fernandez, for instance, whom you met earlier today. Harmon and I were both tutoring her. She comes from a very underprivileged background—"

"Are all the students you and your husband tutor girls?" Kevin asks, cutting short my transparent virtue-signaling.

I consider. Surely either Harmon or I have tutored a male student, but I can't for the life of me think of one at the moment. "Well, you know," I say, "we're still sixty–forty female to male. Haywood only went coed in the late nineties, as you must well remember, Officer Bantree. You were one of the first male students." I look at Officer Gough to see if she knew Kevin went to Haywood but her face is carefully neutral.

"Where did your husband work with Lila?" Bantree asks.

"Where?" I parrot.

"At the kitchen table? In the living room?"

"In his study mostly," I say.

"With the door closed?"

"Honestly, I don't recall," I say in an offended voice that doesn't sound like my own. I sound like one of the wives at those cocktail parties telling the caterer she hasn't replenished the drinks promptly enough.

"You don't remember whether the door would be closed or not?"

"No."

"Do you remember what time you got home from picking up your son last night?" Officer Gough asks.

"Yes," I say, dizzy at the quick change. "I already said. Three-thirty—"

"And where was your husband at that time?" Kevin asks.

"At home, of course."

"Where at home?" Officer Gough asks. They're trading off now in a brisk rhythm that I imagine they've practiced. Trying to wear me down.

"Upstairs in the guest room."

"The guest room?" Kevin repeats, eyebrow raised.

I sigh and look from Kevin to Officer Gough with an I-can't-believe-I-have-to-go-into-this expression. "When I got Rudy's text, Harmon went into the guest room so he wouldn't be disturbed. He gets up early."

"So when you got home he was still in the guest room?" Officer Gough asks.

"Yes."

"Did you check?" Kevin asks.

"Check?" He's managed to make it sound absurd. As if I didn't trust Harmon. "I didn't have to check—" I begin, but then realize the trap I've strayed into, and start to feel angry. I could say that I heard Harmon walking from the guest room to our room, but that suddenly doesn't seem definitive enough. "He came back to bed when I got home." I can feel myself blushing but I stare at Kevin defiantly. Let him think I'm blushing because of the great sex I had with my husband.

Kevin gazes back at me with a neutral expression. "So you were in bed with your husband from three-thirty until . . ."

"Until six-thirty when he got up to jog."

"And you're sure about this, Mrs. Henshaw?" Kevin asks.

"I think I know who I share my bed with, Officer Bantree," I say with confidence, but as the words come out I can't help thinking about the man I shared my bed with *before* Harmon. How well had I known him? How good a judge of men am I?

Bantree looks down at his notebook. I expect him to ask me about the sweatshirt but instead he asks, "Lila was working on some kind of history project with your husband?"

"Yes." This is easy. "Lila had written an essay for a joint project for both our classes." I start to explain, happy to be on the firm ground of pedagogy. "When the workers began renovations on Warden House they found boxes of records from the old refuge. Harmon had the idea of working with the students to catalog the papers, for each student to choose a case study to write about. Lila chose a sixteen-year-old girl named Cora Rockwell who was arrested on the streets of Boston for prostitution and remanded to the Refuge for Wayward Girls. She became a housemaid in the warden's house and eventually head matron and Haywood's first headmistress. It's just the kind of success story that the school likes to promote. Harmon thought Lila's paper would win the contest the historical society holds. They award a scholarship for the best essay about local history."

"I know," Kevin says. "I won it senior year."

"Oh," I say, trying not to look too surprised. I must have already left with Luther before the winner was announced. "That's—"

"The thing is," Kevin says, cutting off my eighteen-years-too-late congratulations, "the essay was due yesterday and according to Haywood Hull at the historical society, Lila never submitted hers. Nor was there any sign of the paper in Lila's room."

"Oh," I say, confused. "It wasn't like Lila to miss a deadline. Did you check her laptop?"

"Her laptop was gone," Officer Gough says. "You wouldn't know where it is, by any chance?"

"Or," Kevin asks, leaning in, "what's become of this paper Lila was supposedly working on with your husband?"

CHAPTER TWELVE

The interview is a blur after Kevin's question about Lila's essay. All I can think about is all those hours Lila spent in Harmon's study, all those trips to libraries and archives in Augusta and Portland, all those afternoons they spent in the basement of Warden House looking through old school records.

The girl has a real knack for historical research, Harmon would say after one of those afternoons. *I wouldn't be surprised if she went on to doctoral work with this. She could write a dissertation on this topic.*

I had thought the glimmer in Harmon's eyes was from getting the chance to do real history again. When I met him he was a newly minted PhD from Brown. He'd come back to Rock Harbor to take care of his aging mother and was teaching at the state university while searching for a permanent, tenure-track position. He talked enthusiastically about his dissertation on the early colony at Rock Harbor, which he hoped to turn into a book once he got a permanent job. But after two years in the job market he got discouraged. *Why take a low-paying job somewhere in the middle of nowhere to teach bored freshmen?* he'd groused to me. The truth was he loved Rock Harbor, loved the house he had inherited from his mother, loved *me*. And I didn't want to move. Rudy was settling into our life at Haywood—or so I thought—and Jean had said she'd give me a teaching job when I finished my BA.

So Harmon took a teaching job at Haywood instead. *The students there are smarter than most of the ones I'd teach at some second-rate state school, present company excepted,* he'd said, *and we can teach together.* I'd thought it was a romantic idea and for the most part Harmon seemed satisfied teaching at Haywood. The students were bright, they all loved him, and if he was a bit of a big fish in a small pond, that suited his temperament.

Working with Lila, though, reminded him of what it would have been like supervising a graduate student on a real research project. Or so I thought. What if that glimmer in his eyes had come from something less *academic?*

I couldn't begin to explain to Kevin and Officer Gough why Lila hadn't submitted her essay to the historical society. And I was so flustered that when they showed me the Haywood sweatshirt—bagged in plastic like evidence in a crime, which of course it was—all I could manage was "All the students and teachers wear those. How can I tell one from another?" I couldn't summon up a picture of Lila cutting carrots. All I could see was Lila following Harmon into his study, Lila getting into the car with Harmon to go look at some archive. *Of course there was a paper,* I tell myself, *it was just lost.* But I still couldn't completely rid myself of the idea that all the time

Harmon had spent with Lila might have been about more than helping a student.

Bantree must have smelled the fear on me. He asked me a bunch of questions about when I met Harmon that I could barely focus on. What did that have to do with Lila? And then he finished with: "Do you maintain that your husband was in the house when you got home and that you're sure that was at three-thirty A.M.?"

"Of course I do!" I snapped.

When they let me go I went straight to the ladies' room and threw up, an image of Lila chopping something bloody playing through my head. There must be an innocent explanation for why she hadn't turned in the essay. My students were always handing in their papers late.

But not Lila. Lila's papers were always on time.

I rinsed my mouth out and splashed water on my face. My reflection in the mirror looked like a corpse. Luther had always praised my pre-Raphaelite ringlets and delicate Botticelli skin—but that kind of skin doesn't age well. There were dark smudges under my eyes and red blotches on my cheeks. My hair was stringy and damp. I looked like the drowned Ophelia in the Millais painting.

Like Lila must have looked when they found her on the rocks.

An image of a crab crawling out of Lila's pink mouth sends me back to the toilet even though there's nothing left for me to retch but a yellowish bile that looks like sea spume.

When I come out Morris is waiting for me. "There you are," he says brightly before turning down his mouth with a moue of distaste. "It looks like they put you through the ringer! But you did good. They've let Harmon go. He said to tell you he'll meet you back at the house."

He may as well be commending his Cavalier King Charles Spaniel for fetching a ball. I've performed my wifely duty, which is my only purpose, as far as Morris is concerned. If I veer from it—try to protect Rudy at Harmon's expense—I'll be on my own. I can only pray that I don't have to make that choice.

BY THE TIME I reach the house I've convinced myself it's ridiculous to be upset about the whereabouts of Lila's paper. It means nothing. If it were important the police wouldn't have let Harmon go. I pull into the garage next to Harmon's Subaru, which is parked perfectly on his side. Like Lila, Harmon is a perfectionist. He probably saw something in Lila's essay that needed more work. He'll have an explanation.

When I enter the house I can tell from the silence that Rudy isn't home. Harmon is in his study, seated behind the Stickley oak desk, looking out the bay windows onto a real bay view. The cloud cover has lifted just enough to light up the bay and fill the room with honey-colored light. I never once questioned why Harmon and Lila worked in here; it's the most beautiful room in the house. *It feels like anything you wrote here would turn into gold,* Lila had once said, twirling her delicate hand in the light that reflected off the bay and poured in through the old mottled-glass windows. For a moment I want to back out; I don't want to bring any more trouble into this room with its shelves of old books and framed prints of historic buildings and maps and portraits of Henshaw ancestors. The eighteenth-century judge Elias James Henshaw gazes down at me from his portrait above the fireplace with a look he might have given to one of the girls he sent to Haywood for *indecency*. When I look from the portrait to Harmon the family resemblance is jarring. He looks older than I've ever seen him before; for a moment I don't recognize him.

But then Harmon manages a small, sad smile and familiarity washes over me. "I was afraid you weren't coming back," he says. "I was afraid you"—he leans forward and covers his face—"that you believed those terrible, terrible lies."

I go to him, sliding into his lap and pushing his hands away from his face to kiss his wet cheeks. "I don't believe any of it," I tell him. "You could never . . . you're not like that. For heaven's sake, I had to ask *you* out and you wouldn't go until I wasn't your student anymore."

Harmon groans. "Your Kevin Bantree brought *that* up. *Did I make a habit of dating my students?*" He gives his imitation of Kevin's flat, working-class accent.

"I was already a grown woman with a child when we met and there were only seven years between us . . . what do you mean *my* Kevin Bantree?"

Harmon leans back in his chair, forcing me to readjust my balance. "He made a big deal of you two having gone to school together. He asked me if I knew what happened to you after you left Haywood and if I knew who Rudy's father was."

A splinter of ice lodges in my throat. I recall Kevin asking me when I met Harmon, but I hadn't understood why. "What the hell does that have to do with Lila?"

Harmon shrugs, casual, but his eyes are still locked on my face. "I think he was trying to make the case that I was a serial pedophile. That I seduced *you* when you were a high school senior."

"That's absurd," I say. Still, I shift off Harmon's knee and perch on the edge of the desk. Suddenly sitting on his lap feels . . . *suggestive*. "You were in grad school at Brown when I was a senior at Haywood."

"Yes, but no one really knows where you went when you left Haywood so people speculate."

I look down at Harmon. He's still looking at me, but the reflection of light from the windows has reached his eyes so I can't read his expression. Why would Kevin Bantree be asking about where I was after high school? Is he trying to find out who Rudy's father is because he plans to make a case against Rudy if he can't make one against Harmon?

"Bantree said that Lila didn't submit her paper to the historical society." The words spill out of my mouth like yolk escaping a cracked egg. "Do you know why?"

Harmon raises his hand in front of his face. I suppose it's to shade his eyes against the glare but it looks like he's warding off a blow. "I've no idea. I gave her some final suggestions three weeks ago—minor details, really, a few sources I thought she should double-check, some grammatical issues . . . and then I didn't hear from her. I had assumed she turned the essay in to the historical society. It's a shame. It would have been something to commemorate her. She'd done fine work . . ." His voice falters and he covers his eyes. "She had so much promise."

"Don't you have a copy of the paper?"

He lowers his hand and gives me a pained look. "No. Why would I?"

"I mean . . . don't you have some of her corrected drafts? You've been working together for *months*." I spread my hands out to indicate the scene of all that work, as if the darkening room could bear witness to the words written in it. But the Henshaw ancestors aren't talking, the books on the shelves stand like mute guards, the thick, old-fashioned blotter on the desk absorbs ink spills and secrets alike. There's no laptop or computer in sight because Harmon doesn't use one. He writes his letters and papers by hand and gives them to the school secretary—or me—to type up.

When I work with a student on a paper, they often send it to me by email and I make corrections and comments in an electronic file. *And* I always ask my students to submit an electronic copy of their paper to Turnitin so I can check for plagiarism.

I can always tell if a paper is plagiarized, Harmon says.

But I can't. Maybe it's because I've told too many lies over the years to spot them in others. But at least if a student loses a paper—their hard drives are always crashing; they never back up anything—I have a copy on my computer.

"I wrote comments on her drafts and she took the drafts home with her. I didn't think I needed a record of our work together." Cold has seeped into his voice along with the dark creeping over the room. Harmon hates having to explain himself almost as much as he hates modern technology.

"I just thought . . . it's a shame . . . what was the paper on anyway? I mean, I know she was writing about Cora Rockwell but neither of you ever said much about it . . ."

"Lila was afraid someone else would steal her idea," Harmon replies curtly. "She'd found something interesting in the records while researching Cora Rockwell. Several girls in the late 1950s gave birth at the Refuge ten or more months after they were admitted."

"Ten months?"

"In other words they got pregnant *at* Haywood. Lila believed there was a guard, or teacher, or janitor—*someone*—who was assaulting the girls at Haywood."

"Assaulting?" I hear Noor Saberian's voice—*Call it what it is.*

"Okay, *raping.* Some of those girls also went missing afterward and then there was that girl who went missing from the school in 1963. Lila thought that disappearance might have been connected to the pregnant girls. She was looking into employees who worked at the Refuge and later at Haywood when it became a school. She thought she'd found a source who could help."

"What source?" I ask a bit too eagerly. If Lila had gotten involved with some stranger perhaps that was who killed her. And if it were a stranger I wouldn't have to choose between protecting Rudy or Harmon.

"She wouldn't say. She was very secretive about it—and then I stopped hearing from her. I figured she was too busy exploring her source, but now . . . Now I wonder if she hadn't pursued that source and perhaps run into trouble in the process."

"Did you tell Kevin Bantree that?"

Harmon laughs, the first lightening of his mood since I came into the study. "Officer Bantree was singularly unimpressed by the details of historical research. He seemed skeptical that the paper existed in the first place."

He raises one eyebrow and shifts his leg so that it rubs

against mine. "He did seem interested in the alibi you had given me and asked why I hadn't mentioned you joining me in the guest room. Of course I told him it was none of his damned business. I'm chagrined to admit, by the way, that I don't recall that middle-of-the-night tryst you told Kevin about."

I blush, embarrassed to think that Kevin Bantree must have conveyed this detail to Harmon or, worse, to Morris. To hide my face I slide down into his lap and into the warm circle of his arms, where I always feel safe. This is my husband, I tell myself, he would never do anything *untoward* with an underage girl. Why would he when he has me? Harmon has pointed to the most logical third possibility: that someone else other than Harmon, and other than Rudy, hurt Lila. Someone she met while trying to find out what happened to those missing girls.

CHAPTER THIRTEEN

I'm relieved when Rudy texts to say he's spending the night in the dorm. Harmon and I need a quiet evening alone. We haven't had enough of those since Lila and Rudy started hanging out at the house.

I heat up a beef stew that's been languishing in the freezer during Lila's vegan regime, open a bottle of Malbec, and tune the radio to a classical station. Outside a cold rain falls—that brief showing of sun a false promise—but inside the solid walls of our two-centuries-old Colonial it's bright and warm. *Safe*.

We go to bed early. Make love. Slow and tender at first, as if we were both respecting the proximity of death, but then fiercely, as if that reminder of death is urging us on. Forcing us to reassert life. We are still alive. We are still here.

I'd been amazed after leaving Luther at the lake—after leaving him *dead*—that I had been able to go on to have a life, even enjoy everyday things again: crisp fall days, the smell of the ocean, my students' fresh faces. I told myself it was because I had to go on for Rudy's sake, but when I met Harmon I had to admit that I wanted a life for myself too, and that a bit of the joy I found in living was that I had survived Luther. He hadn't dragged me down into that lake with him.

I tell myself now that I will survive this too.

I fall asleep for a while but then startle awake with a sense of panicky dread. *Where's Rudy?* is my first thought. I get up and go into his room even though I've remembered that he's in the dorm. I just need the comfort of his things around me. I sit on his bed, releasing a smell of unwashed sheets and boy musk—and feel something hard beneath my hip. It's his laptop. *See?*—I'd like to point out to Kevin Bantree—*he's got nothing to hide, nothing he's worried about me finding.*

I open it up. I'm not spying, I tell myself, I'm just trying to find out more about Lila. A screensaver of the X-Men appears with a password request. I punch in the security code he uses for everything—LOGAN110—his favorite X-Men hero plus his birth date. The screen opens to the last website he visited. I'm braced for the possibility of porn, but it's only a site for X-Men fans, and I'm touched that it's something so innocent.

I open his email but find very little that's not spam or school-related. Kids don't use email anymore, my students have informed me. They use Snapchat, Instagram, Tumblr, most of which won't show up on Rudy's laptop. But there is a messaging app that mimics the one on his phone. I hesitate before opening it. This, more than anything I've done so far, feels like a violation, but then I remind myself that the police are no doubt already reading Lila's texts with Rudy and that's all I'm here to see.

When I open the messaging app I get a screen showing everyone Rudy's texted with recently. I see the text I sent him last night. *On my way!* I know the exclamation point was courtesy of the messaging app, but still it looks callous now. Lila was being murdered while I drove to campus in my comfy, seat-heating Subaru.

There are three other texters on the screen: a group text from Jill telling students when to show up for theater rehearsal, Lila, and an Unknown Sender. What a spare life my son leads, I think with a pang. Surely he should have more friends than this! Is it because he's had to keep so much to himself over the years? I've never been sure how much he remembers of what happened that day at the lake. When I worked up the nerve to ask him once he said he remembers being sick in the hospital and dreaming that he was underwater.

Sometimes, he said, *I hear a staticky noise in my left ear and I think that's what it is—the sound of being underwater.*

He says he doesn't have any memories from before the hospital.

I click on the last message from the thread with Lila. It's from Rudy last night—or rather early yesterday morning—at 5:30 A.M.

Where are you? You're freaking me out!

I wonder if the police have Lila's phone and have read that. If so, it only shows that he was worried about her.

I scroll upward through a dozen more of the same—all the texts on Rudy's side of the screen.

What's wrong?
What did I say?
I know there's something you're not telling me!
Can we talk?
Where are you?

All sent after they fought in the woods. None answered. I scroll farther up until I find the last text Lila sent to him. It's from three weeks ago.

What you did was unforgivable. Period. What's left to talk about?

Shit. What had Rudy done? And what would the police make of that if they were reading Lila's texts? I scroll up through the back-and-forth bubbles—the ones on Lila's side long and pendulous, on Rudy's side short blips—trying to make sense of the argument in reverse. I finally give up and scroll to the beginning of the thread. It starts with a seemingly innocuous text from Rudy:

Hey where you been? You left rehearsal without saying goodbye

Sorry, Lila had responded with a sad emoji face, *busy. Roommate drama and then my source on that history site came through.*

Your source?
You know, the one I told you about!
You mean your stalker?
*Not a stalker! Probably a fifty-year-old librarian bored
    out of her skull.*
How do u even know it's a girl
Cuz why would a guy call themselves that?
Sexist
No just real. Would you brag about that?

When there was no immediate response from Rudy, Lila had added: *Hello? Earth to Rudy? Did I hit a nerve?*

No, he finally responded, *I'm just worried about you. Are you meeting up with your source IRL?*

Got to. The clue is in a diary she has for me.
He
*She. Anyway we're meeting in a LIBRARY. What's she
    gonna do? Brain me with the OED?*
OED?
A big book dummy. GTG see u rehearsal tomorrow
    ♥♥♥

Then the next day there was another text from Lila:

*I can't believe you did that that's such a violation of
    privacy after all the times I listened to you complain
    about your mom's snooping*
I was worried about you . . .

*That's no excuse that's what your MOM says! Forget it
    I can't even text right now I'm so mad!!!*
Can't we just talk?
*What you did was unforgivable. Period. What's left to
    talk about?*

Something needles the nape of my neck, something . . . *icy.*
I click on the Unknown Sender on the text screen. There are
only two conversation bubbles, one on each side. On Rudy's
there is a question: *Are you IceVirgin33?*

And then the answer on the other side: *Why don't you come
find out?* Followed by a pin on a map of Portland.

I look at the time stamp on the message and that needle
penetrates my spine and floods my veins with ice water: 4:36 A.M.
Unknown sent that taunting message only an hour ago.

I pick up my phone as I leave Rudy's room, fumbling with
the Find My Phone app on the dark stairs. While the compass
floats back and forth I open the garage door. One of our matching Subarus is gone. I look down at the phone. A map of coastal
Maine appears, white fingers probing into blue water.

Look at that, Harmon said in disgust once when he looked
at my map app, *they can't even figure out Maine geography. They
can't tell the water from the land.*

That must be it, I tell myself, willing my heart to stop pounding. It's just a glitch that makes it look as if Rudy's phone is at
the bottom of Casco Bay.

CHAPTER FOURTEEN

I should, of course, go upstairs and tell Harmon. I should certainly ask for his permission to take his car. But I do neither. Harmon's car keys are in the bowl by the front door (where mine were, making it easy for Rudy to have taken them) and I pluck them out stealthily lest their jangle wake him. I'm just trying to spare him the aggravation, I tell myself as I change into jeans and a sweatshirt from the pile on the dryer. He needs his sleep after the stressful day he's had, I think generously as I get behind the wheel of his Forester. I hope he'll forego his morning jog and that I'm back before he wakes up, I promise myself as I tap in the location IceVirgin33 provided. Only thirty-eight minutes, my phone tells me. *See,* I imagine telling my Luddite husband, *technology has its uses.* As I back out of the garage, though, I remember that dot pulsing off the coast and feel as if I'm once again diving after Rudy into cold water. Only this time I'm afraid he may have gone deeper than I can follow. He is, after all, going to meet a dead man.

Because that must be who IceVirgin33 is, I finally admit to

myself as I follow the dark coastal road: Luther. Luther was obsessed with that Hans Christian Andersen story. He'd named his son after the hero. Of course it's the name he would use to lure our son back into his orbit.

This is not the first time I've wondered if Luther is really dead. In my nightmares he swims away and lurks under the dock, waiting for his chance to spring out of the dark and drag us down to a watery death like the ice virgin does in the story. I wake from those nightmares screaming and kicking the sheets away—kicking Harmon away—gasping for breath, bathed in icy sweat.

No wonder Harmon often sleeps in the guest room.

The only way I can comfort myself after those nightmares is to ask myself why, if Luther was alive, he hasn't come for Rudy.

But here's the answer. He's been waiting for the perfect time to ruin us. Waiting for the best way to infiltrate our lives, to destroy the fragile peace I've worked so hard to build. And how better to do it than through Lila: trusting, idealistic Lila. I imagine him lurking on the Internet looking for a way to reach Rudy and then finding Lila. He had reached out to her, offering help with her historical project and . . . what? The thought of Luther Gunn in the same room with Lila turns me cold despite the seat warmers, despite the flush of orange spreading over the bay as I cross the bridge into Portland. I think back to the text messages I'd read. Lila thought that IceVirgin33 was an old lady librarian. She must have come down here to meet her. What would she have thought when she found a middle-aged man (Luther would be fifty-three by now)? Would she have been put off by him—or was Luther still as charming and handsome as he'd been at thirty-six? Had he seduced Lila? Is that why she'd been acting so strange these last few weeks? What would Luther have told her about Rudy? I wonder as the cool robotic voice of the map app guides me through the streets of downtown Portland. What would he have told her about me?

You have arrived at your destination, the map app announces. I pull up behind my green Forester, which is empty, and look up at a three-story Federalist townhouse painted creamy white with black shutters and a hand-lettered sign reading CORA ROCKWELL HOUSE. I pick up my phone and switch to Find My Phone. Rudy's blue dot appears at this location. I get out and walk over to the other Forester. Rudy's phone is lying on the tan leather seats. I feel a chill run down my spine. When does a teenager ever voluntarily give up his phone?

"Excuse me?" I turn to find a young woman with dark heavy bangs in a red duffel coat. "Do you know whose car this is? It's parked in the director's spot and he'll have a fit."

"Do you work here?" I ask.

She nods. "I'm the librarian."

"What's the director's name?" I demand.

She pushes her bangs aside as if that will give her a clearer picture of me. "Hamish Pierson?" Her voice goes up at the end as if it's a question. I'm about to ask if she's asking me, which is what I do when my students put question marks at the end of their statements, but it occurs to me that might not be the best way to get her help. The director's not Luther—or if he is Luther he's using a fake name.

"This is my car," I tell her, "but my son drove it here. Without permission," I add with a sigh. "My husband's going to be very angry. I was hoping I could find my son and get the car back before my husband notices."

"My dad would have my head if I took his car without permission," she says, her eyes widening beneath the heavy curtain of her bangs. She's youngish—mid to late twenties—and stylish in a self-consciously nerdy fashion: heavy tights, black and white saddle shoes, carrying a vintage book satchel.

"Did you see a young man leave the car?"

She shakes her head. "It was here when I got here. Can you call your son?"

I point to the phone on the car seat. "That won't do much good." I don't tell her that I tracked Rudy here. It won't endear her to me. I can see her working it out, though, and it gives me an idea.

"I had a feeling he was coming here because it's where his friend was recently doing some research. Lila Zeller? Did you meet her? She's—*was*—a senior at the school where I teach."

"The girl who died." She covers her mouth with a gloved hand. The gloves are white cotton with red buttons at the cuffs. "I heard about it on the radio. She had just asked for copies of all the Bagleiana, ironically."

"The what? And ironic how?"

Two red spots appear on her cheeks, perfect matches to the buttons on her gloves. "I didn't mean to sound so . . . *cold* . . . We call the materials related to the Bagley disappearance the Bagleiana—it's our most popular draw, and also a professional obsession of mine; it's really why I'm here. Noreen Bagley was sixteen when she disappeared and it happened at the same location . . . only . . ."

"Lila didn't disappear," I finish for her.

"Well," she says, "Noreen Bagley didn't really either. Her body was found a year later."

"Oh," I say, thinking that Luther didn't include that detail in his campfire story. "I didn't know that they found her."

"A lot of people don't," the young woman says. "Lost girl always sounds better than dead girl."

I have no real response to this so I glance back at the parked car with Rudy's phone in it. I could go looking for him, but where would I even start? He'll come back . . . and if he doesn't . . .

"I'll wait an hour," I tell her. "And yes, I'd love to see the . . . what did you call it?"

"Bagleiana," she says, pressing her red-lipsticked lips together. Her eyes are bright beneath her heavy bangs, unable to hide her delight. I have to admit I'm intrigued as well. A cult surrounding a missing girl. Maybe what I am is jealous. No one ever formed a cult around *my* disappearance.

MY GUIDE INTRODUCES herself as Lucinda Perkins as she shows me into the townhouse. It's cold inside, as these New England buildings are. She switches on lights, cranks the heater up, and turns on an electric kettle, all while chattering about "the Bagley affair," as she calls it.

"Of course it's not as famous as the Bennington Triangle but I think that's because Shirley Jackson wrote a book based on *that*."

I vaguely recall hearing about the Bennington Triangle in a course I took on horror fiction. "That was about . . . a college sophomore who went missing?" I ask as Lucinda offers me a seat at a round oak table in a room that looks more like a nineteenth-century parlor than a library. Loud floral wallpaper in shades of green and pink covers the walls, clashing with a William Morris patterned rug. It's like being inside a Victorian candy box.

"Paula Jean Welden, age eighteen. She took a hike on the Long Trail and was never seen again alive. A statewide search ensued. Her father was a rich designer, so he had the money to spend. Noreen Bagley's father was a well-to-do Boston doctor but he'd recently remarried and didn't seem particularly interested in pouring money into a search for her. It was assumed she'd run away." She peels off her red coat to reveal a plaid skirt and a white blouse with a Peter Pan collar. She looks like a schoolgirl from the late 1950s. She keeps on the white gloves as she removes file folders and boxes from a black lacquered cabinet.

"Missing girls aren't all the same; the rich ones get much more attention than anyone poor. But a lot of girls go missing every year; they always have. When Cora Rockwell was the matron of the Refuge she kept track of them. She was headmistress at Haywood when Noreen went missing."

"Lila Zeller was writing a paper on Cora Rockwell," I say. "My husband was helping her."

Lucinda places a book in front of me. It's covered in a sober green cloth, frayed at the edges to reveal the cheap cardboard underneath. "Cora Rockwell's diary," she says. "I've bookmarked the relevant sections."

I start to open it but Lucinda slaps down a pair of white cloth gloves on the table before I can. "If you don't mind." It's a command, not a request.

I pull on the gloves and open the book to where Lucinda has placed a slip of paper. The lined pages are filled with a round schoolgirl-ish script. The first entry is for November 10, 1963.

The Maiden Stone has claimed its latest victim, it reads, *another girl has gone missing.*

CHAPTER FIFTEEN

Lucinda Perkins makes a pot of tea while I begin reading. She uses a teapot and loose tea, and puts out china cups and English biscuits. She turns on the radio, tuned to the local NPR station, which features classical music and hosts who speak in muted tones. When I look out the bow window to check that both Foresters are still there my eyes fall on the floral wallpaper, the framed pictures of girls in old-fashioned dresses, and arrangements of dried flowers and needlepoint samplers. I feel like I've traveled back to another era—to a school matron's parlor sometime in the middle of the last century. Back to 1963, five years after the Refuge became a school for girls and Cora Rockwell became its first headmistress.

The Maiden Stone has claimed its latest victim; another girl has gone missing.

She sounds exactly like the kind of woman who would pick this dreadful wallpaper and collect dead flowers. Entering her world feels like squeezing into a closet full of mothballs and mildewed shawls, but it's where Lila went before me, so I take a deep breath and follow.

The Maiden Stone has claimed its latest victim; another girl has gone missing. Noreen Bagley. At first I have to admit I barely noticed she was gone. Most of the girls went home for Fall Break and when Miss Jessym informed me that Noreen wasn't in her English class Monday morning we agreed she might have chosen not to return.

"She hasn't really been fitting in, has she?" Jessym remarked. "I'm not sure she's cut out to be a Haywood Girl."

I refrained from asking what exactly that meant since a scant five years ago a Haywood Girl was one who'd found herself in trouble. Jessym previously worked at Miss Porter's and can be a bit of a snob. Noreen's father, while quite well-off, is what Jessym would call *nouveau riche*. I did have to agree with her, though, that Noreen has not made a smooth transition to Haywood since the tragic death of her mother last autumn. She's known to frequently burst into tears during chapel, pen lugubrious poems in English class, and mope around the woods collecting fern specimens for her Nature Book. It seemed all too likely that she had simply decided not to return after the break.

When I called her father he didn't at first seem

to know if Noreen had gone back to school or not. Which seemed strange until he explained that he had been out of town himself and Noreen had been staying in their Back Bay townhouse by herself.

"Father seems rather uninterested," I remarked to Jessym.

"I hear he remarried—a rich widow from Providence. Did you try the housekeeper?"

I called the house again and after a long rambling speech from a Mrs. Hughes determined that Noreen had taken a train to Portland on the last Saturday of the break. Jessym and I went to her room then. She has a single in West Elm, rare for a junior but she had a letter from her family doctor saying she gets migraines and often needs to lie quietly in the dark. It was a lonely room—no pictures on the wall, just Latin declensions and French history dates thumbtacked to the wall. And a list of girls.

Barbara Hampton

Priscilla Barnes

Shirley Eames

"Who are they?" Jessym asked.

"Wayward girls," I said, taking the list down. No one needed to see that. "Girls who ran away."

"Hm," Jessym said, "perhaps they gave her the idea of running away herself. Perhaps when she got to the train station she decided to take a train somewhere else. I sometimes look at the departure board in South Station and think, Wouldn't it be jolly to take the *Silver Meteor* to Miami or the *Lake Shore Limited* to Chicago?"

"What would you do in Chicago?"

"Oh, I wouldn't stop there; I'd keep on going. To New Mexico or California. Somewhere *warm.*"

"I don't see Noreen Bagley thinking anything was jolly," I said, looking around at the bare room. "And she has the kind of skin that splotches in the sun."

I have to admit, though, that I was encouraged by the idea that she'd gone missing en route to Haywood. It's been hard enough establishing a reputation for a school founded on the bones of a refuge for fallen girls. Mr. Haywood, our director, has been most particular in the selection of girls—only from the best families, he insists—and has appointed his nephew, Haywood Hull, to look over the application letters himself.

Already the girls are spreading rumors about the Maiden Stone. I caught Sloane, the groundskeeper, telling stories about girls who went missing when we were still a refuge, and I had to speak very sternly to him. I would have fired him but of course I needed Mr. Haywood's permission for that and he, tenderhearted man that he is, said he knew the family and didn't want to see his six children go hungry.

"Maybe he should have left his wife alone if he couldn't feed all those children," Jessym remarked.

It was Sloane who found Noreen's suitcase stowed in the luggage room. Then Miss Bealle, out leading her class on a nature walk, spotted Noreen's red cap perched on the Maiden Stone. One of the girls remembered Noreen knitting the cap in Home Economics, botching the reindeer pattern so all the deer looked lame. Another girl said that Noreen had been so upset when the senior girls told the story of the Maiden Stone that she hadn't slept for a week.

"Suddenly they all have a story about Noreen Bagley when they probably couldn't have recalled her name a week ago," Jessym observed.

It was interesting, I thought, that Jessym had gone from thinking of Noreen as a girl from "not the right family" to an object of sympathy, but then, I'm beginning to notice that what I thought was snobbery is a protective defense.

"We'll have to search the woods," I said.

Woody Hull, who's home from Harvard, organized the search parties and volunteered his own hunting hounds to help. I took him to Noreen's room to select a piece of her clothing to give his hounds the scent. Poor boy. He looked so embarrassed when he saw Noreen's room; I don't think he's ever been in a girl's room! But he's been most generous with his time. I recalled that he had organized nature hikes for the girls when it was a refuge.

"Are you sure that's all generosity?" Jessym inquired. "Perhaps he simply likes being surrounded by pretty girls."

"Most of those girls weren't very pretty," I pointed out. "Or very nice. I should know; I was one of them."

Mr. Hull's efforts were rewarded with sad results. A red duffel coat was discovered in an inlet on the oceanward side of Maiden Island, a single black and white Oxford shoe came in with the tide on Kennebec Beach, and a white kid glove was found in a lobster trap. It seems likely, therefore, that Noreen hiked out to Maiden Island and then either fell from a cliff or tried to cross the causeway when the tide was coming in and was swept out to sea.

"Poor girl," Jessym remarked with surprising fondness. She's not only not as snobbish as she pretends to be—she's not as hard-hearted either. When I told her my own history she responded quite warmly.

"You should be proud of what you've accomplished coming from where you do. These girls are lucky to have you."

"Noreen Bagley wasn't lucky," I replied. I can't help thinking that I failed her. Like those girls who suddenly remember things about Noreen it comes to me now that she asked me about the Maiden Stone once. She said she was writing a paper on local folklore for Mr. Hume's class and wanted to know if any girls had gone missing during my tenure as matron of the Refuge.

I may have been a bit brusque. I don't encourage the girls to dwell on the school's history. What could these pampered daughters of the rich know about those girls who came to the Refuge as a last resort?

"Certainly there were girls who ran away," I told her, "but nobody much cared what became of them. They were lost before they came here."

I told Jessie what I'd said and she told me not to be so hard on myself. She also told me in her usual offhanded way that she'd miss me if I went missing and I wasn't to go moping about Maiden Island. Then she made a totally inappropriate remark that I won't set down here but that cheered me up considerably.

I spoke with Mr. Hull the next day and he told me that they were calling off the search. "Poor girl," he said, "I wonder if she knew when she made that list of missing girls that she'd be the next one on it?"

I couldn't sleep that night. I kept picturing Noreen taking the train to Portland a whole day early because she wasn't any more at home in Boston than she was here. And when I did sleep I had dreams of Noreen's list of the other missing girls, the names floating on the waves, then back on her wall. All night I took that list down, put it back, chased it on the waves, and followed it down to the salty depths.

In the morning I knew what I had to do. I went to see Mr. Haywood and tendered my resignation. We discussed my severance package. I'm quite satisfied with the results. I've had my eye on a house in Portland, near enough to keep up with my former colleagues and students, but far enough to be able to live quite independently. I've asked Miss Jessym if she'd like to share my retirement. "It's not Florida or New Mexico," I told her, to which she replied, "It might as well be."

And so.

I packed up poor Noreen's belongings to send to her father but when I phoned to ask what address I should ship them to, the housekeeper informed me that Mr. Bagley had moved house to Providence and is selling the Boston house. "I don't see that he'd want the girl's things," she told me. "Better to give them to charity."

Perhaps it would be better but I can't bring myself to do it. I'll bring Noreen's things with me to Portland along with some other souvenirs of my time here at Haywood. Some might say it's ghoulish to hang on to the past, but I think it's the least I can do. After all, if I don't remember these girls, who will?

THE NEXT PAGE I turn to is empty and I feel an echo of that emptiness in my own heart. I remember that when Luther told this story around the campfire I'd identified with Noreen—a motherless girl whose father had remarried, whom no one cared enough about to look for. But one person, at least, did care enough to keep her belongings.

"Did Cora write anything else about Noreen Bagley?" I ask Lucinda Perkins, who is standing by the window, her hands folded in front of her as if waiting for someone. "Did she ever learn anything more about what happened to her?"

"No," she says, turning to me. "She never kept a diary again. But I think all this"—she waves her gloved hand at the room— "was a tribute to Noreen and the other lost girls."

I get up to take a closer look at the framed photographs on the walls and the objects arrayed on the tables and in glass cases. The photographs are all of young girls, some in posed groups standing in front of the Haywood gates, or seated in classrooms, playing hockey, dancing around a maypole, skating on a frozen pond. But there are also photographs of girls stirring huge vats of laundry and girls lined up in identical canvas smocks, their faces grim and starved looking. These photographs are from the Refuge, not the school. The individual portraits are labeled: *Barbara Hampton, Priscilla Barnes, Shirley Eames.*

"These are the girls on Noreen Bagley's list," I say.

"Yes," Lucinda says, "the girls who went missing from the Refuge. Cora became obsessed with them. She clipped out newspaper articles." She motions to a framed article with the headline "Girl Runs Away from Refuge" and another titled "Mystery of the Maiden Stone Still Lingers." "All these samplers too were done by the girls. Here, this is Noreen's Nature Book."

The book is in a glass display case, open to a page with pressed wildflowers, their names written in an awkward schoolgirl's hand. Arrayed in the same case are a red knit cap, a single soiled glove, and a black and white saddle shoe.

"Are those . . . ?"

"The cap that was found on the Maiden Stone and the glove that washed up on Kennebec Beach. We've got the coat too, but it started to smell so the director put it away."

"Why in the world did she keep all this?" I ask.

"That's the question, isn't it?" Lucinda asks with a coy smile. "She writes that it's because no one else will remember the girls unless she does, but I think she felt responsible for what happened to them." Lucinda takes a step closer to me, her eyes shining. "Noreen came to Cora asking questions about the missing girls and Cora brushed her off. Then Noreen went missing. I think Cora saw that as a warning: Ignore the missing girls at your peril! Frankly, though, I think it makes more sense the other way around."

"The other way around?" I ask, beginning to feel dizzy. I feel like all the girls are looking out of the photographs at me. *You could have been one of us,* they seem to say. That is, if anyone had missed me when I went away with Luther. My own father didn't even try to find me. When I called him after I came back to Haywood he said he'd assumed I'd get in touch when I ran out of money. We haven't been in touch since.

"I mean," Lucinda says, "Noreen Bagley was asking questions about the missing girls and she went missing. Now that girl Lila Zeller was asking about the missing girls and she shows up dead."

I shiver at Lucinda's choice of words. *Shows up dead.* What a ghoulish way of putting it. This whole place is ghoulish. I'm suddenly anxious to be gone. "Would it be possible for me to get a copy of this section of Cora's diary?"

Lucinda bites her lip. The two red spots return to her cheeks. "Well, the director's not here to ask but . . . I suppose since you're connected to Haywood it would be all right. Just wait here a moment."

She leaves the room, those hard-soled saddle shoes clattering on the parquet floor in the hallway. I look at the photographs while she's gone. There's one of the cliff at Maiden Island and a framed newspaper article about Noreen Bagley's disappearance with a picture of the girl. She's squinting at the camera from under heavy bangs, wearing a blouse with a Peter Pan collar and a plaid skirt under a duffel coat. She looks like she's flinching, as if someone just said something mean to her, or as if she knows something bad is going to happen to her. That it will take three days before anyone will even notice she's gone.

"At least they *did* notice," I say aloud to her.

"What did you say?"

I turn, embarrassed that I've been caught talking aloud to a photograph of a dead girl, and it's like Noreen Bagley is standing in front of me. The same heavy bangs, Peter Pan collar, plaid skirt, and saddle shoes. Lucinda Perkins is dressed just like Noreen Bagley—down to the white kid gloves, which I realize now match the soiled one in the display case. She's turned Noreen Bagley into a fetish. This whole place has made Noreen and the other girls into a cult—a museum of lost girls.

"Here's the copy," she says, handing me a manila envelope. "I was wondering if I could ask for something in return."

"What?" I ask warily. Does she recognize me as one of the lost girls that belong in this creepy museum?

"Since you were Lila's teacher you might have something of hers. Might you consider donating some memento—a handwritten essay or piece of clothing—to the museum? After all, she's part of this story now."

What I consider is slapping Lucinda's painted doll's face, but before I can respond I catch a flicker of movement from the window. One of the Foresters is pulling away from the curb. I've been so busy with this nonsense that I missed Rudy coming back.

I snatch the envelope out of Lucinda's hand and grab my coat. "Lila's story is her own," I say. "You can leave her that at least."

CHAPTER SIXTEEN

When I get outside I find a note under my windshield wiper. *Don't bother following me.* The words smear in the rain as I read them. *I'm going straight home.*

Crap.

I try Rudy's phone but it goes to voicemail. I could tell him it was a coincidence that I showed up here. That Lila had mentioned the Cora Rockwell House and I'd come to see if its employees could shed any light on her last days—

At seven in the morning? I imagine him saying. *Stalker.*

The back of my neck prickles with the shame of being caught in the act. It feels like being watched—

I look up from the phone with the sudden feeling that I *am* being watched. The windows of the Rockwell House glare back at me, opaque in the rain. I can't see through them, but I do catch a movement in one of the street-level windows, like a shark moving through murky water. I turn around and see a black Saab turning the corner. I hadn't noticed it approaching. Had it been idling across the street with someone inside, watching me?

Could it be Luther?

I get in, start my car with shaking hands, and pull away from the curb without stopping to put on my seatbelt. The Forester pings indignantly. I turn the corner and spot the Saab three blocks away, idling in the rain at a green light. It moves as soon as I do—or at least that's what it seems like. I imagine Luther inside, watching for me in his rearview mirror, smiling as he sees me take the bait.

On the island, Luther taught me how to fish. *You have to stay completely still until you feel a bite, then reel her in smoothly and steadily. Don't give her a chance to get away.*

When I think back to how things began between me and Luther I see how he lured me into his orbit, bit by bit, dangling praise and acknowledgment—a word or two on a paper, a smile at the end of class, a concerned question, a brush against my arm, a private conference, chance meetings on woodland paths . . . I thought I was pursuing him. But he had been steadily reeling me in, like a fish caught on a hook.

As he is now. He goes slow enough for me to keep pace with him on the slick streets, stopping at stop signs but speeding through yellow lights so I won't get too close. I follow as if pulled by a hook in my gut through increasingly seedier and emptier streets. Where is he leading me? What will he do when we get there? And why am I following despite the sick feeling in my stomach? If it really is Luther in that car, do I want to confront him at the end of some dark alley?

We're near the waterfront now. I can smell the sea. The Saab turns and turns again, always threatening to vanish in the murky gray rain, leading me through a maze of tight, narrow streets. I only have time to glimpse the rear lights through the rain at each turn. Is he trying to lose me?

I make a turn and the Saab is no longer in front of me, but there's only one way to go now. Down to the water. I open the windows to clear the fog from my head, and the smell of the ocean floods in with a gust of rain. I have the feeling that he's leading me straight into the water. That he's going to plunge into the bay and dare me to follow. The scary thing is I have the sick feeling that I will.

I come out onto a street facing the water. The Saab is across the street. As I watch, it begins to move away. For a second I have the feeling that it is floating on the water—and it is. It's on the flatbed of a ferry leaving for one of the islands in the Casco Bay. As it vanishes into the fog I read the license plate.

IceVrgn33.

I DRIVE HOME feeling as frozen as if I had followed Luther into the bay. Luther must have been the one driving that car. He is alive. And he's made contact with Rudy. It's my worst nightmare—or at least it was my worst nightmare until Lila died only yards away from where Rudy last saw her. Did Luther get in touch with Lila first? Was he trying to contact Rudy through her? And did she tell Rudy that she'd met his father? Did she pass on something Luther said that so upset Rudy that he lashed out and she fell to the rocks below?

The scene plays out in my head as I drive through the drizzle and fog back to Rock Harbor. Lila met Luther online and he lured her down to the Rockwell House with the promise of the missing girls. Was it a coincidence that he'd reached out to

Rudy's girlfriend, or had he been lurking at the edge of our lives looking for a way in? He shows her the Cora Rockwell diary and uses it to broach the subject of who he really is: Rudy's long-lost father. He'd spin a version of the tale in which I was the harridan who stole Rudy away from his father. Would Rudy believe it? Is that why he's been so distant with me? The thought of Luther anywhere near Rudy makes me sick to my stomach.

When I get home I'm relieved to see my car in the driveway, but then I see a police car next to it and my heart jolts in my chest. I park crookedly next to the other Forester even though Harmon will be upset that I didn't put his car in the garage.

When I enter through the front door I hear voices coming from the dining room. Rudy's voice, plaintive and pleading. His back is to me as I enter the dining room. He's seated on one side of the table. Kevin Bantree, Officer Gough, and Harmon are lined up on the other like a firing squad.

"What's going on?" I demand. "Shouldn't there be a lawyer present?" I look at Harmon. "Why are you letting him talk to the police without a lawyer?"

"Hold on, Tess," Harmon says. "I think you should get your facts straight before you charge on in."

This is something Harmon often says to his students. Right now it feels patronizing. "An accused's right to a lawyer is a fact," I counter.

"I think you should stop and listen to your husband," Kevin Bantree says. "No one has accused Rudy of anything. He called me to share some information."

I look down at Rudy. He doesn't look at me. I notice that the table is covered with papers. Copies of newspaper articles with the now familiar photograph of Noreen Bagley and copies of lined handwritten pages that I recognize as Cora Rockwell's diary.

"What's all this?" I ask.

"Rudy was just telling us," Harmon says with the exaggerated patience he uses for a tardy student. "If you sit down I'm sure he'll be happy to go over it again for you."

I sit down next to Rudy, aligning myself with him. I want to ask about Luther but instead I say, "What did you find, Rudy?"

He drags the photo of Noreen Bagley over without looking up at me. "Lila was writing her paper about one of the girls who came to Haywood when it was still a refuge for so-called fallen girls. She had this idea that a lot of the girls who got sent there weren't even pregnant, they were just . . . you know . . ." His cheeks turn red. Maybe that's why he won't look at me. He's embarrassed to be talking about sex in front of his mother.

"Promiscuous?" I supply.

Rudy nods, turning redder. "Yeah, she said it didn't even have to be like the girls were sluts or anything just, like, they flirted or wore sexy clothes or talked back . . . like how they put girls away in those Irish Laundromats."

"The Magdalene Laundries," I supply.

"Why don't we let Rudy tell the story," Harmon says. "He's been doing an excellent job."

Rudy astonishes me by giving Harmon a grateful look and then, still not looking at me, goes on, "Yeah, so what Lila noticed was some of these girls had babies after they'd been at the Refuge for more than nine months, which meant they weren't pregnant when they got there. Lila thought that maybe someone at the refuge was raping these girls. Then some of these girls disappeared. No one made much of a fuss about them disappearing because they were just . . . you know, *bad* girls and everyone assumed they must've just run away or something. But then Lila read about a girl named Noreen Bagley who went missing *after* Haywood became a school. People did make a fuss about her. Lila had this idea that maybe the same person who had been raping those girls also killed Noreen Bagley. So she looked at the records to see which employees were there while the girls were getting pregnant *and* when Noreen Bagley went missing, and she found three people: a janitor, a groundskeeper, and the matron of the Refuge, who became the headmistress of the school. Lila found a site online dedicated to the lost girls and that led her to a museum in Portland that belonged to the headmistress, Cora Rockwell. So she went down there and found Cora Rockwell's diary. She was really excited about it but when she came back she wouldn't talk about it. I . . . I think she was upset about something she found out."

I notice that Rudy doesn't mention the fight he had with Lila about the librarian. Or that Lila had stopped talking to him.

"So after what happened . . . after Lila died, I thought maybe she'd found out something bad about someone, like who had raped those girls back then and killed Noreen Bagley."

"Anyone old enough to assault a girl in the 1950s would be pretty old by now," Kevin says.

"Yeah, exactly," Rudy says. "Here, look . . ." He sifts through the pages until he finds one with a big marker circle around a couple of sentences. "It says here that Mr. Haywood put his nephew in charge of picking girls for the school. His nephew was—"

"Woody Hull," I say, unable to stop myself. I'm remembering the time I went to his office. How *small* he made me feel.

"Just because Woody Hull was at the school doesn't mean he had anything to do with those girls," Harmon says.

"But this does," Rudy says, grabbing another page. His voice falters the way it does when he's proud of himself, a hairline crack in his joy. I wonder sometimes if my son will ever feel pure, unblemished happiness without doubting himself. "See here where she quotes him saying that thing about the list of missing girls in Noreen Bagley's room? And then Ms. Rockwell dreams about the list, putting it up, taking it down. Something bothered her about it. I didn't see it at first, but when I read it over I realized Ms. Rockwell took down the list before she showed the rooms to Hull so . . ."

"Woody Hull couldn't have seen that list unless he'd been in Noreen's room before," I say.

"Exactly," Rudy says, rewarding me with a quick, feverish glance.

"That's not enough to accuse a man of rape and murder," Bantree says.

"There's more," Rudy counters. "See how Ms. Rockwell goes to Mr. Haywood the next day. She suddenly decides to retire. She's even picked out a fancy house in Portland. How does an unmarried schoolteacher afford a house like that?"

Rudy grew up hearing me complain about the low salary of a teacher; I'm briefly gratified to hear that something I said sank in.

"She could have had family money," Officer Gough says.

"But she didn't," Harmon says. "Cora Rockwell was a wayward girl herself. She came from abject poverty."

"Yeah, so what if she told Mr. Haywood that if he didn't pay up she'd expose his nephew as a rapist and a murderer?"

"This is all conjecture," Kevin says. "There's nothing solid here to prove Woody Hull had anything to do with those girls in the fifties and sixties and nothing to tie him to Lila's death."

"Lila would have submitted her paper to him," I say.

"He says she didn't," Officer Gough says.

"You can at least check to see if he has an alibi for the time Lila was killed," Harmon says.

"I can," Kevin says, rising to his feet. "And I will, but I wouldn't get your hopes up. He's in his seventies and none too fit. I doubt he can even walk to the Point."

Officer Gough gets up with him but she's looking down at Rudy. "This was some pretty impressive detective work," she tells him. "You should think about a career in law enforcement."

I expect Rudy to roll his eyes or smirk but he instead gives the young woman officer a grateful look that makes me envious.

Before he leaves, Kevin turns and says to Rudy, "Lila sounds like an extraordinary young woman. I promise I'll find who did this. In the meantime, I ask that you all keep this to yourself. And no more playing detective." He looks from Rudy back to me as if he knows what I've been up to. "Whoever killed Lila could kill again." He holds my gaze when he utters this warning, then turns and leaves.

CHAPTER SEVENTEEN

As soon as Kevin Bantree and Officer Gough leave Harmon turns to me. "I was worried sick when I came down here and found both cars missing." His face is ashen, deep lines carved around his eyes and blue shadows beneath them. He looks like he hasn't slept at all.

"I'm so sorry," I say. "When I saw that Rudy had gone I didn't think. I just took your car and followed him."

"How did you know where he'd gone?" Harmon asks.

"Yeah, Mom," Rudy chimes in, his bloodshot eyes accusing. "How'd you know?"

"I tracked your phone," I say, meeting his gaze. "I think your taking my car without asking merits a tracking."

"And you didn't think to let me know?" Harmon asks.

"I . . . I didn't want you to be mad at Rudy."

"Because that's the immediate reaction of everyone in this family," Rudy says. "'It must be Rudy's fault.'"

I'm going to point out that in this case he *had* taken my car without permission, but Harmon speaks up first. "You're right, son. You've taken the blame for a lot that's not your fault. I want you to know that I'm proud of the way you're trying to find out who hurt Lila. She was a remarkable young woman and she deserves justice."

Rudy nods and looks down, his hands gripped tightly in his lap. He's trying to keep from crying.

"That's all any of us want." I give Harmon a pleading look but he's looking down at his watch.

"I promised Bill Lyman I'd proctor his physics exam at noon so I have to go." He picks a piece of lint off his tweed jacket and straightens his tie. Harmon is always complaining that students use their phones to avoid making eye contact, but he has his own repertoire of avoidance techniques. He makes me wait several moments before he looks at me. "We'll talk later," he says, giving Rudy's shoulder a squeeze but pointedly avoiding touching me at all.

As soon as Harmon closes the door, Rudy gets up to go too.

"We have to talk," I say, reaching my hand out to touch his arm.

"There's nothing to talk about," he says, batting my arm away. "You didn't just stalk me; you read my texts."

"How—?" I begin but then I see by the flash of hurt in his eyes that I've just admitted to it. "Rudy, you have to understand how scared I've been for you. I . . . I saw that name IceVirgin33 on Jill's Twitter feed and I was afraid of who it might be."

"Say it," Rudy spits out. "You were afraid it was my father, who you said was dead. You were afraid you'd be exposed as a liar."

"I thought he *was* dead!" I cry, shaking at the confirmation that Rudy has indeed met Luther. "Don't you remember? When we left the lake he tried to stop us."

"I don't remember that," he says, shaking his head. His hands are balled into fists at his sides, his whole body tense with rage.

"It was awful," I say, trying to make my voice gentle to soothe him. "Your father . . ." *How to begin?* "Your father loved you very much," I say finally, "but he needed us to be perfect and when we weren't he grew angry and struck out at us. He wasn't safe to be around then. Whatever Luther has told you about me, or about Lila, you can't believe everything he says. He's very good at spinning stories."

Rudy doesn't answer at first, but I can see his fists relaxing. He's nodding, as if he'd already figured out what I'm telling him. Rudy is a smart boy, I remind myself, maybe he's already seen through Luther's act.

"Funny," he says, "that's what he said about you, that you were good at making up stories. He said that's what drew him to you in the first place—your creativity and imagination. And for your information, he does blame himself for getting involved with a teenager, but he said you seemed so lost and vulnerable. And then you came and told him you were pregnant. He couldn't let you face that on your own. Only later did he wonder if you'd gotten pregnant deliberately so that you'd have someone to look after you."

"That's not—" I begin but Rudy goes on, and I'm so mesmerized by this alternate account of my life that I can't summon any more objections. Even secondhand, the story Luther has spun is irresistible.

". . . By then he was afraid to leave you alone with me. He

said you tried to drown yourself when you were pregnant and that you caused me to be born prematurely. He said you were obsessed with becoming a writer and would ignore me while writing in your notebooks. That your imagination, which he'd always admired, had gotten out of control and become para- noia. That you accused him of breaking my arm when it was really your fault."

"That's not true," I object. "He made you climb a tree—he had this idea you should come by all these skills naturally— and you fell and broke your arm."

"He said that I was doing fine but that when you saw me you screamed and that's when I fell."

"I was terrified," I say, remembering the moment when I walked out of the cabin and saw Rudy stranded high on a shak- ing branch halfway up the tallest tree on the island. "And so were you."

"Because you made me scared of everything, just like you do now. That's why he tried to stop you from taking me away, but then you hit him over the head with an oar."

"I—" Once more I begin to object but then I remember that this is exactly the story I was going to tell Kevin Bantree. Do I really want to tell Rudy the truth?

"He said he almost drowned," Rudy goes on. "He dragged himself to the dock but because you'd taken the only boat, he couldn't get to the mainland. He was afraid to swim to shore because he was suffering a concussion. He had no way to get off the island. He stayed there, running out of food and wood, half crazy with fear that you had hurt me. He would have died except that a hunter found him—half starved, suffering from hypothermia—and took him to a hospital. When he recovered he got work as a logger up north. He felt like he'd failed us so totally that he didn't deserve us. But he never stopped thinking about me." He reaches into his pocket and takes out a carved wooden fox. "He's been carving animals for me all these years. When he gave this to me I suddenly remembered him carving these for me. I remembered him."

The tenderness in Rudy's voice shatters something in me. All these years I've protected Rudy from the truth of who his father was and now he's given him the love he's so rarely shown me.

"Do you remember him throwing the otter in the fire because you'd disobeyed him?" I ask bitterly, the words tumbling out of my mouth before I can stop them. "Do you remember asking me to hide the rest of the animals?"

Rudy looks up at me with haunted eyes. "He says you threw the otter in the fire and then hid all the rest of the animals."

I gasp. "Rudy, that's not true!"

"How can I believe anything you say when you've lied to me my whole life? You've lied to everyone. You told Harmon my father was a fisherman you hooked up with for a couple of weeks. You told Jill Frankel I saw a therapist in Boston when all we ever did was go to the Natural History Museum."

"What else could I do? I thought Luther was dead. I didn't want the police investigating his death."

"So you were protecting yourself." The hurt and accusation in his eyes are excruciating. The last time I saw that look he was huddled in the prow of the rowboat, watching his father grab me to pull me into the water to drown me. Maybe it's time he heard the truth.

"No, honey," I begin, my voice hoarse as if the words that have been unsaid for so long are rusty and barbed in my mouth. Can I really say them now? But if I don't—if Rudy believes Luther's lies—he'll be in greater danger than if he knows the truth. "I wasn't protecting myself; I was protecting you. I wasn't the one who hit Luther over the head; it was you."

I remember Luther's hand on my arm, pulling me into the water, and then the dull thud of wood hitting bone and Luther's hand loosening. When I looked up, Rudy's face looked like *he* had been struck. Then his whole body crumbled, like a puppet whose strings have been cut, and he fell into the water, vanishing beneath the blood-slick surface. I plunged in after him, diving blind, deeper and deeper, flailing my arms back and forth to find him . . .

Until my fingers grazed something—the lightest flutter of silk that might have been a trout's scales or lake grass sliding through my fingers, but that I knew were my boy's curls—the silky hair I loved to comb with my fingers—

I grabbed a hank of hair and dragged his limp, dead weight up, kicking with numb legs, my lungs burning, stars exploding in my brain. When I broke through the surface the air ripped through me, strafing my lungs, but Rudy was limp and deathly quiet. The boat was floating a few feet from us, the dock yards away. It would have been easier to swim back than to get Rudy and myself into the boat but I couldn't go back. I imagined Luther lurking beneath us, waiting to punish Rudy for what he'd done. I couldn't risk that.

Somehow I managed to drag us both into the boat. Rudy landed hard against the floor, cold and boneless as a fish. I fell on him, thumping his chest, then pressing my mouth to his and breathing air into his lungs.

Please please please, I prayed, *I'll give you anything.*

I don't know if I was praying to God or bargaining with the Ice Virgin Luther worshiped. What I do know is that I would have traded my soul to banish the cold from Rudy's flesh. I sometimes think I did. That I breathed some part of myself into his lungs that day, a part of myself I never got back.

When Rudy finally coughed up lake water into my face I wrapped him in my jacket and sat him in the prow of the boat. The sun was low in the sky and the temperature was dropping. I had to get Rudy someplace warm, someplace safe. I retrieved the oar floating in the water and rowed toward the store, keeping my eyes on Rudy, who sat huddled and shivering in the prow three feet away but as distant as a star in the sky.

That's how far away he looks now, absorbing the blow of what I've told him. I take a step forward and he flings up his arm to ward me off. "Liar! I didn't do that. I don't remember doing that."

"You only did it to save me," I say. "And I was wrong to keep it from you all these years. I was trying to protect you. But Luther isn't right, Rudy. Some kinds of love are selfish. He's dangerous. He manipulates people. Why else would he have made contact with Lila? He was trying to get to us through her."

"She contacted him. He'd posted something on a history site about the Noreen Bagley disappearance and she started writing back and forth with him. She met him at the Rockwell House and he showed her the diary. She guessed right away that Woody Hull was responsible for Noreen Bagley's death. She emailed Luther the night of the play and said she couldn't live with lies anymore. He was afraid she was going to confront Mr. Hull so he came up here, only when he got here he realized she had also figured out that he was my father and she'd gotten him up here to bring us together. He said he didn't want to surprise me like that so he left, after making her promise not to confront Woody Hull. *That's* what Lila and I fought about. I knew she was keeping something from me and she wouldn't say what. Luther explained that it was because he'd asked her not to tell me about him yet—" Rudy's voice breaks. "Don't you see? He was trying to leave us alone but after Lila died he realized that she went ahead and accused Woody Hull of the attacks on those girls and the murder of Noreen Bagley, and he killed her. Luther said he thought I had a right to know."

There are so many holes in this story I'm not sure where to start. Clearly Rudy has fallen under Luther's spell, as I once had. "Oh, honey," I say, stepping forward and reaching for him. "You can't trust him."

Rudy's face contorts with rage. "At least *he* believes I'm innocent. At least he doesn't think I killed Lila."

I feel as if I've been slapped. "Honey, I don't think you killed Lila."

"No? Then why did you come in here demanding a lawyer for me? Why did you assume that I was being accused?"

"I was only trying to look out for you—"

"Well, stop it!" he yells, his voice shaking with anger. "What has looking out for me ever done but made things worse? If you had just told me the truth in the first place we would have known Luther was alive. I could have grown up with a father. I wouldn't have grown up feeling like a freak."

"Oh, honey, I'm so so sorry. You're right. I should have told you the truth. I see that now. But you have to understand that I did everything I did out of love for you."

Rudy snorts, his face twisted in a cruel smirk. "What was it you just said? Some kinds of love are selfish? I think you were talking about yourself."

He starts walking for the door. I reach for him one last time and he yanks his hand up and pushes me away. I lose my balance and stumble against the table by the door. Everything goes flying—the crystal bowl, the loose change and keys, the potted African violet. I hit the floor with the rest of the junk. Rudy walks right past me and out the front door. I want to crawl up in a ball and cry but I can't; I have to follow him. I have to try again.

As I get to my feet, though, I hear a step behind me, coming from the kitchen. I turn around and see Harmon standing in the kitchen doorway with his favorite travel mug in his hand. "So," he says with a weak smile, "I guess Rudy's father wasn't an itinerant fisherman after all."

Then he turns and walks away, leaving me standing in the flotsam and jetsam of my shipwrecked life.

CHAPTER EIGHTEEN

had sometimes imagined how I would tell Rudy the truth
about his father. It would happen at some mythical time when
I sensed he was ready. Flush from a victory in ice hockey, perhaps, or after a day at the beach. Driving home we'd pick up donuts
and hot chocolate and park at the scenic overlook above the bay.
We'd both be looking straight ahead at the water so it would be
easier to begin. I'd start by telling him the story of the Ice Virgin.

I've heard that one, Mom, he'd say.

But did you know, I'd counter, *that it was your father's favorite
story?* I would tell him that his father was an English teacher,
that he was smart and handsome and that I fell in love with him
at a vulnerable time in my life. I wouldn't make excuses for the
decisions I made. *We're all responsible for our actions,* I'd say. *Or
as you kids put it, you got to own your own shit.* I'd imagined that
would earn me a smile.

Then I'd tell him that the reason "The Ice Virgin" was Luther's favorite story was that the hero's heart was frozen by his
childhood encounter with the Ice Virgin. *I don't know what*

happened to your father—he never spoke of his childhood—but I think something damaged him. Something left him with a frozen heart and he loved that story because it offered a cure. Rudy would be still and quiet, the way he was when we stood in front of those glass cases in the Museum of Natural History, and I would tell my story to our reflections in the car windshield.

I think that Luther believed that love could thaw the frozen part of him, and it did for a while. When he saw a vulnerable girl he could shelter, when he held his newborn son in his arms, I think his heart thawed. I think he loved us both very much but he needed us to reflect back the picture of himself he had created. I had to be the grateful girl he had saved. You had to be the perfect son who was one with nature, untarnished by civilization because he was raising you in the forest. He thought you should be able to swim the moment he threw you in water and climb trees when he told you to.

I'd push up his sleeve—for once he would let me—and show him the scar from when he fell from the tree. I'd push up my own sleeve and show him the burn mark from the hot fire poker. "He never meant to hurt us," I'd say, "but his anger made him strike out."

In no version of my story did I ever imagine that I would tell him that he had struck Luther to save me.

But that's the world I'm living in now. Of all the horrors of the last hour, that comes to me now as the worst. I kneel on the floor, sweeping up dirt and broken roots and petals as if I could fix what's broken by picking up the pieces. How can I ever fix what I've done? Somewhere inside Rudy is the memory of that moment when he lifted the oar and brought it down on his father's head, and now I have unlocked it.

I sweep the dirt into a dustpan and carry it into the kitchen, thinking everything through. Luther has gained Rudy's trust by giving him an alternate story that explains Lila's death. He's convinced him that Woody Hull is the killer—senile Woody Hull. How likely is that? I'd *like* to believe it. Woody Hull is a misogynistic, domineering bully. He responded to my attempt to report abuse by belittling and intimidating me. But I'm not the only one he hurt. He also fired Luther.

Sanctimonious hypocrite, Luther had called him, *like he isn't leering at all of you all the time. I bet he's screwed half a dozen Haywood girls over the years. He's definitely fucking that mealy-mouthed secretary of his, Jean.*

Ugh, I'd responded, sickened at the thought of balding, middle-aged Headmaster Hull leering after young girls. As if that made him any worse than Luther just because Luther was younger and handsomer. They were both predators. It had enraged Luther, though, that Hull had gotten away with his sins and was in a position to make Luther pay for his. He would want to punish Woody Hull.

And Lila had given him that opportunity.

I stand in the kitchen, still holding the dustpan full of dirt, suddenly cold. Cora Rockwell's diary was certainly an intriguing document. I could imagine Luther reading it with a keen eye, discerning the suggestion that Woody Hull was responsible for Noreen Bagley's death. But if he—a disgraced teacher—had come forward to accuse Woody, he'd be dismissed as a vindictive predator seeking revenge for his firing. But if an idealistic young girl like Lila brought the diary to light . . . Lila was the perfect vehicle for Luther's revenge. I can see him luring her to the Rockwell House, showing her the diary, letting her come to her own conclusions, knowing she'd confront Woody Hull—

And when she did Hull would have been furious. I remember the claw-like grip of his hand on my arm in the chapel. If they'd been standing on the Point he could have struck out at Lila and she could have fallen—

But why would Lila agree to meet him in an isolated spot? Wasn't it more likely that she'd meet Luther? Rudy said that Lila had asked Luther to come up the night of the play, the night Lila died. Maybe he said he wanted to meet Rudy and Lila agreed to facilitate. Maybe after Lila and Rudy fought he walked back out to the Point with her. Maybe they fought— and Luther pushed her from the Point.

My hands are shaking so hard that dirt falls from the dustpan. I have to tell someone what I suspect. But who? Kevin Bantree has no reason to believe me. He doesn't know Luther—

But Jean does. She was assistant to Hull when Luther worked here. Luther despised her and I believe the feeling was mutual. Jean will believe me that Luther is engineering the situation to incriminate Woody.

I dump the rest of the dirt in the garbage, not caring that I've left some on the kitchen floor. I have a bigger mess to clean up. I grab my coat and keys—and my book bag, which still contains Rudy's birth certificate, the domestic violence report, and the hospital report and picture. My head feels clear now despite the little sleep I've gotten. Once I've discredited Luther, Rudy will have to see my side of the story. And as Luther pointed out, I was always a good storyteller.

CHAPTER NINETEEN

My mood continues to brighten as I drive to campus. The rain has cleared, leaving a warm spring day—the kind of weather that transforms everything. There's so much water here in coastal Maine—folded in between fingers of land, seeping up from bog and fen—that the whole land reflects the sky. The bay, which was a dead gray yesterday, is now the iridescent blue of a crow's wing. The sun glitters on the manicured green lawns and gilds the old bricks of nineteenth-century Main Hall. Looking at it, you'd think the founders of the Refuge for Wayward Girls had only the best intentions in mind. It's an impressive building—perhaps a little foreboding—situated on prime Maine coastal property. Jean has told me, though, that when the Refuge closed and became a school the buildings were decrepit.

Roofs leaking, mold in the walls, rats in the basement. There was no indoor plumbing in the "cottages" where the girls lived, and those rooms were squalid and freezing. There was one nurse on staff for a hundred girls. When the influenza struck in 1918 more than thirty girls died. Only an influx of money from the Haywood family was able to restore the buildings to anything like usable and the maintenance is still a nightmare. I have to beg Woody for more money every year.

How will the accusation against Woody Hull affect the school's budget? I wonder. There are other benefactors, but none as significant as the Haywood family estate, all of which passed to Woody Hull when his uncle died in the late 1960s. Would the school survive financially, let alone in terms of reputation, if its chief benefactor and former headmaster is publicly accused of assault and murder?

Perhaps I shouldn't care so much. When I first came to Haywood I hated it. I felt like I'd been sent here as punishment, like those fallen girls who were sent here for pregnancy and promiscuity, and it felt foreign and intimidating. The girls all spoke a language I didn't understand—a prep school lingo full of references to other prep schools and vacation destinations and family connections that might as well have been the Latin that everyone mysteriously had to take. I didn't make friends. I struggled in every class but English, where my love of reading and Luther Gunn saved me.

Or destroyed me. When I found all the letters of dismissal that Luther had received before he came to Haywood I was too shocked at first about what they said about *him* to think about what it meant about *Haywood.* How had Woody Hull hired a man who'd been dismissed four times before? What kind of a man would do that? A man who was an abuser himself? A man capable of murder?

If Woody Hull had still been headmaster I would never have

come back here, but by the time I returned Jean had taken over. She had breathed new life into the school—modernizing the curriculum, pushing for more scholarships for low-income and minority students, diversifying the reading materials, and hiring younger and more progressive teachers from diverse backgrounds. And she had welcomed me back, first as an assistant and then, after arranging for a scholarship for me to go to college, as a teacher. Haywood under Jean has been a haven for me. As much as I'd be happy to see Haywood Hull go down I owe Jean a warning about this threat to the school. And if she can help me redirect attention to Luther Gunn, all the better.

I park in one of the visitor spots in front of Main, where prospective parents park, instead of the faculty lot behind Duke Hall. Purple and yellow tulips are blooming in an island of green grass, celebrating Haywood's school colors. A tasteful swath of ivy adorns the façade—*bad for the brick but it makes the parents imagine their children going to an Ivy League college,* Jean says—matching the green patina of the mansard roof. The brass insignia of Haywood—a Greek goddess bearing the fruits of learning—gleams on the old oak doors. I feel calmer already walking through the heavy doors into the hush of the carpeted foyer. Haywood has managed in just over half a century to shed its humble beginning as a refuge for wayward girls. *I have been able to reinvent myself here.* Surely Haywood and I will survive this crisis as well after Luther has been put away.

Jean's office is to the right of the entrance, down a short hall lined with tasteful sepia photographs of Haywood girls. Many are the same photos I saw hanging at Rockwell House, pictures of girls in classrooms or playing lacrosse, or dancing around a maypole, but absent are the photographs of girls stirring huge vats of laundry or lined up to look like prisoners. It is possible to look at these and imagine that Haywood has been a school for the privileged since the nineteenth century. Not that Jean has ever tried to hide Haywood's "humble origins," as she puts it in speeches and newsletters. She likes to stress the legacy of service and progressive ideals concordant with Haywood's mission to educate modern women. As if Haywood is somehow an extension of the Refuge.

Jean's assistant, Maryanne Galluci, is on the phone in the anteroom outside Jean's office. Maryanne was my replacement when I went from secretary to teacher, and I trained her. She's a much better secretary than I ever was and is handling the call with more aplomb than I would have managed.

". . . I completely agree with you, Ms. Wyatt, but I can assure you that the police are handling the investigation and security on campus is excellent. If, however, you want to take Dakota out now . . ." Seeing me she rolls her eyes. "Well, yes, I imagine return airfare from Gstaad *is* expensive. I'm sure Dakota has friends she could stay with . . . No, I'm afraid I can't tell you which of her friends might be going home early, that would be confidential . . ."

Is she in? I mouth, pointing to Jean's door. Maryanne covers the receiver on her headset and whispers, "For you, yes. She needs a friendly face."

I leave Maryanne to Dakota's mother and knock gently on Jean's door. I feel guilty that I'm getting in because Maryanne thinks I'll be a relief from the pressures Jean's under— especially when I see her. Bathed in the glow of her computer screen, Jean's face looks like it's aged ten years since yesterday. Her well-cut and highlighted hair is standing up on end and she's wearing the same blouse she wore to the chapel, only now it's wrinkled and limp. I picture her up all night answering emails and calls from anxious parents.

"Oh, thank God," she says, barely looking up from her screen, "someone sane. Just hold on while I finish this." She taps her keyboard briskly and finishes with a flourish. "There! I've sent out a campus-wide memo declaring the Point and its environs off limits and I've given Jill Frankel permission to go ahead with *The Crucible* memorial performance tonight. Honestly, I think it's a bizarre idea, but at least it will keep those girls busy until we can ship them home."

I remember that Jill was scheduling rehearsals last night before receiving permission but I don't tell Jean that. "I'm sure it will be fine. They need some kind of ceremony. Besides, this way I'll get to see it."

"Yes," Jean says absently as she looks up at me. "Dear Lord, Tess, you look worse than me. Are you all right? On top of everything else it must have been horrible having Harmon questioned by the police. I hear they dropped that line of inquiry once you gave him an alibi. As if Harmon would hurt a fly!"

I'm momentarily taken aback by Jean's knowing that Harmon was questioned, but then I remember that Jean is Morris Alcott's cousin. He must have told her—even though that seems like a violation of lawyer-client confidentiality. Or someone else told her. Jean's lived in Rock Harbor all her life; she knows everyone.

"They may have a new suspect," I say, pausing to see if Jean's heard about Woody Hull, but her eyes widen and she reaches a hand out to me.

"It isn't Rudy, is it?"

I flinch from her well-meaning touch. "No! Rudy was home in bed when Lila was killed. But he did give the police this information and I thought you should know—"

I explain as clearly and succinctly as I can about the Rockwell diary, Lila's research paper, and Rudy's conjecture that Lila thought Woody Hull was responsible for assaulting the Refuge girls and for Noreen Bagley's death, and that Woody killed her when she accused him of those crimes. I try to tell it as impartially as I can, curious to see how Jean will assess the story. When I'm done she lifts one eyebrow.

"That's one imaginative story," she says.

"I know. Frankly, I'd believe Woody Hull assaulted those girls and even that he killed Noreen Bagley. I don't think I ever told you, but I had a very unpleasant encounter with Woody Hull before I left here."

She makes a face. "I'm not surprised . . . he didn't . . . ?" The eyebrow lifts higher. It takes me a moment to realize that she's asking me if Haywood Hull sexually assaulted me. Blood rushes to my face.

"No—" I begin, but then I remember how Haywood Hull looked at me and called me a *slut* and how *dirty* I felt when I left his office. I'm not so sure that what he did *wouldn't* be considered sexual harassment in today's climate of #MeToo and #TimesUp. Still, it pales in comparison to what I have to tell her. "But there's something else . . . It's about who I think fed this story to Lila and then Rudy . . . do you remember Luther Gunn?"

Jean's face pales. "What's he got to do with this?"

"He was in contact with Lila and now Rudy. He gave Rudy the Rockwell diary. I think he's trying to get revenge on Woody Hull for firing him."

She shakes her head. "After all these years? Why would he do it through Lila and Rudy? That doesn't make sense." She rakes her hand through her hair. Her eyes flick rapidly back and forth as if searching for the truth. I can see I'm losing her. Jean is a practical, rational woman. Without the information I'm withholding from her my story *doesn't* make sense.

"There's something else I have to tell you. Something I've kept from you." She goes still, as if waiting for a blow. I take a deep breath. "Luther is Rudy's father. When I left here after my senior year I left with him."

I tell her the whole story, making no excuses for my poor choices and my cowardice. When I get to the part about the day we left on the boat I consider not telling her that Rudy was the one to hit Luther. I've kept this secret for so long that it feels almost impossible to say it aloud, but again I feel that if I don't tell the whole truth my story doesn't make sense.

"He protected me," I say when I'm done. Something in her softens; I guess she's thinking of her own daughter, whom she was unable to save. "But that was why I couldn't tell anyone. I thought Luther was dead. I was afraid that if anyone knew the truth, Rudy would have to live with the burden of being his father's killer."

"You could have told me," she says, her voice low and strained.

"I know," I say, "but you had already done so much for us. I didn't want to place that burden on you. But I'm sorry, Jean.

I've betrayed your trust with lies. I wouldn't blame you if you wanted nothing more to do with me. But I had to tell you now because Luther's *not* dead." I tell her about the IceVirgin33 tweets and Instagram posts and the text I saw on Rudy's phone, not bothering to apologize for spying on my son—Jean's daughter was an addict; she understands the need to keep tabs on a troubled teenager—and describe going down to the Rockwell House and following the Saab with its *IceVrgn33* license plate. I tell her about confronting Rudy and his account of meeting Luther. I don't tell her about how angry Rudy got or how he pushed me when he left, which was only an accident, after all, but I can see by the flash of sympathy on her face that she guesses how it went.

"Luther was good at turning a narrative to his advantage," Jean says when I'm done. "I remember when Woody called him in to fire him. I was sitting right out there and Woody left the intercom on so I could hear everything." She sees my stricken look and quickly adds, "Oh, don't worry; I had that system changed years ago and I'd never be so clueless. Woody made it a point of pride not to understand how the phones— let alone the computers—worked. That was for peons like me." She smiles and I realize how much patronizing bullshit Jean has had to put up with from Woody and the other blue-blooded men on the school's board. "Anyway, I listened because I wanted to know what really happened. I knew that Woody was likely to sweep it all under the table. He'd done it before . . ." Her voice trails off for a moment, then she shakes herself and goes on. "Luther denied having anything to do with Ashley Burton but I could tell from the way he said it that he was playing Woody. He was all but hinting that there might be other girls. He said at one point, 'You know what these girls are like, Woody, they get their schoolgirl crushes on us and then they're disappointed when it doesn't work out according to their fantasies.' I thought at the time, What a conceited prick! but Woody actually laughed. Then he said, 'Nevertheless, I'm afraid I'll have to let you go,' and Luther . . ." Jean leans toward me. "Luther said, 'No worries, I was ready to leave anyway. But I do trust you'll give me a recommendation. I'm sure you don't want me to bring up that Rockwell diary business.'"

"He knew about the Rockwell diary back then? That must mean he suspected Woody of assaulting those girls and used it to get himself a recommendation." The old boys' club complicity of it sickens me.

"Apparently. I didn't really understand what he meant, but five minutes later they were out here shaking hands and Woody was asking me to type up a letter of recommendation for Luther. I thought it was disgusting at the time, but now . . . well, maybe there is something in the story Rudy told the police."

The part I'm trying to absorb is that Luther left here with a letter of recommendation. He could have gone to another school—but not with a seventeen-year-old pregnant girlfriend. "Maybe," I say, "Luther fed that story to Lila to get back at Woody, but when Lila refused to confront Woody, Luther killed her."

Jean nods. "I can certainly see Lila agreeing to meet Luther on the Point more readily than Woody Hull. Why don't you tell the police that?"

"Bantree will just think I'm trying to protect Harmon—or

Rudy. But if you tell them that Luther had reason to retaliate against Woody, and that he's the kind of man who would kill Lila, they'll take you seriously."

Jean gives me a sad smile. "I think you underestimate yourself, Tess. I've always wondered why you don't have more self-esteem. Now, knowing how Luther Gunn took advantage of you, I think I understand better. I think it's time you confront that. I'll be happy to corroborate your assessment of Luther but you have to tell the police what you've told me first. Otherwise you'll always be living in Luther's shadow."

All the heat I've generated with my confession is quenched in ice water. I know Jean is administering the tough love response she'd give to any of the students under her charge— I *know* she's right—but it still makes me feel chastised and rebuked.

"Okay," I tell her. "I'll go to Bantree as long as you'll back me up about Luther."

"Of course," she says, grasping my hand. "That man is a menace. I wouldn't be surprised if he came after me next."

"Why?" I ask, remembering that Luther didn't like her.

Jean smiles bitterly. "Oh, because that letter? I typed it as Woody requested but then I tore it up in front of Luther's face."

CHAPTER TWENTY

A s I leave Jean's office Maryanne looks up and gives me such a look of pity that I wonder if she's overheard what I told Jean. Just because Jean *thinks* she's fixed the phone system doesn't mean that an adroit assistant doesn't have ways of knowing what goes on in her boss's office (I'd had). I feel small and shamed at the thought of wholesome soccer mom Maryanne knowing my sordid past.

But then Maryanne points to the headset and mouths *Anat Zeller* and I realize that the look of pity on Maryanne's face is for a bereaved mother and not me and my tawdry history. I press my hand to my chest in commiseration and get out of there before Maryanne suggests that perhaps I might want to offer my condolences to Lila's mother.

I take my car keys out but walk past the Forester. I'm too agitated to drive. I walk through the Main Quad, head down to avoid making eye contact with the students I pass. I'm working so hard not to be seen that I bump into a girl who's also walking with her head down. She drops a pile of bright red flyers and they scatter over the path like autumn leaves. I crouch to help her pick them up and see that it's Paola Fernandez.

"Paola!" I cry. "I'm so sorry. I wasn't watching where I was going."

"It's my fault, Ms. Henshaw," she says, shaking her head so that her long dark hair falls on either side of her face like a curtain. I can't see her face but I can hear from her voice that she's crying. "I was going too fast."

"Oh, honey," I say, reaching for Paola's arm. She evades my grasp by grabbing another errant flyer and then standing up, clutching the red flyers to her chest like a wound she's trying to staunch. "This must be so hard on you. You and Lila were so close."

"I'm not sure we really were," Paola says, her eyes averted. "I mean, Lila was great, but we weren't really spending so much time together in the last few weeks . . . I . . . I feel like it was my fault . . ."

Poor Paola. She really is a little oversensitive. "Don't do that to yourself," I tell her. "Don't put this on yourself. Whatever was going on with Lila these last few weeks, whatever led to what happened to her . . . even if you had known you wouldn't have been able to stop it. Lila was very headstrong."

Paola raises her eyes at this. "Yeah, she was. She always thought she knew what was right."

"She did," I say. "She had a great sense of conviction and justice." *Which Luther would have known how to manipulate,* I think. "The person who did this to her will pay."

Paola nods and looks away again, her eyes filling up with tears. "Yeah, well, I gotta go, Ms. Henshaw. I told Ms. Frankel I'd put these up for tonight's performance."

I look down at the flyer in my hand. Printed in black on red is a figure of a woman in Colonial dress and the words *The Crucible: a memorial performance for Lila Zeller.*

"Wow, Jill didn't waste any time . . ." Then I look more closely at the figure of the woman. Its outlines are a little hard to make out—black on red isn't the best graphic choice—but there's something unsettling about it that takes me a moment to figure out. "Christ, is she out of her mind?"

"Um . . . it was Rachel Lazar's idea. She said it's for emotional impact."

"Give me those!" I tell Paola. She hands over the stack of flyers and wraps her arms around her chest as if their absence has left her cold.

"Please don't tell Ms. Frankel I gave them to you. She offered me extra credit for putting them up. I got a B-minus on her final so I could really use the help."

"I'll tell her I took them down myself," I say, holding up one of the flyers so that the figure on it seems to flap in the wind. Which is fitting. It's not just a picture of a girl in Colonial dress; it's a picture of a hanged girl swinging from the gallows.

"ARE YOU OUT of your mind?"

I slap the flyer down in front of Jill Frankel. I've found her in the theater, standing onstage, in front of a raised platform that serves as the gallows. Four girls are lined up in front wearing placards around their necks that say WITCH. I belatedly realize I should have asked to speak to Jill privately instead of confronting her in front of students.

Jill looks briefly toward the girls but doesn't suggest they go; she doesn't seem to mind an audience. "Do you have a problem with the flyer?" she asks with studied innocence.

"Yes," I say, trying to modulate my voice for the benefit of the girls onstage, who include Dakota Wyatt, Rachel Lazar, Samantha Grimes, and Sophie Watanabe. "I don't think an image of a hanged woman is appropriate for a memorial performance for a young girl who died tragically."

"Lila wasn't hanged," Rachel Lazar says.

"That's not the point," I say, and then, in a lower voice to Jill, "Perhaps we should discuss this in private."

"You're the one who stormed in here onto *my* stage," Jill says. "And I don't believe in hiding the truth from my students." She glances at the girls, two of whom have taken their cell phones out of their pinafore pockets. "Go ahead and take five," she suggests. The girls slouch off to the stage wings, still close enough to hear.

I take a breath and try a different tack. "Look, I understand you're trying to honor Lila."

"I'm not, really," Jill says. "I'm trying to expose the hypocrisy and corruption that led to her death."

"What do you mean? We don't know who killed her."

"Don't we? Lila was clearly troubled about something. I tried to talk to her but she was too frightened to tell me what it was. But I know it had something to do with that history paper she was writing for your husband."

"Why do you say that?" I ask, ignoring the sneer on her face when she says *your husband*. I've always suspected that Jill was jealous when I married Harmon. She was closer in age to him and I'd overheard her once say, *He likes them young.*

"Here, look at this." She takes out her phone, taps, scrolls, and hands it to me.

Is Lila Zeller the latest victim of the Maiden Stone disappearances? I read. It's a tweet by someone called LostGirl99 with a link to a site called "Lost Girls of the Maiden Stone." I skim the tweet, which asserts that Lila was researching the disappearances surrounding the Maiden Stone when she was killed. *Could Lila have found out something about the person responsible for those disappearances—or was she a victim of the Maiden Stone's malice?*

"This is ridiculous," I say. "Where did you even find—" But as I scroll farther down I see where Jill got this post. It's been retweeted by IceVirgin33. "How do you know him?" I demand, holding the phone out.

"Who? Oh, IceVirgin33? I don't know . . . I think I met him in a theater group in Portland." Her eyes slide up and to the left, a clear sign she's lying.

"You've met him in person? Luther? Did he ask you about me and Rudy?"

Jill seems taken aback. "What? Why would he? He asked me about *me*, about *my* life and work. Believe it or not, Tess, it's not always about you."

I'm briefly flabbergasted that vain, drama queen Jill Frankel is painting me as the self-absorbed one here, but then I recall how when we were housemates Jill would spend many an evening alone, drinking wine and surfing through dating sites. *It's hell being single in the boondocks,* she would complain. I can imagine how flattering Luther's attentions could be.

"I'm sorry, Jill, I didn't mean . . . it's just that Luther and I have a history—"

"I know," she cuts in. "He told me all about it. Honestly, Tess, how could you keep a father from his own son all these years? It explains so much about Rudy."

"You don't know what you're talking about, Jill," I say, trying to keep my voice under control.

"Don't I? I lived with you for six years, remember. I watched that poor boy playing make-believe games that were always missing a father figure. He was isolated, moody, and violent even as a boy and I've watched him grow into a maladjusted teenager hungry for love and acceptance."

"And did you also introduce Luther to Lila?" I ask.

"Lila?" Jill looks confused. "I don't know what you're talking about."

"Luther met with Lila in Portland."

"Did he?" She's trying to act nonchalant but I can tell that this has taken her by surprise. "Well, I suppose he saw Lila's tweets on my feed and followed her. He must have offered to help with her research. He's quite a brilliant historian. He's writing a book on the Maiden Stone disappearances."

"You don't think it's a little creepy that a fifty-three-year-old man befriended an eighteen-year-old girl online and offered to meet her? Has it occurred to you that he might be the one who killed Lila?"

"What a terrible thing to say about your own son's father!"

Jill is so loud that several of the girls in the wings look up from their phones and turn in our direction. "Luther said you were weirdly overprotective. I offered to talk to Rudy about him—"

"You stay the hell away from my son," I say, stepping toward Jill. She steps back and bumps into the gallows, causing the wood to creak and the nooses to sway.

Rachel Lazar comes running across the stage like she's afraid I may be assaulting her drama teacher. She's holding up her phone. Maybe she's planning to take a picture for evidence. I turn to her, ready to seize the phone, but then I see she's holding up a picture for Jill and me to see.

"Look! They've got Lila's killer!" she cries.

I am terrified for a moment that it will be a picture of Rudy, but it's a picture of Woody Hull being led out of his house by Officer Gough. He's scowling at the young female officer as if he can't quite believe he's being arrested by a woman. Although I still have my doubts that Woody Hull killed Lila I can't help but feel a teeny twinge of gratification that the miserable old misogynist is getting taken down a peg.

Any satisfaction I might feel at Hull's downfall, though, is punctured by an icy splinter of fear when I see that IceVirgin33 tweeted the picture. Luther was at Woody's house—only two blocks away from mine—taking that picture today. Where is he now? Is he with Rudy?

"You see," Rachel says, "it's like I told you. Lila was being sexually assaulted."

I look at Rachel. She's scrubbed her customary kohl and blue lipstick off, leaving her face unnervingly naked and exposed. "Mr. Hull is just being questioned," I say, hardly believing that

I'm speaking up for Woody Hull. "We don't know anything yet. We certainly don't know that he assaulted Lila."

"What else could it be?" Rachel asks, her blue eyes wide and earnest. "That guy is a creep."

The rest of the girls have gathered around, drawn by Rachel's exclamation. "My cousin who went here?" Samantha Grimes says. "She had a friend who said he groped her during an assembly. He's an old pervert."

I look around the circle of girls. With their faces scrubbed clean of makeup and their hair pulled back under close-fitting bonnets they all look alike. All I have to do to join them, I realize, is tell them my story. Woody Hull called me a slut when I tried to tell him I was being assaulted by a teacher here. I would not be surprised to hear that he's assaulted other girls.

But I can't do it. And it's not because I think Woody Hull deserves due process or that I'm frightened by how quickly everyone has jumped on this bandwagon that was set in motion by Luther Gunn. I don't tell my story because I'm ashamed of it. Mixed in with my fear of Luther is a sick sense of shame that everyone will find out that I was a stupid girl who let herself be molested by her English teacher.

"I think we need to get all the facts before we rush to a verdict," I say primly, as if I'm giving a lecture on proper research procedure. "And check our sources." I tap the phone on Ice-Virgin33's name to underscore my point and nearly drop the phone when the screen opens to a photo of a deep ice chasm, the figure of a girl falling into its maw. I have a feeling it's meant to be me.

CHAPTER TWENTY-ONE

As I walk back to my car, Haywood's bucolic campus feels like the set of one of Rudy's games—a two-dimensional cover for lurking peril, only instead of zombies or alien monsters, Luther might be hiding behind the stately oaks and ivy-covered buildings. He is orchestrating all of this—Lila reading the Rockwell diary, Rudy accusing Woody Hull, the picture of Woody being led away by the police. What will he do next? Who will be the next target of his revenge?

I pause in front of Main Hall. Should I go back to Jean and tell her about the photograph of Woody? But she made it clear that I have to bring my story to the police. So that's what I'll do. I'll go to Kevin Bantree and tell him everything, no matter what it exposes about me.

THE VILLAGE OF Rock Harbor looks particularly pretty as I drive through it. The storefront windows sparkle in the sun and reflect the bright blue of the bay. Baskets of petunias and geraniums hang from the cast-iron lampposts, flags printed with sailboats and lobsters snap in the breeze, salt air mingles with the smell of blueberry muffins wafting out of the bakery. The village is gearing up for the summer tourist season, shedding the dark shroud of the winter months. Harmon, like many locals, often bemoans the coming of the tourists, but it's always made me feel lucky to live in a place people want to vacation in.

Now, though, I feel like I don't really belong in this sunnier version of Rock Harbor. I'm part of the town's darker, colder shadow. Once I tell Kevin Bantree my story, how long will it be before the whole town knows that I ran away with my teacher—a sexual predator? For all the town's fascination with its dark history—the Indian massacres and early colony, the influenza epidemic and lost girls—those stories are meant to be part of the past, told on candlelit ghost tours or sold in glossy paperbacks to be read on rainy weekends. The lost girls aren't meant to come back.

But here I am.

I park and walk toward the entrance to the police station, but before I reach it the door flings open and Woody Hull bursts out as if he's fleeing a burning building. His face is lobster red, tufts of hair sticking up on his bald scalp like scorched grass, his tweed jacket fanning the air behind him like a fiery backdraft. He lurches straight at me and grabs onto me as if I could save him. "It's a witch hunt, I tell you," he gasps and then, a dull spark of recognition flickering in his bleary eyes, he spits out, "You! Have you come to spread your filthy lies? I could tell a thing or two about you, you little—"

"That's enough, Woody." Morris Alcott grasps Woody's elbow and yanks him away from me. "Remember what I said about not talking to *anyone*?"

"You're his lawyer?" I ask. I shouldn't be surprised; they're all part of the same boys' club. But the thought of Harmon and Woody having the same lawyer makes me feel a little sick.

Morris opens his mouth to say something but stops when the door to the station opens and Kevin Bantree appears. "Is everything all right out here?" he asks. "Did you need something, Ms. Henshaw?"

"I need to talk to you," I say, separating myself from Woody and Morris. Morris takes a step with me, hissing an admonitory *"Tess!"* but then Woody mutters something under his breath that sounds like *slut* and Morris quickly retreats to take charge of his client. I watch them go and then turn to Kevin. He's holding the station door open for me.

"Could we talk someplace else?" I ask.

"If you have evidence to give it would be better if you give it here on the record," he says sternly.

"It's not evidence," I reply. "More like . . . *background*. And I really, really don't want to sit in that room again feeling like a criminal."

He starts to speak, his face still stony, but then taking me in—I must look a wreck—he softens. "I think I know a place where you won't feel so . . . *criminal*."

WE WALK AWAY from the village along the coastal path, up to the overlook above the bay—the same place where I'd imagined telling Rudy the story of his father. Sitting on a bench facing the bay I can imagine I *am* telling it to Rudy. That I have a chance to start over.

Kevin is a good listener. He lets me tell the whole story from the time I left Haywood to the day I left the island. When I get to that part I tell him the truth: that Rudy was the one who hit Luther over the head. I tell him about seeing the Ice-Virgin33 tweet and reading the texts between Lila and Rudy. I'm glad I don't have to look at him while confessing to spying on my own son. It makes me feel, suddenly, the differences between me and Kevin. Although we're the same age, I have a seventeen-year-old son and he has no children. It makes me feel older.

I tell him about my visit to the Rockwell House and following the Saab with its *IceVrgn33* plates. "He gave Rudy the diary and encouraged him to think that Woody Hull killed Lila," I say. "And then it wasn't enough to draw your attention to Woody; he's posted a picture online."

I open my phone and go to Rachel Lazar's Twitter profile to find the picture of Woody Hull being led away by Officer Gough. There are 119 retweets. Kevin scrolls through them quickly, then hands me back my phone without comment.

"I don't care about Woody Hull," I say. "He's a mean old man and I'd believe he molested students; I'd even believe he killed Noreen Bagley back when he was a young man. But I can't see Lila going to the Point with him or him being able to overpower her."

"He didn't," Kevin says bluntly. "He has an alibi. A night nurse who says he was in bed between three-thirty and six-thirty A.M. Given how much his nurse dislikes him, I don't see her lying to protect him."

"Then it has to be Luther," I say. "Rudy says he came up the night of the play. Lila told Luther that she was going to go ahead and confront Woody—but then she tried to get Luther to meet Rudy. At least that's what Luther told Rudy. But Luther could have been using Lila to set up Woody, but when Lila wouldn't go along with it he killed her and now he's trying to make it look like Woody killed her."

"But he'd have no way of knowing whether Woody had an alibi or not," Kevin points out.

"It doesn't matter. The accusation is enough to ruin Woody's reputation." I scroll through the tweets on Rachel's feed. "Listen to this one from a class of ninety-six alumna: *Always knew he was a creep. Everyone in my class avoided being alone with him.* And here's one from a 1981 alum: *He molested my roommate at the junior prom.*"

Kevin nods. "We've already started getting calls from women who want to give evidence against him. You're right that this will ruin him, but I can imagine another motive for Luther."

"What?" I ask.

Instead of answering he looks at his watch. "Come on, I want to show you something." He gets up and starts walking along the coastal path toward Haywood. I have to hurry to catch up with him. I'm nervous about being seen on campus with a police officer—what if someone posts a picture of us?—but the coastal path is empty of students. Jean's email declaring the peninsula and Maiden Island off-limits seems to have worked. The few students sunbathing on the lawn in front of Duke Hall are too far off—or too zoned out on sunshine—to notice us as we skirt the parking lot between Duke and Warden House.

Kevin pauses at the end of the lot. "Is this where you picked up Rudy?"

"Oh . . ." I'm taken aback by the question. Has he brought me here to check Rudy's alibi? "Uh, yeah. I parked right here." I point to the empty spot in front of Warden House. "Rudy and I lived here when we first moved to Rock Harbor and Rudy's still fond of the place."

Kevin looks up at the decaying old house as if wondering why anyone would be fond of such a broken-down wreck. "So Rudy was waiting here when you got here?"

"Yes," I say, wary now of saying too much.

"And that was at three-fifteen?"

I nod. "Thereabouts. Remember I showed you the text from Rudy on my phone? I got that at just after three and I left as soon as I got dressed. I noticed it was three-oh-six when I left the house and it's only a ten-minute drive from there."

"Uh huh. Did you happen to notice the tide?"

"The tide?"

"Yeah." Kevin turns to face the coastline. "You can see the water from here. Did you notice how high the tide was and whether it was going in or out?"

I pause to think. I remember that when I first got to the path I could hear the water, but after I went behind Warden House and came back I didn't hear it. When I reached the Point I could see the bare rocks of the causeway gleaming in the moonlight. But of course I can't tell Kevin that I went to the Point. He's trying to trick me, I think, into giving away that I went out to the point, but I won't fall for it.

"No," I say, "I didn't notice. I just picked up Rudy and left."

Kevin holds my gaze for a moment as if giving me the chance to change my story, then turns back toward the water. "Me, I grew up here. My father and grandfather and his father were fishermen. I helped out on the boat during the summers, so I'm always noticing the tide. See how you can see the tip of that pointy rock there?" He points to a sharp rock standing a couple of yards off the shore. "Locals call that the Ebb Stone because when it appears you know you've got fifteen minutes before the causeway is clear. Come on." He smiles, like the boy he's recalling, shrugging his shoulder toward the path. "We have just enough time."

Just enough time for what? I want to ask, but I don't say a word as we walk, afraid now that I will give something away. Besides, Kevin seems happy enough to do the talking.

"I used to race the tide when I was a kid. As soon as I saw the Ebb Stone appear I'd start out from my house and cut through the back of campus—did you know I grew up two blocks behind where you live now? You can make it here in five minutes on foot, quicker than driving along the coast road. Rudy could have made it home faster by walking than waiting for you."

The introduction of Rudy in the narrative makes the back of my neck prickle. I shrug off the chill. "I always tell him to call if he wants a lift home. I'd rather come get him than have him wandering the town in the middle of the night."

Kevin ignores my parental philosophy and goes on, "Me, I

could barely stay put when I was that age. I couldn't sleep. It felt like I might *miss* something. When I saw the Ebb Stone from my window it felt like a dare. If I started out from my house I could make it to the Point just as the tide cleared the causeway. There's nothing like that moment when the sand and rocks are laid bare, when you're the first one to step on land that was under water only moments before. Like an explorer being the first to step foot in an undiscovered country."

I glance at Kevin. "I remember that from Senior Seminar," I say. "You played Hamlet."

"And you played Ophelia," he says with a wistful smile. "That phrase—the 'undiscovered country'—always makes me think of this."

We've reached the end of the path. We're below the Point—where Rudy was waiting for me that night—and the rock causeway leading to Maiden Island stretches out in front of us. There's still a corrugated film of water over the rocks, but as we watch it withdraws, as if pulled by a magician's hand, leaving bare gleaming rock and sand. I can almost hear the *suck* of the tide retreating, like an indrawn breath—a gasp—and I notice that I'm holding my own breath. This is what I saw when I came out here to get Rudy. I didn't see Lila's broken body. She must have been pushed from the Point *after* we left.

I let out my breath, relieved.

"Come on," Kevin says, again with that boyish shrug, this time indicating the short steep path that goes down to the causeway.

"Um. I really don't have the shoes for it," I say, pointing at the rope-soled canvas slip-ons I'm wearing. But he's already scrambling down the path, so I follow, keeping a close eye on the slick, seaweed-slimed rocks. When I make it down and look up, I see that Kevin is already striding across the massive flat stones that make up the causeway. I step gingerly on the first stone, skirting tide pools where small fish dart and delicate strands of seaweed wave in the sparkling water. Ever since Luther told our English class the story about the nine sisters who drowned in the incoming tide and turned to stone I've hated walking on the stones. The legend says that when the tides come in, the sisters will pull anyone still on the stones down into the sands to drown with them. Luther said that part of the legend came about because there's quicksand on either side of the causeway.

I look down at my watch and see it's only been fifteen minutes since the low tide point. There's no chance of being caught by the incoming tide. Kevin is sitting on a low ledge just below the Maiden Stone, waiting for me. I walk carefully over the slick stones, trying hard not to think about drowned girls reaching up to pull me into quicksand. When I reach Kevin I look down at my watch again. "Shouldn't we head back?"

"The causeway is clear for three hours," he says. "We have plenty of time. Don't you want to touch the Maiden Stone?" He crooks his head and looks up to the tall standing stone looming above him. Below the narrow ledge he's on there's a deep gap where seawater churns restlessly as if eager to take back possession of its vanquished land.

I shake my head and point at my soaked canvas shoes. "I told you, I'm not wearing the shoes for it. Why don't you tell me why you brought me out here?"

He holds my gaze and then nods as if he's made up his mind

about something. "Okay. I did want you to see something. It's back there." He stands up and leaps nimbly from the ledge to the causeway, leading the way back to the mainland. "The causeway is crossable for three hours," he says. "And Lila was found here." He points to the first flat stone directly beneath the Point. "The man who found her at six-thirty took pictures because he knew that when the tide came in at seven it would destroy evidence. There was blood around her head, staining the rock. So we know she died after three thirty-six, when the tide went out. According to your account you and Rudy were already home at three-thirty—six minutes before the tide cleared the causeway."

"Yes, that's right—"

Kevin cuts me off. There's nothing boyish in his face now. "And you heard Harmon when you got home at three-thirty and you're sure he was home until he went out jogging at six-thirty, so Harmon couldn't have had anything to do with Lila's death."

"That's right," I say, meeting his gaze.

"But," he says, climbing up to the path. "If you were just a little off . . ."

"I showed you the text from Rudy. I left right away."

"I know, Tess," he says, almost gently. "The traffic light camera on the coast road clocks you there at three-twelve." He lets that sink in for a moment and then adds, "And clocks you coming back at four-ten. So my question for you is: What were you doing between three-ten and four-ten?"

I could tell him that Rudy and I sat in the car arguing. But what if that's another trap? What if there's a security camera in the parking lot? It would show me leaving the car and returning with Rudy at four. I have a feeling I don't have too many chances left with Kevin Bantree. And besides, I know Lila's body was not on the causeway when I arrived at the Point so I won't be endangering Rudy if I tell the truth.

"Okay," I say. "Rudy was waiting for me there." I look toward the Point. "It's a place he goes when he feels scared. The safe place, he calls it—"

"*SP*—not 'Student Parking.'"

"Right, only Rudy and I have a pact to keep it secret. That's why he didn't tell you the truth. Remember what I told you about how Rudy grew up; we had to be secretive."

"Uh huh," he says, "so you came out here?"

"Yes," I say eagerly. "I stood right here and looked out on the causeway. If Lila had been dead already I would have seen her."

"And then what happened?"

"Nothing. I got Rudy and we walked back to the car and drove home."

"Arriving home at four-fifteen. That still leaves some time unaccounted for."

What's he getting at, I wonder. I feel as if Kevin is laying a trap for me as dangerous as the quicksand beside the causeway, but Lila's body wasn't here so it shouldn't matter how long I took getting out here.

"On the way out here I heard something off the path and thought I saw something behind Warden House. I thought it might be Rudy come to meet me but it wasn't. I stood there for a few minutes . . . or longer, I guess, maybe ten minutes."

"What was it?" he asks.

"I thought . . ." I hesitate, remembering standing in the circle, remembering the old ghost stories, and wondering if what I'd seen was one of the girls that drowned on the causeway. What if it hadn't been a ghost or my imagination? What if it had been Lila? I could have helped her. Or Luther? I could have stopped him. "It was nothing," I say at last. "A flash of white . . . Just my imagination. So I walked out here to the Point, found Rudy, we talked for a few minutes, and then we left."

"And you didn't see Lila or anyone else?"

"No," I say. "Maybe that flash of white I saw behind Warden House was Luther. I could have stopped him. Or maybe it was Lila. If it was, I wish . . . I wish I'd gone to find her. Maybe I could have saved her."

"If she wasn't dead already."

"I told you, I didn't see her on the causeway. I was standing right here." I look out at the line of stones marching to Maiden Head—the Nine Sisters . . . only something is wrong. I count them. There are only eight.

I feel a deep chill, as if the ninth sister has indeed come to life and is even now coming to drag me under the sand, but what Kevin Bantree says next is worse.

"You can't see the Little Sister Stone from here. It's obscured by the angle of the path. Lila could have been there when you arrived and you wouldn't have known."

CHAPTER TWENTY-TWO

S
o that's why you brought me out here?" I spit at Kevin. "To lay this on Rudy."

"We'd have a good case," Kevin says, his face sad but firm. "We know Rudy and Lila fought—we have their texts from Lila's phone. We know they were meeting and that Rudy has a history of violence."

"That's not fair," I cry, "he's never started a fight. He only strikes out to defend himself when he feels threatened and only because of the trauma he experienced as a child."

"And if he struck out at Lila because she said something that hurt him? She could have fallen. It could have been an accident."

"No," I say. "It wasn't Rudy. There was someone else here that night—that flash of white I saw behind Warden House could have been Lila or Luther."

"But you didn't see who it was."

"No, but . . ."

"So it could have been Harmon."

"What?" A wave of vertigo sweeps over me, as if I'm still standing on the shifting sands beside the causeway. "Harmon was home in bed."

"You don't know that for sure. This revised timeline doesn't just throw out Rudy's alibi; it ruins Harmon's. You weren't home until four-twenty. That gives Harmon over an hour to get here on foot, kill Lila, and walk—or run—home. Assuming you really did check that he was upstairs when you got home."

I try to take in what he's saying but there's a roaring in my ears as if I am underwater. "That's absurd," I say, ignoring his suggestion that I may have lied. "Why would Harmon want to hurt Lila?"

"I can think of at least one reason." Kevin looks almost pained, but I realize now that won't stop him from pursuing Harmon. That's whom he's been after all along. He just wanted me to think he was after Rudy so I'd slip up. And it worked.

"Harmon would never act improperly with a student."

"You were his student," he says.

"That was different. I was twenty-three, I already had a child, and we didn't even date until the class was over. Lila was seventeen. Harmon would never have laid a hand on her."

"Then why did he have Lila's blood on his sweatshirt?"

My mouth goes dry. "There are dozens of ways that could have gotten there. Lila wore that sweatshirt—"

"Cutting carrots?" His mouth twists in a sardonic smile. "I'm familiar with Lawyer Alcott's theory."

All I have to do is tell him that Rudy was wearing the sweatshirt that night, but I can't do it. "You can't prove that she didn't," I say. "I'll swear she did. And you can't prove that it was Harmon behind Warden House. It had to have been Luther. This is what Luther wants. He wants to rip my life apart, first by killing Lila, then taking Rudy from me, and then implicating Harmon in Lila's death. Please don't fall into his trap. There must be something . . . can't you use that traffic camera to trace Luther coming up here?"

"We do have his car on camera before the play that night," Kevin concedes, "but that doesn't prove he was on the Point with Lila."

"At least bring him in—question him!"

"We have," he says. "He has an alibi from the end of the play until after seven the next morning."

So Kevin knew all about Luther before my teary confession. I feel as if I've been set up.

"Who?" I ask. "Who's his alibi?"

Kevin shakes his head. Of course he can't tell me that . . . but he doesn't have to. I already know. It has to be Jill Frankel. I turn around and start walking toward campus. Kevin follows me to the parking lot. "Even if you think you know who gave Luther his alibi, I caution you against approaching him or her. It won't help your husband's case."

I wheel on him, prepared to tell him I'll talk to whomever I like, but then I realize he's right. Confronting Jill won't help right now; I have to warn Harmon about what's coming. "Let me worry about my husband, Officer," I say curtly. "I'm going home now. As you've pointed out, it's a short walk."

I turn, wondering what I'll do if he follows me, but he doesn't. I'm not sure if I'm relieved or not.

HE'S RIGHT THAT it's quicker to walk the back way than to drive on the coast road. Why have I been taking the car all these years?

Because I wore that Forester like armor. *Look at me with my solid Colonial and professorial husband and fancy private school and seat-warming car! Nothing can hurt me—or my son—here.*

But none of that has helped Rudy. I'd thought that Lila would keep him safe—that the safe world she came from would rub off on him—but instead our dark world reached out and took her life. And now it's coming for Harmon.

Without the car to park I come in the front door, which makes me feel like a guest in my own house—no, not a guest, an intruder. But haven't I always felt like I was masquerading as the kind of woman who could live in a house like this, married to a man like Harmon Henshaw?

Harmon is sitting at the dining room table with a stack of books to one side and one spread out in front of him. When I come in he looks up over his gold-rimmed reading glasses, which have slipped to the end of his nose. It's a quaint professorial look that catches at my heart. I have imagined growing old with this man whose trust I have betrayed. I have to come clean now—about *everything*.

I pull out a chair and sit down. "I'm sorry I didn't tell you the truth about Rudy's father . . . about Luther," I say, hating to even say his name in this house. "It's no excuse, but I want you to know that it wasn't because I didn't trust you. I told myself I was protecting Rudy, but I think now I was ashamed. That if you knew how stupid I'd been you'd think worse of me."

"You thought I'd think better of your fictional fisherman?" He raises both eyebrows.

"That seemed merely foolish," I say. "But a person who had lived with a man like Luther, a man who preyed on teenagers, for five years"—I try to find a way to explain how I thought he'd see me if he'd known the truth—"would be *damaged*."

A shudder passes through Harmon's stolid Yankee frame. At first I think I've disgusted him; I was right that his knowing about Luther has changed how he sees me. But then he places his hand over mine. "He's the monster, not you. I've been looking through your yearbook." He points at the book in front of him. It's open to a group shot of the literary magazine staff in the east parlor of Warden House. I'm seated at the center, posed with pen in hand as if I'm about to dash off a poem. I'm beaming. I'd been so thrilled when Luther asked me to be the editor in chief. *You have real talent*, he'd said, and I'd believed him. Luther is sitting next to me with that sulky, amused look he'd so often worn. We're not looking at each other but I can feel the charge between us. Even then it had made me dizzy sometimes. Now it makes me feel sick to my stomach.

"I *met* him," Harmon says, "at some fund-raiser my mother roped me into when I was home from school. He struck me as a smug, pretentious jerk. But I remembered that we knew some people in common so I made some calls this morning. I spoke with Doug Marshall at Choate, who said that Luther was let go under suspicious circumstances. And Arthur Fieldston, who I knew at Brown, says his sister was at Brearley when Luther taught there and it was well known he slept with students. How did this creep get hired at Haywood? And how did no one notice that one of our students vanished with said creep?" A deep flush colors Harmon's pale skin. He's mad—but not at me.

"How could they have known?" I say. "I had graduated. I told my father I was getting a job in Portland." I don't mention that my father had never tried to find me in the five years I was on the island or what he said when I did get in touch with him after. It makes me feel ashamed that my father cared so little for me—as if I hadn't been worth caring about.

"It was their business to know!" Harmon pounds the table with his fist. All the books jump. Strewn across the table are yearbooks going back to the fifties. Harmon's mother, who was a Haywood alumna and board member, kept a yearbook for each year. "It was Woody Hull's business to know. It was the school board's—of which my mother was a member—to know. Why was a man suspected of child molestation let loose to go on his way to molest more children? Why were no charges pressed? Why wasn't he entered into a sex offenders database?"

I imagine an alternate reality in which Luther Gunn was arrested for child molestation. I would have been exposed—shamed—but in the end I'd have been forced to tell my father I was pregnant. He might have disowned me—or maybe he would have helped me. Or Jean might have; I could have gotten that scholarship then and gone through college. Raised Rudy on my own. He would never have had to live with Luther Gunn. How different would he have turned out?

"I tried to talk to Woody but he wouldn't listen," I say quietly.

"He wanted to shut you up," Harmon says. "He was afraid that if it all came out he'd have to answer questions about why he hired a teacher who'd been let go from three schools."

"Four," I say. "I found the dismissal letters when we were on the island. But none of them said why Luther was let go.

Woody could have claimed he didn't know there were any previous accusations."

"Maybe, but I bet he was afraid that once an investigation was opened, others would come forward accusing him. Look at the women who are coming forward now." He moves one of the yearbooks and I see there's a laptop underneath. For a moment I'm confused. Harmon doesn't own a laptop. Then I realize it's mine.

"I hope you don't mind," he says, seeing me stare at it. "You left it open to your Twitter feed. I just wanted to see what people were saying."

"I didn't know you even knew what Twitter was," I begin in a teasing tone, before remembering we're not on teasing terms right now.

Harmon lays his hand on mine. "Have I been an awful prig about things like that? Is that why you didn't feel you could tell me the truth—because I'm such a hidebound old man?"

The idea that Harmon might blame himself for my failure to confide in him breaks my heart. "You've never given me the slightest reason not to trust you," I say, struggling not to cry. "I should have told you in the beginning. I . . . I was too ashamed."

"That's not your fault," he says firmly. "It's *his*." He taps the photograph of Luther. "He preyed on a young vulnerable girl and exploited your trusting nature. It's the part of you I've always loved best—your ability to see the best in people." He pauses and then says quietly, "Maybe I took advantage of you too. After all, I was your teacher. Maybe I'm no better than Luther Gunn or Woody Hull."

"Don't say that!" I cry, moving into Harmon's arms. "You're nothing like them. I was a grown woman when we met—and I practically had to proposition you."

I'd like to stay in Harmon's arms, but remembering what I have to tell him, I move away.

"I've just come from Kevin Bantree," I say. I explain how Kevin demolished my alibi for Rudy.

"That doesn't prove anything," Harmon says angrily. "I don't believe Rudy would hurt Lila."

Harmon's faith in Rudy touches me—and makes it harder to say what I have to say next.

"That's not all. It's not just Rudy's alibi that's been ruined; it's yours. I didn't get home until four-twenty. Bantree says that would have given you time to get to campus and back while I was gone."

Harmon goes very still. "And what do *you* think?" he asks in a low, tight voice.

It takes me a second to understand he's asking me if I think he killed Lila. "I'd sooner believe Rudy did it."

It's not how I meant to put it, but it is perhaps the most effective way I could have professed my belief in Harmon's innocence. I know that Harmon has always believed that Rudy comes first with me. I know he's always tried to understand that. But I also know it's always irked him.

A shudder goes through him, breaking the tension in his face and releasing a single tear. "That's all that matters to me," he says. "That you believe me."

"But it's not all that matters," I say. "You don't have an alibi and Luther does. Kevin wouldn't say who but I'm sure it's Jill

Frankel. She's been seeing Luther all along and I don't think she'll have any trouble lying for him."

"No, I don't see Jill having any trouble lying either."

"What do you mean?" I ask.

He looks embarrassed. "You know I went out on a few dates with her, right? Before you and I started seeing each other?" I nod. "Well, on one of those dates she got very drunk and told me she had lied on her résumé. She never graduated from Yale Drama School."

"No! How did Jean miss that?"

Harmon shrugs. "I'm afraid Jean's missed a lot over the years. You know, this scandal about Woody . . . well, it won't look good for Jean that she's taken all his money for the school all these years. And if there's an accusation against me . . . even if I'm not arrested I don't see her keeping me on."

"It's not going to come to that," I tell Harmon. I take the red flyer from my pocket. "I'll go to Jill tonight before the play. I'll threaten to reveal that she lied on her résumé if she continues lying for Luther."

Harmon shakes his head. "That could be dangerous, Tess. If people found out they might say you're trying to protect Rudy. I wouldn't want you to do anything that might put him at risk."

"I'll just have to take that chance," I say.

His face crumples and I can see he's about to cry. I rush into his arms and hide my face against his chest. I can't look at his expression of gratitude knowing that I'm still keeping the truth about the sweatshirt from him and the police.

CHAPTER TWENTY-THREE

lthough I hadn't gone to the first night's performance of *The Crucible,* I'd gotten a text from Jean telling me that there had been a great turnout. I doubt, though, that the first night was as well attended as this performance. The chapel is packed when we get there, the crowd hushed out of respect for the occasion, and I'm afraid we'll have to stand until I see Jean down in the front waving us toward two seats she saved for us. Harmon moves forward but I touch his arm and whisper for him to go ahead. "I'm going to go talk to Jill."

"Be careful," he says.

I go around the side to the back room. The hallway is full of students; they are also hushed, but perhaps less out of respect than in thrall to their phones. As I pass I see that picture of Woody Hull on their screens and also photos of Noreen Bagley and the other "lost girls." I hear their names too, repeated in a low whisper—Barbara Hampton, Shirley Eames, Priscilla Barnes—like a chanted spell.

I find Jill surrounded by students in the dressing room, giving last-minute instructions. It's not the best time to approach her but it might be the only chance I have before Kevin arrests Harmon. Jill sees me approaching but pointedly ignores me, instead turning to a student with a clipboard and giving intricate lighting instructions, which, from the bored expression on the girl's face, I'm sure she's gone over many times before. I wait patiently until the girl makes her escape.

"I need to speak with you," I say.

"I'm a little busy," she replies. "In case you hadn't noticed."

"Yes, you've got a great turnout, but this can't wait. It's about Luther."

"I don't have to listen to your lies about him," she says.

"I'm not here to discuss his character," I say. "I just want to know if he was here that night for the play."

"Yes, he was." She tilts up her chin defiantly. "We'd spoken quite a bit about it and he was interested in what I'd told him about Lila's production. And of course he wanted to see Rudy's performance. Why shouldn't he come?"

Because he'd had an inappropriate sexual relationship with a student here, I'm tempted to say, but instead I ask, "And did he go home to Portland afterward?"

"No," she says with a smug smile. "He stayed with me."

"Oh," I say, pretending that I'm bothered by this. "All night?"

"Of course all night," she snaps, "not that it's any of your business."

"It's my business if you're his alibi for the time of Lila's murder," I say, stepping closer to her.

She takes a step back from me but then squares her shoulders. "In fact, I *am*. Luther couldn't have killed Lila."

"And you're sure he was with you *all* night? He couldn't have gone out for an hour?"

"I'm quite sure—"

"Because here's something I remember about you from when we were housemates, Jill: you sleep like the dead. Especially when you've had a bit to drink. You used to fall asleep on the couch with the lights on and the television blaring. You once slept through a smoke alarm when one of your candles started a fire. So how can you be so sure that Luther didn't go out for an hour in the middle of the night? And why should anyone believe you when you lied about graduating from Yale on your résumé?"

Her face turns red. "How . . . ?" Then she smirks. "Did your husband tell you that? Did you wonder why he needs you to discredit Luther's alibi so much?"

"Have you wondered," I say, stepping closer to her and lowering my voice, "what he's really doing with you? A man with a history of abusing teenage girls? Do you really think it's *you* he's interested in or"—I look around the dressing room with its piles of discarded female clothing and its aura of teenage girlhood—"or is it your access?"

Her face gets even redder. She's angry but there's also a glint of doubt in her eyes. As I turn to leave I almost feel sorry for her. I remember what it was like to have my idol topple. But pity is quickly swallowed by anger. How many more girls' lives will be ruined by Luther? I have to make sure that Lila is the last.

THE LAST THING I want to do now is sit still in a crowded room and watch a play about hysterical teenage girls. But this is my only chance to see Rudy perform so I squeeze past Martha

James, who's parked her wheelie bag in the aisle and has a stack of papers in her lap, and Jean to the empty seat beside Harmon. A murmur moves through the audience: *Can you believe . . . Didn't think . . . coming here . . .*

I can feel blood rushing to my face, sure the crowd is muttering about me, but then I see that it's Woody Hull coming down the aisle who's caused the reaction. I'm as surprised and outraged as the rest of the crowd. What is he thinking? Hasn't he heard what people are saying? Or is this his idea of brazening it out?

Jean gets up and goes to meet him in the aisle. She's pulled herself together since I saw her earlier in the day—her hair is styled and she's wearing an elegant, tailored blue dress—but her face is etched with fatigue and worry as she bends to whisper in Woody's ear. She is explaining, I imagine, why it is not the best idea for him to attend this particular performance. In response, Woody rears back his grizzled head and brays loudly, "After all the goddamned money I give this school, I think the least it owes me is a goddamned seat!"

"He can have mine," I say, glad to have an excuse not to sit near the front. "I can stand in the back." But Martha James has already gotten up. "I've already seen it," she says, "and I've got so much grading to do. Have my seat, Mr. Hull. Please."

Jean thanks Martha, who stuffs her papers in her bag and then loudly and awkwardly drags it up the aisle. Woody sits down, spreading his legs so far that Jean has to squeeze her knees next to mine. She gives me an exasperated look and whispers, "Did you talk to Bantree?" I nod and mouth *Tell you later* as the chapel is plunged into darkness.

A drum beats, slowly at first, and then faster, speeding my heartbeat with it. A flickering candle appears on the stage, seeming to float of its own accord. I think of the light that legend says shines from the Maiden Stone and I imagine Lila behind that light, her disembodied soul roaming the woods for all eternity, seeking vengeance. Then other lights ignite on the stage and move in a circle, intertwining with one another, braiding an intricate dance around an invisible maypole to the fast and insistent drumbeat. I imagine the lights are meant to be the Salem girls dancing in the woods before they're discovered by the Reverend Parris, the prelude to all the action of the play, but I can't help think it's an allusion to the lost girls and the legend of the Maiden Stone—a conclusion borne out when the backdrop becomes visible. It's a rugged coastline that could be Colonial Salem but is actually the view from campus of the Point and Maiden Island. The light reveals five girls dancing, holding not candles, but cell phones with flickering candles on their screens.

One of the girls steps forward, holding her phone out to the audience. The light from her phone streaks her face with shadow and light, which makes it look like she's wearing warpaint—or blood. I don't recognize Rachel Lazar until she speaks.

"The edge of the wilderness was close by," she announces, quoting a line I recognize from Arthur Miller's prologue. "The American continent stretched endlessly west, and it was full of mystery for them. It stood, dark and threatening, over their shoulders—"

Each of the girls looks over her shoulder. It's as if they're looking at the Maiden Stone.

"—night and day, for out of it—" They turn back to the audience, their faces now dyed red by stage lights. I know the line that comes next: *for out of it Indian tribes marauded from time to time, and Reverend Parris had parishioners who had lost relatives to these heathen*—but I know that Lila had wanted to change it because she thought it was insensitive to Native Americans. We'd had a discussion in class about whether it was ethical to change an author's words. I find I'm holding my breath to hear what comes next—as if I'm waiting to see what is coming out of the wilderness for me.

"For out of it dangers came," all five girls chant, "sometimes not from the wilderness outside but from the wilderness inside our own hearts."

Rachel speaks alone next. "This performance is dedicated to our fallen friend, Lila Zeller, who was lost in that wilderness."

The girls take deep breaths and blow out their virtual candles on a single drumbeat, plunging the stage back into the dark. I find I'm gasping for breath, my heart racing, as if I've been running. Then the lights come up and we're in an ordinary room. According to the play it's supposed to be the bedroom in Reverend Parris's house, but last year the junior class went to a performance of *The Crucible* on Broadway and Lila had been so struck by the production that she decided to emulate it. The girls are wearing traditional school uniforms, which haven't been worn at Haywood for over a decade, and there's an electronic white board at the center of the stage. I feel Harmon shift in his seat and I know what he's thinking: all of this electronic gadgetry is distracting from the spirit of the play.

I see, though, how the board is being used. When the

Reverend Parris asks Abigail Williams if her name in town is "entirely white" and she answers "there be no blush about my name" a text message appears on screen: *OMG did you hear why Goody Proctor fired Abigail Williams? Hint: It has something to do with John Proctor!* [winky-face emoji] The audience laughs, a release of tension that soon evaporates when John Proctor and Abigail square off against each other.

I'm tense the moment Rudy appears onstage, afraid he'll forget a line or falter under the scrutiny of the whole Haywood community. But I've never seen my son so self-assured. He plays John Proctor with a wry charm and confident swagger. It makes him seem older. It makes him seem—

It makes him seem like Luther.

I have always tried very hard not to see Luther in Rudy. It is not Rudy's fault that his father was what he was, and while I don't know what made Luther into the man I knew, I have struggled against thinking it's anything genetic that Rudy could be heir to. And mostly it hasn't been hard. Rudy is gentle and diffident where Luther was brusque and boastful.

Now, though, with Rudy dressed to look older and projecting John Proctor's confidence, Luther is stamped all over him. Perhaps it's inevitable. *The Crucible* was one of Luther's favorite works to teach. He loved talking about the Puritans' fear of the wilderness, the dark sins and secrets that festered in their hearts and ran riot when released. *Puritans had no means like the Catholic confessional to exculpate sins,* he'd say, *and so the trials became a public ritual to air old grievances and confess secret lusts. If I fantasize about some young girl*—he'd looked straight at me—*I'd say she came flying in through my window at night to sit on my chest. If you had a crush on an older man, you might accuse his wife.*

He loved using *The Crucible* as a parable for the persecution of the individual by a corrupt society. He loved John Proctor's speech at the end where he declares he will not sacrifice his reputation to save his life. When Ashley Burton accused Luther of molesting her, he called it a witch hunt. But when I pointed out that he could explain his innocence by revealing his affair with me, like John Proctor does by confessing his affair with Abigail, he said it wasn't the same.

We make our allegories by choosing what part of the story to remember.

Watching the play now it strikes me that the story of persecution Miller fashioned as an allegory for 1950s McCarthy-era communist-hunting is less the point than the story of John Proctor sleeping with his seventeen-year-old servant and then calling her a whore when she accuses his wife of witchcraft. Why was the relationship with Abigail Williams even in the play? In real life Abigail Williams was eleven and John Proctor was sixty. It feels like victim blaming. Like a convenient way to discredit an accuser. Hadn't Woody Hull also called the accusations against him a witch hunt?

I look over to see Woody Hull smiling smugly. *That's* why he wanted to come to the performance. *See,* I can imagine him saying, *it's all the fault of these hysterical girls.*

Lila's production lends itself to this interpretation. The girls' accusations against the townspeople appear as texts and tweets on the white board. When John Proctor confronts Abigail, the other girls circle them, taking pictures with their phones that appear on the screen, and when John Proctor confesses his affair with Abigail a Snapchat banner appears with the headline: "John Proctor is a lech!"

I glance over at Harmon to see if he's enjoying the sly critique of Internet culture and am shocked to see that there are tears streaming down his face. Is he thinking about how the police accused him of "untoward" behavior? While guilty Woody Hull is watching this play as a vindication of his innocence, innocent Harmon is seeing guilt. It makes me angry. For the first time watching this play, I am squarely on the side of those girls who found their retribution where they could. Only when John Proctor is led away do I remember that this is what could happen to Rudy.

There's a drumroll that signals the execution and then the gallows appear. The five girls who started the accusations stand in front of it. They're wearing placards around their necks that read WITCH. This was not in the original play but it is powerful; I suppose it signifies that we are what we accuse others of being.

Samantha Grimes steps forward and turns her placard around. The name Priscilla Barnes is written on it.

"I'm Priscilla Barnes," Samantha says. "I was born in 1937 and remanded to the Haywood Refuge for Wayward Girls in 1952. I gave birth to a baby girl ten months later. My baby was taken from me and put up for adoption. I disappeared from Haywood in November of 1954. The records say I was a runaway but no trace of me has ever been found."

She steps back and Paola Fernandez steps forward, turning her placard around to reveal the name Barbara Hampton. "I was sent to Haywood in 1955 because my stepfather raped me. I didn't give birth until I'd been here a year and a half, though. My baby died in childbirth and I disappeared two weeks later. No one ever saw me again."

"This wasn't in the first night's version," Jean says under her breath. "Did you know about this?"

I shake my head, wondering if Luther fed this idea to Jill.

The third girl steps forward. Her placard reads SHIRLEY EAMES. "I got sent here in 1958 by a judge in Boston because she didn't know where else to send me. I'm black, you see"— there's a ripple of giggles because the girl playing the part, Sophie Watanabe, is not black—"and Protestant and all the good orphanages in New York are for Catholics and Jews. I had a baby here who was taken from me and then I vanished. My record says 'Suicide' but if that's so, where's my body?"

Dakota Wyatt steps up next, holding out her placard: NOREEN BAGLEY. "By the time they found my body on Kennebec Beach my eyes had been eaten out by crabs. 'Accidental death,' it says in my record, but isn't it funny that I'd had a list of these girls"—she points to the three girls on her right—"in my room and that the man who found my body was Woody Hull." She points down into the audience and a spotlight appears on Woody's bald head. The murmur in the audience grows and I notice now that it's accompanied by a low drumbeat.

Rachel Lazar steps forward, but she doesn't turn her placard. "I noticed that all three of the missing girls were part of a hiking group that Woody Hull led," she says. "Woody Hull also was in charge of the search for Noreen Bagley. Cora Rockwell, the headmistress at the time, records in her diary that Woody

Hull knew there was a list of the missing girls in Noreen's room even though Cora had taken it down before she showed him the room. I took my suspicions to Woody Hull and then"—she turns the placard around to reveal Lila's name—"I was found dead beneath the Point."

"I was at home in bed!" Woody yells, struggling to his feet. "The police have exonerated me!" He shakes his cane at the stage, blinking in the spotlight.

"Who the hell is manning the lights?" Jean mutters, getting to her feet.

"This is a witch hunt!" Woody yells, turning to face the audience. He looks like he's playing the part of Angry Old Man yelling at kids to get off his lawn. Jean reaches for his arm and he swings the cane at her, catching her on the cheek. Someone screams. Harmon is pushing past me, trying to get to Woody, who is now lumbering up the aisle, head down, like a bull charging. The spotlight stays on him—who the hell *is* manning it?—turning his bald skull an angry red.

Harmon is right behind Woody, reaching for him as he stumbles and goes down. There's a loud thump that I think is the sound of Woody's body hitting the floor but then realize is the drum. *Who the hell is still drumming?* I push past Jean and through the now-crowded aisle. Harmon is kneeling beside Woody, pushing his hands down on Woody's chest, trying to breathe life into Woody's slack mouth even though anyone can see from the vacant, fixed stare on Woody's face that he's gone. With his sweat-drenched face, and ooze coming from his mouth, he looks like he has drowned on dry land.

CHAPTER TWENTY-FOUR

Harmon keeps administering CPR long after it's obvious there's no use. I want to tell him to stop, but I know Harmon; he has to do something. He'll do this until the EMTs arrive. I look up to ask the crowd if anyone has called 911—and see *him*.

He's leaning in the doorway to the balcony—of course, I think, *he* was manning the lights—arms crossed over his broad chest, looking straight at me. *Luther.* A spark ignites inside me, like a small electrical fire caused by a faulty wire, as our eyes meet. He smiles. The ease of it infuriates me. Then he turns and walks out the front door.

I am up and following him before I know that I mean to, drawn by that slow easy smile as if by a leash. I follow him out the door into the night. He's standing on the edge of the woods, his white shirt glowing in the moonlight, lighting a cigarette. When he sees me he shakes out the match, tosses it to the ground, and walks into the woods. He's taunting me, daring me to follow him. I'm shaking, but it's no longer with anger; it's with fear. The monster who stalks my nightmares is *here* and, as in a nightmare, I am being drawn forward into the last place I should go.

I *won't* go. I'll call Kevin Bantree. I take out my phone—

But what if Luther's gone by the time he gets here? What if this is my only chance to get Luther to admit to killing Lila? What if this is my last chance to save Rudy *and* Harmon?

Instead of calling the police I set the voice memo to *record*.

Then I follow Luther into the woods. Even without the glimpses of his white shirt I'd know how to follow him. The path he's taken leads to Warden House. He's taking me to the clearing where we used to have our bonfires, where Luther told his stories to a circle of enraptured girls. *Girls,* he once told me, *are so easy to scare.*

When I emerge into the clearing, he's lounging on one of the stones in the circle, his long legs stretched out in front of him. "Tess," he says, as if it's been twelve minutes instead of twelve years since we've seen each other last. "I was hoping you'd come. We have a lot to talk about."

"Yes," I say, sitting down on the stone next to him. Being so close to him makes my skin crawl but I want to make sure the phone picks up his voice. "You must be satisfied seeing Woody destroyed."

He shrugs. "Aren't you? He was a pompous old ass and he was horrible to you. Or have you forgotten?"

"I haven't forgotten anything," I say. "But I didn't want him dead."

"Me neither," he says, grounding his cigarette out under the heel of his boot. "It's too good for him. He should have to account for his sins, watch his reputation crumble."

"Is that why you're here? To exact revenge?"

He shakes his head. He doesn't wear his hair as long as he used to but it's still full enough to fall over his brow in the same silky waves I love on Rudy. I notice glints of silver in the moonlight. Otherwise he doesn't seem to have aged at all. "All I did was show that girl Cora Rockwell's diary."

"Lila? You met with her?" I ask.

"She responded to a post I wrote on a local history site and started following me on Twitter. We started talking online and she asked me for help on her research project. All I did was tell her about Cora's diary and suggest she go to the Rockwell House in Portland. I've been doing research there. After the island I went back to grad school and finished my doctorate." He must see my surprise. "What did you think, Tess? That I was moping around mourning for you all these years? Yeah, it was a shock to have the mother of my child try to kill me, but in a way you did me a favor. Your departure was a wake-up call. I knew I had to get my life together if I ever wanted Rudy to be a part of it."

I want to point out that it wasn't me who hit him over the head with an oar, but I remember that we're being recorded and I'd rather not spell out Rudy's guilt. "So you found a way back into our lives through Lila," I prompt.

"As I said, she asked to meet with me after I told her about Cora Rockwell's diary. I've long wondered if Woody Hull had anything to do with those deaths but I didn't think I had enough to prove it. Lila did, though. The minute she read that diary she wanted to confront him. I urged her to be careful but she was quite headstrong." He smiles. "She reminded me of you."

"Lila was *nothing* like me," I spit out. "She was confident and radiant. I didn't have any of her poise and direction at that age. If I had, maybe I wouldn't have been such an easy target for you."

Luther regards me silently for a long moment, his eyes gleaming in the moonlight. "Is that how you see it? You think I was drawn to you because you were weak?"

This isn't what I want to talk about, but I can't resist confronting Luther with the truth. "I was a total mess. My mom had just died of cancer and my father sold my childhood home and remarried. I was in a strange place where I felt like I didn't belong and you—you flattered me and dangled the promise of love and comfort in front of me. You took advantage of a vulnerable teenager to make yourself feel big and important."

He stares at me, his eyes huge dark holes in his pale face. "Tess"—I can't help it; I shiver when he says my name—"I know what I did was wrong but I wasn't drawn to you because you were *weak*. I was amazed by how strong you were despite all the hardships you'd been through. And the way you took all your grief and pain and put it in your writing. I . . . I think I wanted some of that strength for myself. I've realized since then that *I* was at a very vulnerable place. I was diagnosed with bipolar disorder a few years ago and I see now that I was in a manic stage when we met and then I descended into a severe depression on the island."

"You threw Rudy into the lake," I say, anger making my voice shake. "You broke his arm—"

"That was an accident," he says. "He fell from a tree—"

"Which you made him climb," I spit back.

"He only fell when you screamed. You made him fall."

"Is that what you tell yourself?" I demand. "Was what happened to Lila an accident too? Did you *accidentally* push her off the Point?"

He leans forward. "Is that what you think? That *I* killed Lila? God, Tess, what happened to you? This life you're leading—the good little wife and schoolteacher in your white house and station wagon—has it made you *blind*? That girl was infatuated with your husband; she couldn't stop talking about him."

"Harmon wouldn't hurt a fly," I say, "and he would never take advantage of a student. He doesn't need his ego bolstered by an awestruck teenager."

"Why not? Because he's got you to do that? Do you tell him that it's fine to teach high school after spending ten years getting a PhD? And if Harmon's so unthreatened, why have you abandoned your writing? Are you afraid he'd be jealous if he saw how much talent you have?"

"Like you were?"

He recoils as if stung, but then he nods. "You're right. I *was* jealous. You had more talent in your little finger than I ever had. So why did you abandon it, Tess?"

I can't help it; I feel a tingle of pleasure at his praise—and then a sickening lurch at the realization of how easily he can still play me. "Maybe because the only person who ever praised me turned out to be a child molester. Maybe because making a living and raising a child on my own hasn't left me a lot of time for hobbies."

"Or maybe because you're living a lie," he says. "Rudy told me about the stories you made up—about living in Portland and hooking up with a seasonal fisherman. This whole persona you've adopted is not who you really are. Even Lila saw that."

"Lila?" I say, surprised.

"Yeah, she said you were a really cool woman but you'd buried your own dreams to raise Rudy. She thought that was why you were always hovering over Rudy, that it was an excuse not to pursue your own dreams."

I blink, stung by this picture of myself. I remember Lila asking me if I'd always wanted to be a high school teacher. I talked so passionately about authors and books in class—had I ever wanted to be a writer? Why had I given it up? And all the time, while I turned over my kitchen to her messy, vegan casseroles and proofread her college essays, she was judging me—

And then I see what Luther is doing. What he's always done. He's spun a story in his own image. It's a distraction. I need to take control.

"When was this?" I ask. "The night of the play? I hear you were up here."

"Of course I came. I wanted to see *my son*." He says the words so tenderly that I am momentarily disarmed. But then I remember how he demonstrated his love when we were on the island. How he pushed Rudy to satisfy his own ego even if it meant putting Rudy in danger.

"And spend the night with Jill Frankel? Does she know you left in the middle of the night to meet Lila? What happened,

Luther? Did you think you could manipulate Lila the way you manipulated me? Did she threaten to tell Rudy you'd been using her to get to him? She wouldn't have been as easy to intimidate as I was. Lila would have fought back. You'd have to throw her from the Point to keep her quiet."

Luther's face looks ravaged in the pitiless moonlight, as if I've ripped off the protective cellophane wrapping that seals in his emotions. I've made him see himself for what he is, but I feel no triumph. There's too much of Rudy in his face for me to hate him anymore. I feel a terrible kind of pity for him, and the aching realization of what it will do to Rudy when it comes out that his father killed his girlfriend. "If you confess," I say, offering the only solace I can, "they might believe it was an accident."

"Oh, Tess," he says, leaning closer to me so that his face is only inches from mine and sliding his arm around my waist. I want to move away but I'm afraid that if I show fear I'll break the moment and he won't say the words I need him to say. *Confess!* I want to shout as the judges demand of John Proctor. "You're right. Lila was nothing like you. She was a naive child and I . . ." He lowers his voice to a whisper as if he can't bear for even the trees to hear his confession. His lips touch my lips and then brush across my face to my ear, where he whispers the last words so low I feel them more than hear them, as if they're branded on my flesh. I have to squeeze my eyes shut and clench my nails into my palms to keep from screaming.

When I open them he's gone. Vanished. As if he were one of those spectral visitations the villagers of Salem were so prone to in the winter of 1692. I almost think I imagined him until

I hear a rustle at the edge of the clearing and turn—but it's not Luther, it's Harmon, his face so stricken it's clear he saw Luther too.

"Tess," he says, "what were you doing? Why were you with him?"

"I was trying to get him to confess," I say, getting to my feet.

"And did he?" Harmon asks. "Did he confess to killing Lila?"

I gape at Harmon, thinking about everything that Luther said—everything I have recorded—and realize that he never gave himself away. It was almost as if he knew I was recording him. Even his last words: *Lila was a naive child and I—*

He had leaned in and whispered in my ear. I'd been so braced for a confession that I can hear it—*I murdered her*—but what he'd said was: *And what I want now is a woman.*

CHAPTER TWENTY-FIVE

Harmon is quiet for most of the drive home. I can tell he's angry because he's got what Rudy calls his I'm-so-disappointed-with-you look on his face. I understand now why it drives Rudy crazy. It's as if an impenetrable glass dome has been lowered down over his whole body, cutting off all access. I feel like nothing I say or do will reach him. When we pull into the garage, though, I try.

"I wanted him to admit to hurting Lila," I say, "to help you."

"Oh," he says dryly, "is that what you were doing with your mouth? Kissing him to get a confession?"

"I didn't kiss him!" I have to keep myself from wiping my mouth to erase the stain of his lips on mine. "He kissed me. I didn't want to move because he was about to confess."

"Oh, Tess." Harmon looks at me the way he looks at Rudy when he tracks mud into the house or misuses the word *literally*. "You're smarter than that. Why would he confess to you? He was either using Lila as bait to seduce you again or—" He grimaces and covers his eyes with his hand.

"Or what?"

"Or you're using Lila as an excuse to see him again."

My stomach turns at the thought even as I feel a guilty pang at the way I'd momentarily preened under his praise.

"That's a horrible thing to say! You're suggesting I *wanted* him to seduce me when I was seventeen—"

"No," he says, holding up one hand to silence me. "Of course you're not to blame for what happened when you were seventeen; I'm the one who told *you* that earlier. But you're not seventeen now. You're a grown woman who went into a secluded spot with a serial child molester. You have to ask yourself why."

"I told you—"

"I don't need you to prove my innocence," he cuts in. "And if that's really what you wanted, you would tell the police who was wearing that sweatshirt earlier in the night."

My mouth goes dry. "What?"

"Please, Tess. I figured it out. The sweatshirt smelled when I put it on. I thought you'd just forgotten to wash it. When Morris told me about the blood on the cuff I figured that Lila must have worn it sometime. But that's not what happened, is it? Rudy was wearing that sweatshirt when you picked him up. You gave him the clean, dry one that was on the radiator because God forbid Rudy have a moment of discomfort. You put the sweatshirt Rudy had been wearing on the radiator to dry and then you let me wear it to jog. You *let* me wear it to the police station and when they found bloodstains on it you didn't tell anyone—not me, not my lawyer, not Kevin Bantree—that Rudy was wearing that sweatshirt when he saw Lila. So let's be clear about who you're protecting here, Tess, because it's not me. You went to that monster to protect Rudy—I don't even blame you for that—but you let him kiss you because for some sick, twisted, messed-up reason you still want him."

He turns and opens the car door. I start to stop him but what can I say? I can't deny that I lied about the sweatshirt, and a person who would do that is a monster. And a monster might well be drawn to another monster.

WHEN I GO upstairs Harmon is in the guest room with the door closed so I go back downstairs, too agitated to even contemplate sleep even though I'm so tired the backs of my eyes ache. I go instead into the dining room, open up my laptop, and search Woody's name on Twitter to see what people are saying. Some tweets suggest that he was unfairly hounded to death over unproven allegations but these are quickly shouted down by those sure of his guilt.

> *He got what he deserved.*
> *If he wasn't guilty why was he so upset by the accusations?*
> *It's about time there was justice for those lost girls.*

This one was tweeted by LostGirl99, whose tweet I saw earlier in the day on Jill's feed. When I click on her profile picture to get a closer look I find a photograph of Noreen Bagley against a backdrop of peeling wallpaper that I recognize from the Cora Rockwell museum. Her bio says that she is a "tea lover, history devotee, and searcher of lost girls," and that she manages a website called "Lost Girls of the Maiden Stone." I recall that the site was linked to a tweet I saw before. I click on the site now and find atmospheric shots of Maiden Island in the fog, pictures of the girls who went missing, excerpts from Cora Rockwell's diary, and theories of what happened to the girls. Three weeks ago LostGirl99 posted a picture of Cora Rockwell's diary with the caption: *Do the secrets of the lost girls lie here?*

Lila had replied to the post: *Where can I read it?* and Ice-Virgin33 responded: *The Cora Rockwell House. PM me and I'll tell you more.*

So there it was; that's how they were connected. Luther was telling the truth about that. I scroll back to the top of the page. The most recent posts make a case against Woody Hull. There are photos of a young Woody leading hikes with the Refuge girls, old newspaper articles about his efforts to find Noreen Bagley, and links to stories about Woody's donations over the years to Haywood Academy and the Rock Harbor Historical Society.

Why has Woody Hull given so much money to the school and scholarship program over the years? one post asks. *Since his retirement in 1999, Woody Hull has given increasingly more money to scholarships for underprivileged girls both to attend the Haywood school and go to college after graduation. Does he do this out of the goodness of his heart? Or is someone extorting hush money from him to keep his crimes hidden?*

I click on a link and find myself looking at a picture of Woody Hull and Jean Shire at a fund-raising event for the school. The caption of the article is "Headmistress Shire accepts generous donation to scholarship program." Below, LostGirl99 has posted *How has Jean Shire gotten Woody Hull to donate so much money to underprivileged girls? What does she know?*

I scroll down through the comments:

> *Wasn't she Woody Hull's assistant before she became headmistress?*
> *How could she not have known what he was?*
> *If she knew and didn't report him she is just as guilty as him.*
> *She's his enabler . . . his cover-up . . . his pimp.*

I feel a sudden chill that makes me look up at the window across from me. The curtains have been left undrawn—a chore Harmon usually attends to before going to bed—and I feel suddenly exposed. I get up to draw the drapes but pause at the window, my hand frozen on the cord. *The scholarship.* Jean got me that scholarship even though it had been six years since I graduated from Haywood and my academic record was pretty dismal.

I'll pull some strings, she'd told me with a flip of her well-manicured hand. I'd been in awe of her then—of her elegance and competence and enlightened vision for the school. *Places like this,* she told me, *can't just be for the children of the rich. Haywood can do so much more; it can change lives.*

I'd worked with her on the outreach program to inner-city schools. She'd extended the scholarship program to bring minority and underprivileged students to Haywood and then send them to college—all bankrolled by the Haywood family fortune.

If I ever wondered how she did it, I attributed her success to her persuasiveness, her driving ambition, her charm.

Not to blackmail.

But what if there is something to the rumors? What if she *had* used something she knew about Woody to make him fork over the money for those scholarships? Would that really be so bad? Look at all the young people she had helped, students like Paola Fernandez, who had come out of a poor school in Yonkers and was going on to Mount Holyoke in the fall. Maybe I could help Jean put together a list of all the students who had benefitted from those scholarships to counterbalance the accusations—

But I see another list in my mind.

Priscilla Barnes
Barbara Hampton
Shirley Eames

Was there any counterbalance to those dead girls? And for all I knew there might be more. Girls that Woody mistreated over the years, predatory teachers he overlooked—

Like Luther. Had Jean known about me and Luther? Had that been one more thing to hold over Woody's head as leverage to get him to give me that scholarship?

No, I can't believe that, I tell myself as I pull the drapes shut. Jean was a mother; she'd never stand by and watch another young woman be victimized. I'm letting myself be carried away on a tide of speculation and gossip. I'll talk to Jean myself tomorrow.

I turn away from the window to the warm lamplit room, safe now behind closed drapes, but the laptop reminds me what an illusion that is. No closed drapes can shut out the world flooding in through *that* window.

CHAPTER TWENTY-SIX

've only managed to get a few hours of sleep when my phone alarm goes off. I set it for six so that I can get to campus to talk to Jean before anyone else gets in. Jean's always in her office by seven. I'm hoping that she's sticking to her routine even though she's being trashed on the Internet.

When I get downstairs I'm surprised to find Harmon up and sitting at the dining room table, drinking coffee and eating cereal like it's a normal day. I'm even more surprised to see that instead of reading his customary *Boston Globe* he's looking at my laptop screen. It's on the tip of my tongue to complain that he's invading my privacy but after our fight last night I can't do it. How can I complain that he's invading my privacy when I'm withholding evidence that could exonerate him?

"Are they still going after Jean?" I ask after I've poured a cup of coffee and sat down at the table.

He looks up at me over the rims of his glasses. His eyes are bloodshot. He hasn't gotten much sleep either. "I'd be tempted to call it a witch hunt but I think that phrase is getting overused these days."

I shudder, recalling they were Woody's last words. "Poor Jean," I say.

He nods and turns the screen so I can see it. "Where do they get all these pictures?" he asks. "There are photos of Jean and Woody going back to the eighties, long before the Internet or digital cameras."

"People take pictures of old photos with their phones," I say, scanning the photos. "But also, Jean had some students digitize old newsletter and yearbook photos for the school's website, so some of these could be from there." There's one of a young Jean standing next to Woody at some outdoor party. His arm is around her and she looks uncomfortable. "I don't understand why these are supposed to be so incriminating. Jean was Woody's assistant. She couldn't help it if he wanted to pose next to her at parties."

"Some of these posts suggest she might have been sleeping with him."

"That's ridiculous," I say, recalling Luther making the same spiteful suggestion, "*and* misogynistic—as if the only way a woman can attain power is by sleeping with a man."

"It's rumormongering at its worst," Harmon agrees with a look of distaste on his face. "But I do remember there was talk when she was made interim headmistress. It was meant to be temporary, did you know that? Woody resigned without much notice and the board appointed Jean interim headmistress because she knew how things worked. They planned to do a nationwide search for a new head of school but then Woody Hull threatened to withdraw his funding if Jean was replaced."

"Oh!" I say, surprised. "I didn't know that."

"Very few people *did* know, only the members of the board and whomever they told—as my mother told me. But someone is spreading that information now. Would you happen to know who IceVirgin33 is?" He turns the screen toward me so that I can see the latest tweet: *Why did Woody Hull blackmail the Haywood Board into keeping Jean Shire as headmistress? What hold did she have on him?*

"Oh my God," I say, "that's awful."

"Yes, but the question is how did this"—he gives the screen a look of disgust— "*person* know? Who is this IceVirgin33?"

I could say that I'm not sure but that would be disingenuous. "It's Luther," I say reluctantly. "He's been interacting with Jill and Lila online and then he texted Rudy to lure him down to Portland."

But Harmon doesn't seem upset by my mentioning Luther. "That makes sense. Luther's uncle was on the board. He might have heard about the rumor from him." He makes a face. "I'm sorry about the things I said last night. Seeing you two together . . ." His voice cracks and I'm alarmed to see that he's on the verge of tears.

"I only wanted to get him to confess," I say. "I wasn't just thinking about Rudy, but you're right. It was wrong of me not to tell Kevin about the sweatshirt. I . . . I just couldn't bear the thought of them arresting Rudy. But I'll go to the police station today and tell him everything."

"No," Harmon says. "I don't want Rudy involved in this. *I'll* talk to Morris today and ask why they're not looking at Luther.

If, as you said, there's a record of communication on the Internet between him and Lila, they should be looking at him more closely."

I'm relieved that Harmon has turned down my offer of telling the police about the sweatshirt. I know it's the right thing to do but every fiber of my being rebels against the idea of putting Rudy in danger. "Thank you," I say. "I promise I won't let you take the blame for this."

He squeezes my hand. "I know you won't." His assurance touches me; I just wish I knew how I'm going to make good on my promise.

I GET TO campus later than I meant to. Maryanne is already at her desk, glaring at a row of blinking lights on her phone.

"Is she in?" I ask.

She sighs. "She just got off the phone with Chelsea Whittenberg. I was giving her a moment before telling her about the six other calls waiting for her."

"Are they all blaming Jean?"

Maryanne wheels back in her chair to scan the hallway for lingering students, but it's empty. The whole campus feels eerily empty, I realize, as if we were living in the aftermath of an apocalypse. She motions for me to come closer and whispers, "The board's asking her to resign. They want her to fall on her sword, as if the lot of them hadn't known what kind of lech Woody Hull was all along."

"That's awful," I say. "Do you think she will?"

"I don't know," Maryanne says, eyeing the door to Jean's office. "A week ago I'd have said she'd fight it, but the fight's gone out of her. I haven't seen her look like this since Tracy was alive."

"You mean since Tracy died?" I ask.

Maryanne shakes her head. "No, I mean, of course that was terrible, but Jean was actually amazing after that. She came in a week after Tracy's funeral and asked me to get her all the stats for drug addiction in teens and all the studies that identified risk factors for addiction and self-destructive behavior. 'We're going to keep this from happening to other children,' she told me." Maryanne wipes away a tear. "She was a warrior. You know when my Ben got addicted to pain pills after he tore his rotator cuff, Jean got him into the best rehab treatment in the state and made sure the school's insurance policy paid for it."

"I . . . I didn't know . . ." I stammer, thinking of all the times I've envied Maryanne's picture-perfect family.

Maryanne laughs while reaching for a tissue. "We told everyone he was at soccer camp in Michigan. Jean was the only one who knew. Anyway, what I meant before wasn't that Jean was okay after Tracy died, but that she went back to work. There were times, though, when Tracy was alive that Jean would get a call from her or from the police or her parole officer, and you could see the stuffing get sucked right out of her. Those were the only times I'd see her look like she didn't know what to do . . . until now." She looks up at me. "Maybe you can help. After all you've been through . . . maybe you can help Jean find the strength to fight this."

The idea that I might be able to help Jean find strength almost makes me laugh, but when I walk into Jean's office I don't feel like laughing. Even though she's facing away from me, look-ing out the window, I can see by the slump of her shoulders that she's given up. I've never seen her like this. I want to turn around and flee—there's nothing I can do for her—but then I remember who's brought her to this and it makes me angry. Lu-ther doesn't have a right to tear down someone as good as Jean.

"This isn't fair, Jean," I say, approaching the desk. "They can't blame you for Woody's crimes."

She turns to me and for a moment I think I've made a mis-take; this isn't Jean. It's a waxwork dummy that's been propped up in her place. Even her voice when she speaks sounds like that of one of those computer-generated avatars.

"But you see, the thing is, I knew."

"What do you mean? You suspected—"

"I didn't suspect; I *knew*. I knew about the three girls he got pregnant when Haywood was a refuge, about how he made them disappear, and that he killed Noreen Bagley."

I sink down into a chair. "How—?"

"When I was his assistant he used to send me down to Port-land to help out Ms. Rockwell—or 'that old bat,' as he used to call her. We became quite close, Cora and me. She explained the 'deal' she had with Woody. She was really a very clever woman. In another age she would have made an excellent CEO or politician."

"The list on Noreen's wall," I say. "Woody knew about it even though he claimed not to have been in the room before."

"Exactly, but Cora had something else. When Noreen's coat washed up on Kennebec Beach, Woody's handkerchief was found in its pocket."

I recall Lucinda Perkins saying the museum had the coat but kept it stored away because it smelled. This, though, presents another explanation. "Why didn't she go to the police?"

"She didn't think she'd be believed. Remember her background; she'd been sent to the Refuge for 'lewd behavior.' She'd risen to the role of headmistress by her hard work but no one forgot where she came from. It all would have come up if she accused Woody Hull—a rich and powerful man—of impregnating and killing those girls. So she blackmailed him instead."

"Her pension and the house in Portland . . ."

"Yes, but so much more!" A bit of Jean's old fire sparks in her eyes. "She made Woody promise to begin a scholarship program for underprivileged girls."

"But she left him *in charge* of a school full of innocent girls!"

Jean nods. "She swore to him that if she ever heard that he touched another girl she'd expose him. That's where I came in. She deputized me as her watchdog. I was supposed to keep an eye on Woody, make sure he never transgressed again. And he didn't."

"But all those allegations on the Internet . . . "

"Oh, I can't swear that he never touched a girl here and there but I'm sure it never went beyond that. Or do you think *every* accusation of sexual misconduct is true?"

I'm shocked to hear Jean ask that question—but then I remember Ashley Burton. "No," I say, "but I think most of them are."

"I think those girls—and women—writing in now had good reason to know there was something off about Woody and and that he behaved in ways that today we wouldn't hesitate to call inappropriate. But if I had brought that kind of behavior to the board ten years ago they would have dismissed it. Even the disgusting things he said to you."

It takes me a moment to realize what she's saying. "You overheard him call me a slut," I say, "and you didn't do anything about *that*?"

She flinches and I immediately feel sorry, but then I think of how I felt when I left Woody Hull's office that day. Would I have run away with Luther if Jean had stopped me and talked to me? "I understand why Cora Rockwell didn't think anyone would believe her," I add, "but why didn't you expose Woody? You come from that world; you would have been believed."

Jean holds my gaze for a long moment and then she tilts her chin up defiantly. "Because Tracy needed rehab and I didn't have the money. Tell me you wouldn't do the same for Rudy."

I open my mouth and then close it—then try again. "I can't. I'd do—I've *done*—worse. But Jean, Tracy died five years ago. Why didn't you expose him then?"

"And admit I'd been taking money from him all these years? My career would be over—it *is* over, now. Chelsea Whittenberg just asked me to resign."

"You could fight it."

Jean sighs. "If I do that it will all come out—the money I took from Woody, the deals I've made, even the one I made for you." At my look of surprise she laughs bitterly. "Do you think Woody gave you that scholarship out of the goodness of his heart? I told him he owed it to you for hiring Luther Gunn in the first place."

This had occurred to me last night but hearing Jean admit that she knew that I'd been with Luther when I came back here still stuns me. "So helping me—giving me a job, getting me a scholarship—that was all so you wouldn't feel guilty?"

She gives me a sad smile. "Oh, my dear, nothing I could do would make up for not looking for you when you left here, but I learned a long time ago to live with the guilt." The smile falters. "Or at least I thought I had." She looks at her computer screen. "But if Luther really did kill Lila . . . Well, I don't know if I can live with that. I've been sitting here figuring out how I got here. I was just trying to do the best thing for my daughter. How could it have led to something so wrong?"

CHAPTER TWENTY-SEVEN

It only takes me a few hours to do what I have to do. By noon I am standing in the clearing behind Warden House, shivering in a light rain. I'd heard on the radio driving back from the police station that there's a nor'easter heading for the coast this afternoon but I didn't want to go home for a raincoat.

The ominous gray chill in the air feels suitable for the business at hand. If I had my students here I would point out that this is an excellent example of the pathetic fallacy—the literary device in which nature mirrors the internal emotional state of the narrator. I have set a storm in motion this morning; now I'm waiting for it to break over all our heads.

"I got your message."

I turn to find Luther at the edge of the clearing. He's dressed as he was last night in a white button-down shirt and jeans, no more prepared for the coming storm than I am. "I figured you'd be checking your Twitter notifications pretty often," I say. Of all the strange things I've had to do this morning, tweeting at

IceVirgin33 was perhaps the oddest. "It must be gratifying to watch your enemies fall."

Luther can't resist a rueful smile. "It *is* gratifying to see the truth come out. All these years Jean Shire has preened as this champion of the underprivileged and now it comes out that she was protecting a sexual predator."

"The same sexual predator who protected you," I say.

"Are we here to tell fairy tales?" he asks, spreading his arms wide to indicate the circle. "Let me guess, your story features a beastly ogre who imprisons an innocent princess. And yet as I recall"—he comes closer to me, entering the circle of stones where he would gather his class and tell his stories—"you weren't all that reluctant to go with me."

"I was seventeen," I say.

"Yeah, yeah, so that makes me a 'child molester.'" He crooks his fingers in air quotes. "But you were no child, Tess."

"And what about Lila?" I say. "Was she grown-up enough for you?"

A muscle on the side of his jaw twitches. "I didn't touch that girl. But no, actually, she wasn't as grown-up as she thought she was. She was so sure she wanted to expose Woody Hull for the lecherous child-killer he was, but then she got scared."

"Are you sure that's why she was scared? Maybe *you* frightened her. Meeting a man here . . . alone . . . at night . . ."

Luther tilts his head and smiles. "Are you recording this, Tess?"

So he *did* know that I was recording him last time. No wonder he was so careful about what he said. I take out my phone and show him the screen. "It's just us," I say. "You can tell me everything. I know how you like a good story."

He smiles, his face relaxed. This is why I brought him here. I knew it would be easier to get him to tell his story in this campfire circle. "Okay, so yeah, I did meet Lila here that night. I saw her and Rudy go out toward the Point after the play . . . don't look at me like that. I was only waiting for an opportunity to talk to Rudy if she told him about me. I hung back here, though, and then I saw her coming back from the Point alone. She was upset—I think she'd had a fight with Rudy— and her hand was bleeding. I gave her a handkerchief and she said there was something she wanted to talk to me about. She asked me if I thought it was always better to expose the truth, even if it might hurt innocent people."

It's such a Lila thing to ask that I feel a physical pang. I can almost see her standing here, posing her earnest question.

"I assumed she was having second thoughts about going public with the paper she'd written, that she wasn't sure she wanted to expose Woody Hull at the expense of Jean Shire. I told her that if a person hid another person's crime, they weren't so innocent anymore."

"That's a good answer," I say. "And how did she respond?"

"She didn't get a chance. We heard someone on the coastal path"—he nods toward the north side of the peninsula—"and she got spooked. She thought it was Rudy and she didn't want him to see us together. We walked that way." He points toward the south coastal path.

"It wasn't Rudy," I say. "It was me, going to meet Rudy on the Point. What did you do then?"

He shrugs. "Nothing. Lila didn't want to talk anymore and I figured I'd better get back to Jill." He grins. "Not that she noticed I was gone. The woman sleeps like the dead."

Luther's enjoying this, taking me right up to the precipice of admitting his guilt and backing away. That's all right. I didn't expect him to get there on his own.

My phone rings and I look down to see a rare picture of Rudy smiling that Lila uploaded to my phone at Christmas. I swipe the screen, switching the call to speakerphone.

"Mom!" Rudy's plaintive cry ruptures the still of the clearing and reaches down into my gut. He could be six crying for me in the night. Every atom in my body wants to run to him.

"I'm here, honey," I tell him, just as I would on those nights when he woke up from nightmares. This time, though, the nightmare is real and I am the cause of it.

"Is it true? Did you really turn me in to the police?"

"No, honey, I didn't turn you in. I just told them that the sweatshirt Harmon was wearing when they took him in was the one you'd been wearing earlier in the night."

"But now they think I killed Lila!" he wails. "They're arresting me."

Earlier Kevin Bantree had asked me if I wanted him to hold off on bringing Rudy in. I'd told him no. The only concession I'd asked for was that Rudy be allowed—and encouraged—to call me. "They're not arresting you; they're taking you in for questioning. Just tell them the truth, Rudy, and it will be all right."

"But how? Lila's blood was on my sweatshirt because she cut her hand on a beer bottle, but they'll never believe that—do *you* think I hurt Lila?"

I look up at Luther, who is staring at me as if I've grown horns. "No, Rudy, I know you didn't hurt Lila. When the person who *did* hurt her comes forward, the police will let you go. Just tell the truth and try to stay calm. I love you."

"Mom!" He sounds so scared that again, all I want is to run to him, but I can't. Not yet.

"I've got to go, Rudy. I'll see you soon." I end the call in the middle of another plaintive *Mom!* It's the first time I've ever hung up on him, and I feel like I've been punched in the gut. Every instinct in my body wants to protect him, but then that's what Jean had thought she was doing when she blackmailed Woody to pay for Tracy's rehab. *I was just trying to do the best thing for my daughter,* she'd said. *How could it have led to something so wrong?*

Because that's what hiding the truth did.

I take a deep breath and meet Luther's outraged stare.

"What the hell have you done, Tess?"

"I've given you the opportunity to save your son," I say.

"By turning him in to the police to protect your husband?"

"I didn't turn him in; I just told the truth. Rudy was wearing that sweatshirt when I met him on the Point. It was soaking wet so I gave him Harmon's—then I left the wet one on the radiator and Harmon took it in the morning. I didn't tell the police because I was protecting Rudy, but I can't protect Rudy at the cost of letting Harmon take the blame for something he didn't do."

"So you did it for Harmon."

"No, I did it for Rudy. When you go to the police and tell them you were on the Point with Lila, they'll let Rudy go. I'm letting you be the hero, Luther. Isn't that what you've always wanted?"

He stares at me open-mouthed for a moment and then tilts his head back and laughs. "You're crazy. You've bet our son's welfare on a hunch that *I* killed Lila. What if you're wrong, Tess? What if Harmon killed Lila? Do you think *he's* going to sacrifice himself for Rudy?"

"I know Harmon is innocent—not just because I know *him,* but also because I know Lila. She'd never let herself be taken advantage of by a man the way *I* did. If Harmon had so much as touched her she would have stopped it; she would have told me. I'm sure of it. But would she have gotten involved in trying to prove that Woody Hull killed those girls? Yes. And would she have hesitated to uncover his crimes if she thought it would hurt Jean? Yes, again."

Luther's face is a mask of rage, transporting me back to those times at the cabin when he would explode at me. "Goddamnit, Tess, you've made up a good story but that doesn't mean—"

My phone ringing cuts him off. I look to see if it's Rudy, but it's Kevin Bantree. I answer it and put it on speaker so Luther will know I'm not bluffing.

"Tess," Bantree sounds like he's out of breath. "Rudy made a break for it. I couldn't stop him. He's running toward the Point."

I'm about to ask him how far away he is, but then I catch a flash of purple and gold on the north path. "I see him," I say. "I'll catch up to him."

Luther's seen him too, and he's already running through the trees, trying to cut Rudy off. But Rudy is fast. He's been train-ing for track all year and jogging with Lila. He sprints forward

when he hears Luther and easily evades him. I follow, screaming Rudy's name, but I doubt Rudy can hear anything above his
own labored breathing and the surge of the sea as we get closer
to the Point. The tide is coming in, crashing over the far rocks
on Maiden Island and spilling over the causeway. I'm relieved
to see it. Rudy will have to stop. Then Luther will have to confess or see his son go to jail.

I hear Kevin behind me and he soon catches up with me.
"Go back, Tess," he says. "Let me take care of this."

I shake my head, but he's already pushing past me. I jog
behind him. When the path angles down toward the beach I
catch a glimpse of Rudy and Luther, who have reached the end
of the peninsula just below the Point. Rudy stops and looks
back. He sees Luther close on his heels, he sees the steep path
up to the Point. He turns to face the causeway, which is already underwater. He'll stop now—

But he doesn't. He leaps from the path down onto the causeway. I lose sight of him because of the slope of the ground, just
as I couldn't see the Little Sister Stone when I was here last—
and I picture Rudy broken on that rock as Lila had been. I cry
out and sprint forward. As I come to the end of the path I peer
out and catch my breath. It looks like the causeway is crowded
by figures in white dresses, as if the ghosts of the drowned
sisters have risen out of the sea. But of course it's just the fog,
pillars of which are drifting across the causeway, blurring the
line between water and sand—and obscuring Rudy. Luther is
on the causeway, leaping from one rock to the next through the
incoming tide following Rudy, trying to save him from drown-

ing. I wasn't entirely wrong. Luther does love Rudy, but will his love be enough to save him?

Kevin has stopped on the path and has his radio out. When I reach him he puts his arm out to keep me from plummeting to the causeway.

"I've called the coast guard," he screams over the crash of the waves. "They're sending a boat and rescue equipment."

I nod, too winded to reply, and take a step back. I've made a terrible gamble and put my own son at risk. There's only one way to make up for that. While Kevin turns away to bark another order into his radio I use his distraction to swerve past him and leap down into the surf.

CHAPTER TWENTY-EIGHT

land to the right of the Little Sister Stone, sinking ankle-deep in wet sand and soaking my jeans to the thigh. The sand clutches at me, pulling me down, and just as I get my balance a wave knocks me over. The drifting pillars of fog obscure my vision and make me dizzy. The slate-gray sky wheels above, as deep and wet as the ocean below. Everything is upside down; I've turned my own son in to the police and I'm counting on the monster of my nightmares to save him. How will I ever find my way in this topsy-turvy universe?

Then a hand grabs my arm and hauls me up onto the stone causeway. "We have to go back," Kevin Bantree yells over the crashing waves.

I shake my head and look east. Through the fog I can just make out Rudy. He's almost reached the island and Luther is two or three stones behind him.

"He'll be safe once he gets to the island," Kevin shouts. "We can wait for the next low tide. They're not going anywhere."

That's six hours. It was only half an hour that Rudy sat in the prow of the lifeboat while I rowed us to shore, and only a few feet between us, but that distance grew to a gulf. If I don't bridge this gap between us now, I may never get my son back. "I have to go," I yell, pulling away from him.

He doesn't loosen his grip. "Then I'm going with you. Stay right next to me."

Where else would I go? I wonder as we make our way across the rocks. The ocean and sky have turned the same green-gray and ice water flows from each. Rain needles down like ice spears thrown by an angry god. The ocean crashes against our legs, each wave a little higher. I can barely feel my feet. The temperature must have dropped ten degrees in the last hour. Even if we make it to the island we might all die of hypothermia by the next low tide. I try to keep my eyes on Rudy, but he's swallowed by the gusts of rain and banks of fog. I can't see farther than a few feet ahead of us. I don't even know if we're still heading in the right direction.

But Kevin does. He keeps us moving forward, navigating the stones as if their map is imprinted in his DNA—and maybe it is. He's a local boy, the son of fishermen. In a fairy tale he'd be the child of Selkies, shape-shifting from seal to human form, protected by the spirits of the sea.

"There!" he shouts in a very un-seal-like command. "They're at the Maiden."

He points and I catch a glimpse of the tall standing stone. It's surrounded by water on all sides now, cut off from the island by a gap of six feet. Rudy is clinging to the stone, balanced on the narrow base around it that locals call the Maiden's Skirt. Luther is below him, standing on the last Sister Stone, up to his waist in water.

The next wave that comes in reaches my ribs and lifts me off my feet. It's almost a relief not to have to struggle against the surf. Maybe I can ride this current straight to Rudy—

But Kevin Bantree yanks me back. We're on the second to last Sister Stone now, just behind Luther, who I can hear above the roar of the waves.

"No one thinks you hurt Lila," he's shouting. "Just come back and we'll work it all out."

"He can't come back," Kevin mutters in my ear. "We all have to get to the island."

"Why not?" Rudy wails into the wind. "I almost killed you when I was only five. I thought I *had* killed you."

My heart breaks at the admission. So he *did* remember. All these years he's carried that with him. I *let* him carry that with him. I struggle out of Kevin's grip and wade toward Luther. "That wasn't your fault, Rudy. You did that to save me," I shout.

Luther turns and looks at me. I can see him struggling with something. His eyes are as dark and shifting as the sea boiling around us. Then he turns back to Rudy. "Your mother's right," he shouts. "I wasn't . . . *right* then. I was sick. I didn't know what I was doing. Thank God you stopped me, Rudy. If I had hurt you or your mother, I'd never have been able to live with myself."

I'm so stunned by Luther's words I wonder if the wind and surf are playing tricks on me. Never in all my nightmares of Luther have I imagined him regretting what he did.

Rudy is staring at Luther with something like hope on his face, but then he shakes his head. "Maybe I'm sick in the same way," he cries. "When I get angry everything goes black. It did that night with Lila. I knew she was hiding something from me. She said she couldn't tell me, that it would destroy too many people. I was so angry that I . . . I threw a bottle. I didn't mean to hit her, but it cut her hand. I tried to grab her but she pulled away—"

He holds out his hand, palm up, as if he's seeing her blood there, loosening his grip on the Maiden Stone—

Luther and I lunge forward at the same time, but Kevin reaches me at the last stone and holds me back so it's Luther who gets to the Skirt and pulls Rudy back. Rudy is gasping. "Maybe I did kill her! After I threw the bottle the next thing I remember, Lila was gone and I was wading through the surf. I don't remember how I got there. What if I did push her?"

"No," Luther shouts. "I saw her after she left you. She was crying but only because she cared for you so much. She was afraid she had hurt you. We went back to the Point to make sure you were all right, but when we got there you had already left. And then we fought. I wanted her to expose Woody Hull but she was afraid that it would hurt Jean and your mother." He looks back at me. "You see, I had told Lila that Woody had let me leave Haywood with a seventeen-year-old student. She couldn't bear to expose you and your mother without talking to Tess first. She started to go after you and I tried to hold her back. I was too rough—I'm always too rough!—and she pulled away and fell. I went down to the causeway but she was already dead. And I left her there. I didn't care who took the blame—but I can't let *you* take the blame, Rudy. Not when it's all my fault."

He looks back at me and I feel a chill acknowledgment pass over the water. He's not just admitting to killing Lila; he's taking the blame for the rest. Then his gaze shifts over my shoulder. "Did you get that, Officer Bantree? Are we clear on who killed Lila Zeller?"

"We're clear," Kevin says. "Now let's get to higher ground."

"Get Tess to the island," Luther says. "Rudy and I will follow. Okay, son?"

Rudy looks at Luther and then at me. "That's why you told the police about the sweatshirt," he demands, his voice suddenly firm in his outrage, "to force him to confess?"

"Yes," I say, knowing he may hate me forever for this, "because I knew your father loves you too much to let you take the blame for something he did."

Rudy glares at me. "You always have to interfere," he says.

I can't argue with that. I let Kevin pull me to the low rocks on the edge of the island. We climb until we're above the water and then I turn to watch Rudy wade through the gap between the Maiden Stone and the island. It's deep there and the waves rush into the gap, churning ferociously like the maw of a hungry mouth. Kevin takes off his belt and tosses it to Luther, who takes off his belt and buckles the two together. He tosses one end to Kevin and they hold a lifeline above the gap to guide Rudy across. The waves crash over his head and I hold my breath until Kevin has his arms around Rudy and is hauling him up onto the rock. I throw my arms around him but he shakes me off.

"Let me go. I want to help Dad," he says, taking the belt from Kevin's hand. But Luther has dropped his end of the belt. He's staring into the churning water, like he sees something in it. Then he looks up, grins, and slides into the maelstrom. Rudy howls a scream that seems to make the stones below my feet shake. It takes Kevin and me both to hold him back from following his father.

CHAPTER TWENTY-NINE

The only way Kevin can convince Rudy not to go after Luther is by promising that he will call the coast guard for help. "I can't do that if I have to worry about you going in after your father," he tells Rudy for the third time. "I need to know that you're not going to do that before I can make that call. Do you understand, Rudy?"

Rudy shakes his head as he's done each time so far. "We have to go in and look for him."

"We can't," Kevin says with supernatural patience. "The currents between the Maiden Stone and the island are lethal. Anything that goes in there gets sucked out to sea. The best thing we can do for your father is alert the coast guard so they can search for him along the path of the current."

I'm afraid that Rudy is going to reject this logic again but this time he nods. "Okay. But you gotta promise to call."

"Absolutely, son. Now let's get you and your mother to shelter." Kevin indicates to me that I should hold on to Rudy's arm.

"Hold on to your mother. The rocks are slippery and she's not wearing very practical shoes."

Rudy looks down at my feet. It's the first time he's looked at any part of me since Luther vanished. "She never does," he mutters, taking my arm and leading me over rocks slippery with kelp and bright orange lichen. We follow Kevin to a shallow cave, where we can sit out of the wind and rain, our backs to the rock.

Kevin squats in front of us and looks Rudy in the eyes. "I need you to stay close to your mom. Her lips are blue. You have to keep her warm."

"Make that call," Rudy says. He still won't look at me but he does squeeze closer and puts his arm around me. I'm grateful for Kevin's strategy. If Rudy thinks he's protecting me, I can keep *him* warm and safe.

Kevin gets on the radio and tells the coast guard that a man fell into the water just below the Maiden Stone off Maiden Island. He even knows the coordinates. The reply is so garbled I can't make it out, but Kevin clearly does. "I'm going back to the shore to look for the boat. You stay here." He looks at Rudy. "I need your promise on that."

Rudy nods—or maybe it's just that his head is shaking from the cold. I realize now that we're not moving that my whole body is shaking. Kevin gives me a worried look. "I'll be right back," he says and then he's gone.

I put both arms around Rudy. "I know you're mad at me and that's okay."

"Th-thanks," he stammers. "I-I don't need your permission to be mad."

"I know. I just want you to know I didn't mean for your father . . . I honestly thought I was helping him by giving him a chance to save you. I knew he loved you . . . and I was right. He wanted to save you as much as I did."

"Can we not talk about this now?" he asks.

I nod. At least I think I do. The shaking is so bad I'm basically nodding to everything. Rudy's body is shaking against mine so hard I can hear his teeth clicking together. I steal a look at him and see that he's sobbing. In my plan to get Luther to confess to killing Lila, I hadn't counted on Luther dying in front of Rudy's eyes. For the second time. What have I done to my son? I find myself praying for the coast guard to save Luther.

"Mom?"

I open my eyes and I'm looking into Rudy's pale blue eyes. Eyes the color of a glacial crevasse. Luther's eyes.

"Mom, don't fall asleep. Kevin says they're sending a boat."

He looks so worried! "It's okay," I tell him, "I'm not cold anymore." Only I'm not sure if I actually say the words or not. When I open my mouth to talk, the words that come out leave my mouth like bubbles that float lazily up to the sky. When I look up I see that I'm far below the water's surface. But that's okay. The Ice Virgin's kiss has given me the power to breathe underwater. She is floating above me, holding out her hand for me. I shake my head. I can't go with her, I have to stay here with Rudy. He needs me. I turn to Rudy to explain this but he's getting to his feet, helping me up.

"It's okay, Mom," he's saying. "The boat's here." He puts his arm around my shoulder and helps me to my feet. He's so strong! My son! Why had I never seen how strong he is? All these years I've been so afraid for him I barely even saw him, but now, through the prism of this deep water, he's clear to me. He's fine. He'll be fine without me.

I feel as if an enormous weight has been taken off my chest, as if the line that's been tethering me to an anchor has been cut. I feel light and buoyant as we follow the Ice Virgin to the shore and all the lost girls join us. They're standing on the water in a line between the island and the mainland. Some dressed in white, some in red. One of them is holding a red cloak out to me, offering to help me into it. *Yes,* I want to tell them, *I'm one of you.*

They help me onto a flat-bottomed boat and seat me in the stern. I look for Rudy and can't find him but then one of the red-cloaked figures squeezes my hand and says, "It's okay, Mom." He sits with me in the stern while the lost girls pull the boat along a rope stretched taut between the island and the mainland.

As we move away from the island I feel as if I'm being pulled back through time. The island vanishes in the fog. I picture that other island, on the lake. It too has vanished. I was never there. The five years are gone. Luther never hurt me or Rudy. Rudy never struck his father. We go back to my last night at Haywood. After my interview with Woody Hull, Jean takes me aside. She tells me that what Headmaster Hull said to me was wrong and asks what's going on with me. I've changed this semester. I'm so quiet and withdrawn. I break down and tell her everything—about Luther, about being pregnant. She calls my father—he yells at me and he's upset but then he breaks down and cries and tells me he'll be there in the morning. We'll work it out. I can have the baby or—

I could not. I know that this might have been the best choice. If one of my students came to me pregnant at seventeen, I would tell her to consider not having it. If I could truly go back in time, would I choose not to have Rudy?

I might as well ask if I'd go back before the very first time Luther came into my tent—

Or six months before my mother found the lump in her breast.

The boat is floating on a sea of fog, tethered between past and future. The tide is wiping the sand below us clean of all missteps and stumbles. All I have to do is let go.

So I do. I rise above the boat and look down. The me in the boat is wearing a ridiculous red suit—a survival suit, I think they're called—but the me in the air feels light and warm. Returning to my body means returning to that terrible cold, the burn of flesh coming back to life, and, worse, Rudy hating me for what I've done. It would be easier to just let go. Rudy will be all right without me. I can see how strong he is. He doesn't need me. Harmon might well be *better off* without me.

I can see one of the red suits leaning over, calling my name, pounding my chest. I can see Rudy's face, tear-streaked, grief-stricken. The fact that he's mad at me won't make mourning me any easier. In fact, as I know from losing my own mother at Rudy's age, it will make it worse. He'll blame himself. And that is what tugs me back. Rudy should get to be angry at me, not mourn me. I owe him that. And that obligation is a thin, unbreakable cord, the thinnest filament tugging an airborne kite that lands me smack back in my body with an explosion of heat and cold and pain. I know how much pain is in store for all of us and I'm ready to bear my share of it.

CHAPTER THIRTY

I awake cocooned in something that feels like a body bag. *I'm dead,* I think, *I waited too long to come back.* When you go missing it's not so easy to return. Maybe you never really do.

My next thought is that death should not hurt this much. Every muscle in my body aches; my skin feels like it's on fire; my throat burns like I've swallowed a gallon of seawater. When I move my head the room spins and a dozen Harmons lean in to say, "You're okay. You're wrapped in heating blankets to restore your core temperature."

I swallow and try to ask for Rudy. Only a croak comes out but Harmon understands me. "Rudy is fine. He had mild hypothermia but he warmed right up. The resilience of youth, right? He's being debriefed by Kevin Bantree—don't worry, Morris is with them and Bantree's assured me that neither I nor Rudy are persons of interest anymore." He looks at me gravely. "You took an awful risk telling Bantree about the sweatshirt. What if Luther hadn't confessed?"

"It was the truth," I try to say, but from the frown on his face I'm guessing he doesn't understand.

"Get some rest," he says. "There will be plenty of time to talk later."

BUT SOMEHOW THERE isn't. Although Harmon comes to collect me from the hospital the next day he's preoccupied and distant. "Jean's resigned and the board has asked me to be interim headmaster. Frankly it's such a mess I tried to turn it down, but Chelsea Whittenberg said if I didn't take it they were considering closing down the school and I just couldn't let that happen."

"No!" I say. "Think of what that would do to the lower classmen—especially the scholarship students. Even though the money came to them dishonestly, it still wouldn't be fair to let them suffer."

Harmon nods. "My thought exactly. I'm talking to Morris about Woody's estate to see if we can secure the donations to the school and the scholarship program. I've asked some of the scholarship students to put together a presentation to the board on what the opportunity to go to Haywood has meant to them. Paola Fernandez is heading it up."

"Good choice," I say. "She's come so far academically this year but she's still so shy. It will be good for her to take a leadership role."

"Yes, and it will be good on her résumé. I was thinking that next year we should start a mentorship program for scholarship students . . ."

We talk about his ideas for Haywood for the rest of the trip home, falling into an easy pattern of trading observations about students and classes. I think we both know that we're avoiding more difficult subjects, but we're also grateful for a diversion. We have these things in common. Perhaps if we can reestablish the patterns of our life together the rest—forgiveness, trust, passion—will come later.

It won't be so easy with Rudy. He's nice to me for about fifteen minutes when we get home, offering to make me tea and finding me a sweater when he sees me shivering, but when he fishes my sweater out of my book bag his original birth certificate, the police DV report, his hospital records, and the picture of Luther holding him as a baby all fall out.

"Why did you keep all this from me?" he demands and then storms off before I can answer.

For the next few days he alternately cries and rages. I make an appointment with a psychologist in Portland. It takes the whole first appointment just to bring her up to speed, at the end of which Rudy throws up his hands and says, "Long story short: my dad was crazy and my mom's a pathological liar who killed him. You probably think you've hit a gold mine."

"I think we have a lot of work ahead of us," the therapist—a woman who reminds me of an older Lila—says, "but you've taken the first step by coming here."

Rudy rolls his eyes and replies, "Whatev," and lopes out of the office. I shiver and huddle into my cardigan.

"How are you feeling?" she asks me.

"Cold," I say. "I just feel cold all the time."

I can't seem to warm up. Even though the weather is finally settling into summer I'm still wearing long-sleeved shirts and sweaters. I take long hot showers and sleep under a down quilt.

I feel like I never really came fully back into my body, as if a part of me is still hovering over the cold waters off Maiden Island. Or that I've been turned to stone like the tenth sister, doomed to stand sentinel over my own bad choices for all eternity.

KEVIN COMES TO visit me at the end of the week to "tie up some loose ends." I make us hot tea and wave him into the living room, where I've got the gas fire going. We sit on the couch; I curl into the corner while Kevin leans forward so he can reach his laptop on the coffee table.

"I've been going over Luther's online activities in the weeks leading up to Lila's death," he says, opening the screen to Ice-Virgin33's Twitter profile.

"You don't have any doubt that he killed Lila, do you?" I ask, pulling a knitted throw over my legs and shivering at the sight of the icy crevasse on the screen. "You heard him confess."

Kevin keeps his eyes on the screen. "My report of Luther's confession is compelling, but since we don't have a written confession I'd like to see more corroborating evidence before I close the investigation. We did find a handkerchief with traces of Lila's blood in Luther's apartment in Portland."

"*That* seems pretty compelling," I say, taking a sip of tea.

"Yes, but it's also consistent with Luther's first story to you about meeting Lila in the clearing and then leaving her. Didn't he tell you that he noticed her bleeding hand and gave her a handkerchief?"

"He was taunting me," I say, sorry now that I told Kevin what Luther had said in the clearing. This *telling the truth* is cumbersome sometimes. "He told the real story when he had to."

"Some would say he was coerced."

"Do *you* say that?"

"I don't like loose ends," he says, nudging the laptop so it is aligned with the edge of the coffee table. I recall the boy who lined up his pens and notebooks in class.

"Life isn't always so neat," I say.

"No," he agrees, leaning forward to click on a link at the side of the profile page. IceVirgin33's message history appears. "We were able to access Luther's message history with Lila on his Twitter account. Lila responded to a tweet of Luther's about the lost girls of the Maiden Stone and then Luther suggested they continue their conversation in private messages on his Twitter account. Here's her message to him:

Hi! I'm doing a paper on Cora Rockwell and the history of the missing Haywood girls and it sounds like you may have some ideas for me.

And his reply:

That's a long and complicated history. How much time do you have?

"The messages go on like this for a couple of days . . ." Kevin says as he scrolls through a long thread of messages. "He's careful not to seem too eager to meet her, but eventually he does suggest she come to Portland."

"I bet he did," I say, leaning forward to read the messages. "That's just how he was with me—cool and distant at first.

Look here." I point at the screen to one of IceVirgin33's messages.

You've got a keen investigative mind. You'd make a good journalist.

Lol. If journalism wasn't dead, Lila had responded, adding a frowning face and a skull and crossbones emoji. *I'm thinking of getting a PhD in history.*

The conversation had smoothly veered into Lila's hopes and dreams for the future, Luther drawing her out and coaxing her to give him more personal information.

"He's grooming her," I say.

Kevin nods. "Yeah, that's pretty clear. Lila was smart, though. When he asks where she's driving from, she deflects him by saying she'll just Google Map directions. But after they met she acts differently. See here . . . she asks him if he's coming to her play."

"So he must have gained her trust when they met," I say, leaning back and tucking the throw under my feet. "Luther was good at that."

"Yeah, but I think he had help. Look at this." He clicks on another box and opens a new message thread. *Hey, I really liked your take on the Portland theater scene. We should meet up IRL.*

"That's Jill. I noticed they followed each other on Twitter. Jill said that's how Luther and Lila connected in the first place, when Lila liked something Luther had tweeted about the Lost Girls."

"Actually, the first contact was a tweet from this person called LostGirl99 that Lila, Luther, and Jill all retweeted. That's what took them all to the site 'Lost Girls of the Maiden Stone.'" He clicks on a link and the page opens up to the site I'd gone to earlier with its moody picture of the Maiden Stone wreathed in mist. Despite the gas fire and the throw and the hot tea—despite the fact that it's seventy degrees outside—I begin to shake.

Thankfully, Kevin is too busy clicking to notice. "The tweet that led Lila, Jill, and Luther all to this site was from Lost-Girl99." He clicks on LostGirl99's Twitter profile with the peeling wallpaper and photograph of Noreen Bagley.

"I saw her before, I didn't realize that was the first contact. My guess is that LostGirl99 is Lucinda Perkins, the archivist at Rockwell House," I offer. "She's obsessed with the Maiden Stone disappearances. She even dresses like Noreen Bagley. And she must know Luther since he was doing research at the museum. You should talk to her."

"I have," Kevin says. "She does know Luther and she was very upset by his death. She called him 'the Maiden Stone's latest victim.'" I'm tempted to laugh but I remember the look on Luther's face when he slid into the water and shudder instead. "But here's the thing," Kevin adds. "She swears up and down that she's not LostGirl99. In fact, she was quite incensed by some 'historical inaccuracies' on the site."

"That doesn't mean she's telling the truth," I say, feeling a wave of nausea. "Can't you track who it was, using IP addresses or something?"

Kevin shakes his head. "The site was created only a few

months ago under a false identity and it was only ever logged into from public computers in libraries and Internet cafés in Portland."

"That sounds like Luther, then."

"Maybe. But I'm not sure why he covered his tracks as Lost-Girl but not as IceVirgin. And then LostGirl's social media accounts were all taken down after Luther died."

"Oh," I say, "that is odd."

This time when I shudder Kevin notices. Or maybe he's noticed all along. Nothing much gets past him. He offers me a second throw from the other end of the couch and then tells me a story.

"My great-uncle Joe had hypothermia after he survived a shipwreck in World War Two. He said it took him near a year before he felt really warm again."

I shiver again, picturing a man floating in the sea, but it's not Kevin's great-uncle Joe I see; it's Luther, whose body has not been found. He resurrected himself once before. Who's to say he won't do it a second time.

CHAPTER THIRTY-ONE

For years I imagined what it would be like to watch Rudy graduate from high school. Whenever I pictured him walking to the podium to accept his diploma I would tear up. I was sure I'd never make it through the ceremony without crying. I hadn't realized that everyone would be crying. When Lila's thirteen-year-old sister accepts Lila's diploma for her, there's not a dry eye in the audience. Instead of throwing up their caps, the graduates toss handfuls of lilac blossom into the air. Then they clasp their arms around each other and sing John Lennon's "Imagine," Lila's favorite song.

Rudy, I notice, is between Dakota Wyatt and Rachel Lazar, and even after the rest of the graduates drift apart I see that Rachel and Rudy stay close together. *Tragedy makes for odd bedfellows,* Harmon had said when I mentioned that Rachel and Rudy were spending a lot of time together. She isn't the friend—or girlfriend, if that's what she is—that I had imagined for Rudy but I'm grateful for the protective stance she's taken toward him.

Rudy Levine is just as much a victim as Lila Zeller, Rachel had posted on Instagram. *We all need to bond together to stop the cycle of abuse.*

Rudy lured his own father to the Maiden Stone to get him to confess, Dakota Wyatt had replied.

When he touched the Maiden Stone Luther vanished, someone else had added. At that point the discussion had verged into conjectures that Luther wasn't really dead.

Perhaps this is the end of the Maiden Stone disappearances, someone called Final_Girl posted. *The Maiden Stone has finally gotten her revenge.*

If I hadn't still felt so uneasy about Luther's missing body I might have found it fitting that Luther, who loved folklore, had become a figure of myth.

Rudy seems ambivalent about entering the realms of Haywood lore. *People need to tell stories,* he told the therapist in our last session, *to make sense of all the crazy in the world.* He doesn't seem to mind the attention of Rachel and all the other drama kids, though. They cling together in a pack as the crowds drift from the outdoor theater into Warden House, where the graduation reception is being held.

I was surprised when Harmon told me that the house was in shape for graduation. "It was Jean's last effort," he said. "She supervised a crew to clean and set up the rooms before she left for Florida." Jean left for her sister's house in Fort Lauderdale while I was still in the hospital. It had hurt my feelings a bit that she hadn't waited to say goodbye, but I understood the instinct to flee. And I can see too that she wanted to make this last gesture to the school. While the restoration isn't complete, the rooms, open to the evening air, are beautiful. The hardwood floors have been refinished to a satin polish that reflects the candlelight. The faded and peeling wallpaper looks oddly elegant, like the worn pelt of an exotic animal. A string quartet plays in the rotunda, the music drifting up the double spiral staircase and out into the clearing, where it mingles with the salt air and the murmur of the surf.

"Can you believe these were our old digs?" Jill Frankel remarks to me on the drinks line. "Harmon's really outdone himself."

I examine Jill for signs of bitterness. She's dressed in an ankle-length embroidered dress, her curling hair piled on top of her head, holding a glass of champagne. "That's nice of you to say," I tell her. "I know you were interested in the job."

Jill shrugs. "The important thing is that we all band together for the students. Look at how they've come together." She waves her champagne glass at a group by the nonalcoholic-punch bowl. Dakota Wyatt whispers something into Paola Fernandez's ear and Paola laughs. Rudy is standing between Samantha Grimes and Rachel, both of whom have their arms around Rudy's waist. "I hear the historical society scholarship is going to Paola," Jill says. "And that it's going to be renamed the Lila Zeller Scholarship."

"Oh, who . . ." I start to ask, but then guess. "Did Jean set that up?"

Jill nods, taking a sip of champagne. "Her other parting gift."

I take a swallow of my champagne to dull the pang I feel at Jean's absence. "She should be here."

"Maybe," Jill concedes, "but someone has to be the scapegoat." She tilts her glass toward a group of well-dressed men and women on the terrace. I recognize Chelsea Whittenberg in a pale lilac sheath and pearls and a trio of men—Morris Alcott, Harmon, and a third trustee whose name I don't recall—in black tuxes and lilac bow ties, lilac ribbons on their lapels. "The board is also starting a fund to support a domestic violence and child abuse shelter in Lewiston. They'll shell out their tax-deductible donations to fund a feel-good distraction and throw one of their own under the bus."

I look back at Jill and notice that she's aiming her glass of champagne at the board members as if it's a loaded pistol. "I'm sorry about Luther," I say.

Jill's eyes widen and a drop of champagne sloshes over the rim of her glass. "What do you have to be sorry about?"

"If I'd come forward about what happened to me, he wouldn't have been free to hurt other women. Lila, of course, but also you. It must be hard—"

"To know that I was stupid and desperate enough to sleep with a child molester?" she hisses, her voice dripping with rage—most of it directed at herself.

"You have a good heart," I say, surprising both myself and her, "and he took advantage of that. Maybe we both need to stop blaming ourselves . . ." I falter, blinking away tears, and then focus on Paola Fernandez laughing at something Dakota is saying. "Or how else are we going to help *them* not make the same mistakes we did?"

Jill chokes back a strangled sob, then wipes her eyes, smearing her mascara. "Shit," she says when she sees the black smear, "I've got to go to the ladies' to fix this." She hesitates, then adds, "Let's go for a drink sometime this summer, okay?"

"Sure," I tell her, "that would be fun."

She sweeps away, her long dress nearly catching fire as it trails past a bank of candles. *Tragedy makes for odd bedfellows,* indeed. I instinctively search Harmon out again. He's talking to a slender young man I can't make out until Harmon turns away and I recognize Kevin Bantree, looking unlike his usual self in suit and tie (a rather florid purple). He's an alum, I remind myself as I watch him watch Harmon crossing the room to the group of students around the punch bowl. That's why he's here, not because he's still harboring any suspicions about Harmon.

I have to admit, though, that I've been anxious since Kevin's visit, with his talk of loose ends and the vanishing of LostGirl99. Which is ridiculous. It's just compulsive (*OCD much?*) Kevin Bantree squaring off uneven corners. I hope he hasn't been spoiling Harmon's night. Harmon worked so hard to pull this together. Being headmaster suits him. As much as he claims not to have coveted the job it's exactly what he needs. Luther was right about that; teaching AP History wasn't ever going to be enough for him. And he's *good* at this. I watch him laugh with the students and sample the punch. "Just making sure it's not spiked," I hear him say as he rests his hand on Paola's arm.

Paola flinches so hard she drops her glass.

Smoothly, Harmon catches it. Samantha Grimes says, "Good save, Headmaster!" as Harmon hands Paola a napkin and makes a joke about his mad catcher skills being wasted in a desk job. As if he can feel me watching, he looks up and meets my gaze. There's something naked and surprised on his face. Then he turns away and saunters out the French doors onto the terrace.

I see Rudy step next to Paola and Kevin Bantree heading across the room to them, but I am already following Harmon, replaying the scene in my head and telling myself I'm wrong. Paola's high-strung. And clumsy. *Remember when she bumped into you and dropped all those flyers—*

Remember how she clutched them to her chest like an open wound and wouldn't make eye contact with you?

Remember all the hours Harmon spent tutoring her, the two of them closeted together in Harmon's study with the door closed?

No, I tell myself, *you wouldn't believe it of him and Lila. Why would you believe it of him and Paola?*

Because Paola is vulnerable—a scholarship girl out of her depth, terrified of failing and disappointing her parents, dependent on the goodwill and financial assistance of men like Harmon.

I catch up with Harmon in the clearing beyond the terrace. "It's such a lovely night," he says. "I thought I'd get some air. Care to join me? If we hurry we'll catch the last light on the Point."

He ushers me onto the path that cuts straight down the peninsula. It's too narrow to walk side by side so he walks behind me, his breath on my bare neck. I shiver and he drapes his tuxedo jacket over my shoulders. Ever-solicitous, gentle Harmon. He wouldn't hurt a fly. I have just imagined what I thought I saw, which was nothing, because there was nothing to see.

When we reach the Point I see that he was right about the light—it catches the lichen on Maiden Island and turns it a fiery orange, like a floating island in a fairy tale. The view is serene and beautiful, nothing like the fog-and-ghost-ridden island of my nightmares. That's all my suspicions are—a nightmare vestige of the trauma I've been through. I turn to face Harmon, ready to make a joke of my suspicions. "You know when I saw you with Paola back there . . ." I begin.

And then I see it on his face. A wince, as if I'd said something in bad taste. "I worry about her," he says. "Sometimes I think it's unfair to take a girl like that out of her community and give her just enough education to make her dissatisfied with where she came from. I wonder if she'll ever truly belong anywhere."

"She looked so nervous when you touched her arm," I say. Weakly. Plaintively. I *want* him to convince me that I didn't see what I saw. (I *did* see something.)

And he seems ready to oblige. "We had a little . . . *misunderstanding*," he says smoothly, his equilibrium recovered. In control. "That's all. Girls like Paola, they don't really get all the social cues. We've spent a lot of time together this semester because I was tutoring her—remember, you asked me to tutor her—and I'm afraid she might have misread my attention to her as something other than what it was."

"You mean she thought you were interested in her . . ." I falter, feeling stupid, like *I'm* the one who has misread the social cues. ". . . *sexually?*"

He makes a face. "I think it was more of a romantic fantasy on her part. A schoolgirl crush. You know how girls are at that age."

Teenage girls have big imaginations, as Luther said.

"I think she's embarrassed," Harmon continues, as I scramble to make sense of what I'm hearing. "She made a bit of a"—he smiles sheepishly—"*profession* of her feelings to me and of course I told her it was completely inappropriate. I tried to be gentle but she still got upset. There were tears . . ." He shudders. "You know I'm hopeless when you women cry." He steps closer and puts his hands on the lapels of his jacket to pull it closer around my shoulders, then rubs his hands up and down my arms to warm me up. "Please don't let this upset you, Tess, not after all we've been through. I really think things are going to be better for us when Rudy goes to college in the fall. And now that I'm headmaster we'll work together to make this a school that Lila would have been proud of—one that includes girls like Paola Fernandez."

I find I'm nodding along. Of course a girl like Paola would get a crush on Harmon—hadn't I?—and as Harmon just pointed out, I had been the one to encourage him to tutor her, just as I'd encouraged Lila to mentor and then room with her—

"Did Lila notice?" I ask.

"What?"

"That Paola was upset?"

His hands tighten on my arms. "Why do you ask that?"

"It's just . . ." I'm recalling the texts between Lila and Rudy three weeks before Lila died. Rudy had asked why Lila had left rehearsal early and she'd texted: *Roommate drama.*

I look around me. The last light in the west skates across the water and catches on the lichen-stained stones of Maiden Island. The Maiden Stone glows gold against a purple sky. In this light it looks like a girl standing straight and tall. Watching us.

"When did this thing happen with Paola?" I ask.

"I told you there was no *thing*," Harmon says, an edge to his voice.

"I mean her getting upset and crying," I say.

He shrugs and looks away from me. "A couple of weeks ago."

"About three weeks ago?"

"I don't really remember, Tess," Harmon says. A warning note has crept into his voice, but it's mild, as if he's asking me not to make a scene in public. But we're not in public. We're alone on a high precipice above the sea. The tide is going out. Soon the rocks will be bare. I notice he's positioned himself farther from the edge. One strong push and I would go over.

Or I can back away from the edge—not just the physical one behind me but the place where my imagination has been taking me. Paola hasn't accused Harmon of any wrongdoing. Luther has confessed to Lila's murder. What more do I want?

Harmon must feel the slump in my shoulders as I relent. He gives me a little shake. "See," he says, "that's what you get for snooping on your son's texts on his laptop."

I start to smile, but my lips feel suddenly frozen. "How did you know I read his texts on his laptop?"

Harmon's mouth also looks as if it's frozen in the half act of smiling. His hands grip my arms tighter. I suddenly see it: the texts that Rudy sent to Lila after they fought—*What's wrong? What did I say? I know there's something you're not telling me!*

"You read Rudy's texts," I say. "And you thought Lila was going to tell Rudy about what happened between you and Paola."

"I told you that *nothing* happened between me and Paola," he growls.

"Paola thought something happened and Lila would have believed her. You saw the texts on Rudy's laptop and you were afraid she was going to tell someone."

Harmon's mouth sets in a firm line, the way it does when a student—or any *underling*—challenges his authority. "All right, Tess, you want to do this? Then let's clear the air. Yes, Lila overheard Paola crying three weeks ago and even though Paola told Lila that it was nothing and she didn't want Lila to do anything about it, Lila wouldn't take no for an answer. She had to climb on her high 'social justice warrior' horse and interrogate me. I told her she ought to mind her own business and get back to work on her paper—I even gave her a little nudge in the right direction."

"What do you mean, *a nudge*?" I ask, my voice shaking. A *nudge* is all it would take right now to send me careening over the cliff. I try to inch forward but Harmon is blocking my way.

"I simply directed her to the Rockwell diary."

"Wait," I say, "I thought Luther told Lila about the Rockwell diary."

Harmon smiles. "Do you think he just *happened* upon Lila? I gave him a little nudge in the right direction too, by introducing both him and Lila to LostGirl99."

I stare at Harmon. "But you . . . you don't . . ."

"Use the Internet?" he asks. "That doesn't mean I *can't*. It was easy to make a website that would appeal to their interests and lure them there with some ridiculous tweets. I let the rest take its course."

"But how did you know Luther?"

He gives me a pitying look. "Please, Tess, do you really think I married you without doing a background check? Morris hired a private investigator, who found Rudy's hospital records in Skowhegan. Then he tracked Luther to Portland—"

"You knew Luther was alive?" I ask, shocked. "And you didn't tell me?"

"How was I to know you thought he was dead?"

"Why didn't you confront me? I *lied* to you!" I think of all the guilt I've felt over the years of keeping Luther a secret from Harmon, while all along he knew. How could I have been so blind? But then I understand. I had been too busy keeping my secrets to suspect Harmon of having his own. As if he can read my thoughts he echoes them with a shrug.

"You kept your secrets from me and I kept mine from you. I knew when you got that text from Rudy you wouldn't tell me what was going on, so after you left our bedroom I took Rudy's laptop into the guest room and checked to see where you were going. I saw Rudy wanted you to meet him here at the Point—yes, I figured out about your 'safe place' years ago. I knew something must have upset him if he wanted you to meet him here. I was afraid Lila might have told him some story about Paola so I ran out there after you left. When I got there I saw Lila in the clearing with Luther. I wanted to make sure she wasn't telling *him* about Paola, but they were talking about Cora Rockwell's diary, so I waited until he left to approach her. I just wanted to explain my side of the story before she went off spreading some half-baked lies about me."

I stare at Harmon, aghast at how calmly he is describing behavior that could only be described as stalking.

"We walked toward the Point on the south path," he goes on. "Lila explaining to me that I had 'intimidated Paola into silence by our unequal power dynamic.' Ha!" He barks a harsh one-syllable laugh. "What drivel these children spout these days!

Then we heard you and Rudy leaving the Point and she wanted to follow you—to tell you and Rudy what Paola had told her, to get it out into the open. I tried to stop her . . ." He passes his hand over his face as if wiping the memory away. "She fell, Tess, I swear. It was an accident. I went down to see if I could help her but she was dead. What could I do? How would I explain what I was doing out here with her in the middle of the night? You know what people would have said—what it would have looked like. So I left her. I thought it would be dismissed as an accident. I didn't know she had cut her hand or that the police would think that was a 'defensive wound' or that you'd leave me Rudy's bloody sweatshirt to wear."

"And when Rudy was taken in by the police after I told them the sweatshirt belonged to him?" I ask. "You didn't come forward then."

"I would have," he cries, looking affronted at my accusation, "but I didn't have time. Rudy ran out here and Luther took the blame. As he *should* have, after what he did to you and Rudy. Don't you see, Tess? It's all worked out as it should have. Luther has paid for what he did to you; Woody and Jean have paid for hiding it. Rudy is a hero! And Paola is fine! I spoke with her the morning after Lila died and all she was worried about was passing her AP Physics final. Which is what she should have been worrying about all along." He steps back and holds out his arms to me. "Honestly, Tess, I'm glad you found out. You kept your secrets from me and I kept mine from you, but now everything is out in the open."

I look at him, at the face I have loved and trusted, at his open arms. All I have to do is step into them and tell him that

I believe him. What difference does it make if it's true or not? I'll let myself believe that nothing happened between him and Paola, that Lila's death was an accident.

I know it won't be that hard because I've lived with lies long enough already. And look at what those lies have done to me and Rudy—and Lila and Paola. If I hadn't been blinded by my own lies I might have seen what Harmon was and protected them from him. I hold up my hand.

"No," I say, "it's not out in the open yet. We'll go to the police and you'll tell them what you've told me. It was an accident. If that's the truth it will hold up. I'll stand by you. I don't care if you lose your job and the house."

He gives me such a beatific smile that I believe I've touched him with my offer. "That's very generous of you, Tess, to be willing to dispose of all the comforts *I've* given you. But I think not."

He steps closer again and grips the lapels of the jacket. Then he snatches it off me, upsetting my balance. I stumble back two feet. Dirt crumbles under my heels, giving way beneath my feet. I fall to the ground and look up to see Harmon looming over me. This can't be right. No matter what I've learned about Harmon in the last few minutes I still can't see him as a man who would physically abuse his wife. But then I see his foot moving back, poised to deliver a kick to my belly, and I am reaching out to grab his foot. My body recognized where the threat was before my mind could admit it. He goes down, screaming as his back hits an outcropping of rock. I lunge past him, but before I can make it to the path I feel his hand close around my ankle. As I go down I cry out and hear an answering cry from the woods.

"Mom?"

It's Rudy. I hear him running toward me. I want to warn him off—what if Harmon goes after him?—but then I see that Kevin Bantree is with him and he's drawn his gun. Harmon releases my ankle and I scramble up and toward them. When I turn back I see Harmon holding his hands up.

"Put that away," he orders Kevin Bantree as if he's still the one in control. "I was trying to keep my wife from jumping off the cliff. You know what a troubled history she has—"

"It's your history I'm interested in, Mr. Henshaw," he cuts him off. "Paola Fernandez has told me everything. I'm arresting you in the murder of Lila Zeller."

Rudy puts his arm around me and leads me away from the edge of the Point while Kevin puts Harmon in handcuffs. I'm shaking so hard Rudy takes off his jacket to give me. I shake my head. I'm not cold anymore; I'm just angry.

CHAPTER THIRTY-TWO

Sometime in mid-June I receive a package from Martha James containing a stack of blue books from my final exam. She had proctored it for me while I was in the hospital and then, after Harmon was arrested for murder, took it upon herself to read and grade the exams for me. Martha's conscientious like that; the board finally did something smart when they made her interim chair after Harmon had to resign. She'd flagged one of the books with a Post-it note that said, *I thought you might find this one interesting.*

It was Paola Fernandez's exam. Martha had circled the last paragraph:

I think it was wrong that they made Hester wear that red A but in the end maybe it was better for her. Mr. Dimmesdale suffers more because he has to keep what he did to himself. Hester wears her shame on the outside so it doesn't eat her up on the inside.

It was shame, Paola told me the week after Harmon was arrested, that kept her from telling anyone when her history teacher touched her and tried to kiss her. "He said I had acted like I wanted him to do those things and I thought maybe I had and just didn't know it. I thought that if I made a big deal of it I might lose my scholarship. When Lila saw me crying I begged her not to tell anyone. When Lila died I was afraid that was my fault too—but then I saw Mr. Henshaw in the chapel and he said he'd been home all night . . . that's what *you* said that day too."

I remembered coming over to Harmon and Paola that day in the chapel and Harmon saying he felt guilty that he'd stayed home when I went to pick Rudy up. I'd replied by saying that I'd come right home. Although I didn't know it, I was giving him an alibi so Paola wouldn't think he killed Lila on her account.

"He manipulated you," I told Paola. "You have nothing to be ashamed of."

Which is more than I can say for myself. I am the woman whose husband sexually harassed a teenage girl and then killed another teenage girl to keep her from talking. What kind of woman marries a man capable of that behavior? How could I not know? I have no answers. All I can think is that I was so busy keeping my own secrets—hiding my own shame—that I wasn't really paying attention.

All my shame is on the outside now.

At first I felt like I wanted to hide under a rock. I told Morris Alcott to sell the house and use whatever he got for it for Harmon's legal fees. He told me that Harmon had a good chance of getting off with only five to ten years for manslaughter: "He didn't really do anything to the Fernandez girl and there's nothing to prove that the Zeller girl's death wasn't an accident."

I told him that he could address any further communication to me through the divorce lawyer I hired.

I rented a little two-bedroom bungalow down by the fishing docks for Rudy and me, but Rudy has been spending most of his time in the dorms. Jill's doing a summer stock production of *Carousel* and Rudy's playing the role of Billy Bigelow. I'm relieved he's got something to keep him busy and glad that Jill's chosen a lighter play for the summer.

"I may never do anything but musicals again," she tells me when we finally get that drink in the third week of June. We meet at the Salty Dog, a waterfront bar full of tourists. "Perfect for the two town pariahs," she says on her third gin and tonic.

"You just dated a sexual predator," I say on my second, "I lived with one and married another."

"Don't forget I dated Harmon too," she points out.

"I guess we both have terrible taste in men," I say, clinking glasses with her. And then, when I'm on my third drink, I ask, "Did you suspect anything?"

"About which one?"

"Either."

She considers. "Well, when you started dating Harmon I thought you were a little young for him, but that might have been me being petty. I *did* wonder why he was content to teach high school, because he'd been a little condescending to me about my doing it. I thought it had something to do with how the girls were so crazy about him."

"They made him feel bigger," I say. "*I* made him feel bigger. I was the fallen woman he rescued."

"Yeah, men are like that, right? If they don't think they can rescue you, they want to tear you down."

"Not just men," I say. "I did the same thing with Paola. I thought I was rescuing her from her impoverished background and instead I was introducing her to a predator."

"And now you're feeling sorry for yourself about it," Jill says with a bit of the old venom in her voice.

I bristle, thinking of a stinging rejoinder, but instead take a sip of my drink and admit she's right. "What else am I supposed to do? My blindness caused Lila's death."

"Stop being so blind, then," Jill replies. "Open your eyes. Life keeps going. Rudy's really great in this play. There will be a whole crew of new girls for you to teach in the fall."

"I'm afraid I'll feel like an imposter standing up in front of a class," I say. "I've been thinking that maybe I should do something else."

Jill shrugs. "That would be a shame. You're a good teacher. To tell you the truth, I think that's why I didn't like you. I was jealous."

I laugh. "I bet you're over that now."

"Well," Jill says with a sly smile, "you're a little easier to take now. You seem a little humbler."

"Oh? And what was I before?"

"A little smug," Jill replies, without a smile this time. "In your big house with your rich husband."

I start to tell her she's wrong, that I was terrified all those years in that house, but then I realize that's what scared looks like on the outside when you're hiding so much shame on the inside. Paola was right: shame eats you up when you have to keep it hidden. Now at least I have nothing to fear.

Or maybe that's the three gin and tonics talking.

I switch to plain tonic water and offer to walk Jill home, but she says she's going to stay awhile. I follow her gaze to the bar where I recognize Brad Sorensen, sunburned and fit-looking. "Oh," I say, "how long has that been going on?"

She blushes. "A couple of weeks. He's a bit of a square but"— she shrugs—"I think I've had enough drama for a while."

Which makes me laugh. I can't imagine Jill Frankel ever having enough drama. I get up, kiss Jill on the cheek, and tell her thank you.

"For what?" she asks.

"For trying to get through to Rudy all those years ago; for giving him a part in the play; for reminding me not to be smug."

She smiles and tosses her head. "Any time. You'll need reminding when you stop feeling sorry for yourself, open your eyes, and"—she tilts her glass back in the direction of the bar—"notice that Kevin Bantree can't take his eyes off you."

I give her another kiss on the cheek and head toward the door. The truth is I'd noticed Kevin about twenty minutes earlier and felt his gaze on me, but far from reading his attention as romantic I'd felt embarrassed. Kevin knows all the worst things about me, and although I'm resigned to living with my shame on the outside, I don't relish seeing it reflected in his eyes. I slip through the crowd and out the door into the cool, salty air.

When my mother was dying of cancer she said there were days when the only thing that kept her going was the feel of the air on her face. I close my eyes and take a deep breath, and when I open them Kevin Bantree is coming out the bar door.

"Caught you," he says.

"That's really not a good joke for a policeman to make," I reply.

"Who's joking? You've been avoiding me since our last interview."

He'd mediated at a conversation with Paola at my request. I'd been grateful to get to tell Paola how sorry I was but it had been painful—Paola's eagerness to forgive me hadn't made it less so—and I hadn't wanted any reminder of it. "I haven't felt much like socializing," I say.

"I hear you've moved into Roberta Malone's cottage down by the docks."

"Do you keep tabs on all your witnesses?" I ask.

He winces. "How 'bout I walk you home. That neighborhood is a little rough."

"I thought it was the neighborhood you grew up in," I say.

"Exactly," he replies, holding his hand out to the sidewalk. I fall into step beside him. We walk in silence past the tourist bars and restaurants, the shops selling blueberry jam and lobster cooking pots, and then into a neighborhood of small clapboard bungalows painted cheerful colors and bearing cutesy names like Sailor's In and Beachy Keen and Sea Plum Cottage. The neighborhood is a bit run-down but it's certainly not "rough." Kevin must have some other reason for walking me home, some ugly detail that's emerged about Harmon that he wants to warn me about. It must be bad if he's taking so long to get to it.

"Spit it out," I say.

"What?" He looks startled.

"Have you found something new? Are there other girls?"

This is what I'm most afraid of, that there will be a parade of girls coming forward now that Harmon's been unmasked. That I will have to face in each one my culpability, my *shame*. It makes me want to flee, to go live in Fort Lauderdale with Jean.

But Kevin shakes his head. "There haven't been any other accusers. Maybe there will be in time, but from what Paola told me . . ." He hesitates, then takes a breath and goes on. "Given how quickly he backed down, I think it may have been Harmon's first advance."

"It wouldn't have been his last," I say.

"No," Kevin agrees, "not if he got away with it. He certainly went to great lengths to hide what he'd done. What's interesting is how well he took to cyberstalking. He must have gotten the idea from spying on Lila's Instagram and Twitter accounts from Rudy's laptop. He wanted to keep track of her and distract her by feeding her the Cora Rockwell diary so he made that 'Lost Girls' website and invented LostGirl99, who followed Jill and Lila and Luther and then sent tweets out that drew them all into the site. When Lila walked out to the Point with him that night she had her laptop in her backpack. He managed to hold onto that after he 'accidentally' pushed her to her death, and was able to look at all the correspondence she'd had with Luther, which I believe gave him the idea of making Luther look like the guilty party. Lucinda Perkins says that Luther had been reading the Rockwell diary for years, but I think it was only when LostGirl99 contacted him that he started thinking of it as a way to ruin Woody Hull and Jean."

"Harmon said he'd done that to distract Lila," I say, wanting to ask what Kevin made of Lucinda Perkins and her Noreen Bagley obsession. Lucinda emailed me a few weeks ago to ask if she could interview me for a podcast she's started about the Maiden Stone Murders, as she calls them. I haven't gotten back to her.

"I think at first that's all he was trying to do but then he realized that he could destroy Woody and Jean in the process and get himself appointed headmaster. He almost got away with it. If you hadn't see him with Paola and realized something was wrong, he might have."

I stop—we're at my house anyway—and turn to face Kevin. "But you said when you arrested Harmon that Paola had told you everything."

The corner of his mouth quirks. "That was a bit of an exaggeration. I saw your face when Paola flinched and I knew you'd seen something wrong. I went over to Paola when you left the room. She was crying and seemed upset that you had followed Harmon outside. She was afraid that you were going to confront Harmon and that he would hurt you. So you see, you solved the case."

I laugh. "Please, Kevin, you would have figured it out. You were already onto it when you asked me about LostGirl99. That may be why I saw what I did."

"Well then," he says, his full mouth smiling now, "I suppose we make a good team."

Then he leans in and kisses me. It's the quickest, lightest touch of his lips on mine, but it shifts something in me, like the moon pulling an internal tide. He looks pleased with himself when he steps back. "There," he says, as if he's just squared a corner and made everything right in the world, "I've wanted to do that since senior year, but you went away before I could."

"Kevin," I say, "I . . . I'm not sure I can . . . I mean, I have a pretty awful track record with men."

He laughs. "Let's hope we can change that."

And then he kisses me again, his lips lingering for a moment longer, that *shift* becoming an insistent tug that nearly knocks me off my feet. "Take your time," he says as he pulls away. "You know where to find me."

Then he's gone, vanished in the fog, leaving me on my doorstep swaying slightly as if a retreating wave had just moved the sand out from beneath my feet.

After a moment I go inside my empty house. I'd taken almost nothing from Harmon's (Rudy had that right; in the end it had never really belonged to us) other than my clothes and books—and the tuck box from the attic. I gave Rudy the wooden animals—a reminder that no matter what his father had done, no matter how damaged and imperfect he was, he'd loved him. (The journals I've stored in a desk drawer for a time when I feel I can face them.)

The two-bedroom bungalow is a quarter the size of the Colonial but it feels large tonight. Kevin's kiss still thrums on my lips, his words reverberating in these empty rooms. *I've wanted to do that since senior year, but you went away before I could.*

What if he had? Would it have made a difference? If I'd known a nice boy like Kevin Bantree liked me would I have resisted the dark pull of Luther Gunn? I imagine a different life for myself: falling in love with a boy my own age, going to college together, marrying, having children—

But not Rudy. I wouldn't have had Rudy. I already know I wouldn't go back if I could. I'd never choose a life that didn't have Rudy in it—

But tonight I sit with the girl I was and wonder who she would have become. When the shells along the windowsills turn white and pink I look out to the bay and see the first light touch the Ebb Stone. I remember what Kevin said about racing the tide and walk out my door.

I cut across campus, hidden by the fog from sight of the dorms. Warden House, newly painted, looms out of the mist. It looks like it might have when it was new and the Refuge had just opened its doors to the wayward girls of New England. I wonder what they felt, transported from the tenements and teeming streets of Boston and Providence and the mills of Lowell and Lewiston. Did they think they'd come to a prison or a refuge? Do we know, always, which is which? For years I'd thought of Harmon's solid white Colonial as a refuge from my past but now it feels like another prison—as much a trap as Luther's island—that chained me to the past with a web of lies.

My life—and Rudy's life—grew off-kilter because of those lies. I wonder what shape our lives will take now that those lies are out in the open. I hope that Rudy is young enough that his future can be righted. I don't think I am. Like the scarlet letter on Hester Prynne's breast, I fear I'll always bear the marks of what's been done to me and what I have done and failed to do.

My students are never sure what to make of Hester Prynne returning to her cottage and taking up the scarlet letter again. They complain that she's giving in to society's judgment of her. But then I read to them from the last chapter: ". . . the scarlet letter had ceased to be a stigma which attracted the world's scorn and bitterness, and became a type of something to be sorrowed over, and looked upon with awe, yet with reverence, too." The most I can hope is that the marks I bear will someday be transformed into something so benign.

As I walk past Warden House, through the clearing and onto the path that runs along the north side of the peninsula, I don't feel alone. The ghosts of all those lost girls—the ones who drowned and the ones who turned to stone; the wayward girls who came here seeking refuge and were betrayed by the people who should have protected them; Noreen Bagley looking for the truth, and Lila, who just wanted to keep another girl from going missing in her own life—walk with me. They are joined by one more—the girl I was before I left with Luther Gunn. The girl who might have kissed Kevin Bantree and gone to college and lived another life. She walks with all the other lost girls to the edge of the land.

We reach it together just as the tide recedes like a silk scarf drawn away from the taut skin of sand and stone. I can feel her, that girl I was, tilting her face up to the sun, inhaling the sea air, her future stretching out before her as unblemished and limitless as this length of virgin shore. I tilt my face to the same sun, breathe with her, and let her go. I can't have her back. All I can do is set one foot onto this sand, which has been swept clean of all that's gone before, and then the other.

ACKNOWLEDGMENTS

As always I am enormously grateful to my intrepid agent, Robin Rue, and the amazing Beth Miller of Writers House for guiding my books to their perfect refuge. Thank you to Katherine Nintzel for captaining the ship, and to Vedika Khanna, Gena Lanzi, and everyone else at William Morrow for leading this book through the mists of production to safe harbor.

I told this story first to my friend Ethel Wesdorp on holiday at a hotel in Wells, Maine, and her interest and enthusiasm set me on my way. A year later my friend Connie Crawford read a first draft in a little cottage on the Kennebec River and steered me clear of many a treacherous shoal. In between I shared the story with Roberta Jean Andersen and Alisa Kwitney on many a walk, and with my daughter Maggie Vicknair over many a cup of tea. My husband, Lee Slonimsky, and stepdaughter, Nora Slonimsky, read the drafts and helped me steer a true course.

Writing this book I have been constantly reminded of all the people in my life that helped me find my way, who kept me from feeling lost, and who remain steady lights in my life today. I am enormously grateful to them all and hope that all the girls—and boys—growing up today can find such true guiding lights on their journeys.

About the author

About the book

Read on

Insights,
Interviews
& More...

Meet Carol Goodman

Franco Vogt

CAROL GOODMAN is the critically acclaimed author of twenty-one novels, including *The Widow's House*, which won the Mary Higgins Clark Award, and *The Seduction of Water*, which won the Hammett Prize. Her books have been translated into sixteen languages. She lives in the Hudson Valley with her family and teaches writing and literature at SUNY New Paltz and the New School. ∾

The Lore of the Lost Girl

I have always liked to read books with a little bit of fairy tale or myth in them. From *Jane Eyre*, with its allusions to "Beauty and the Beast" and "Cinderella," to A.S. Byatt's *Possession*, with its medieval legends embroidered into an academic intrigue, to all of Angela Carter's wondrous and transgressive fairy tales and Kelly Link's surreal slipstream stories, I love when a writer weaves a little magic into an otherwise realistic story.

It's little wonder, then, that I've tried to do the same in my books. There's Greek and Roman mythology in my first novel, *The Lake of Dead Languages*; selkies in my second, *The Seduction of Water*; changelings in *The Other Mother*; and Greek tragedy and constellations in *The Night Visitors*. Fairy tales, legends, and myth enrich and broaden a story for me, and are just plain fun to work with.

When I began *The Sea of Lost Girls* I knew right away that there would be lore. The image that came to me on a beach in Maine, and which became the genesis of the story, was of a young girl standing with a lantern on a fog-wreathed rock as the incoming tide swept around her. I imagined her being transformed into a standing stone in the liminal space between land and sea, where the tides drew new boundaries that were forever blurred by the fog. ▶

The Lore of the Lost Girl *(continued)*

Who was she? What stories would spring up around her? And what truths and hidden secrets were those stories evoking?

I also heard a character (I didn't know yet that it was Luther) saying: *Listen to legends, the truth often lies beneath them.* Why, I wondered, as may you, would we look to legend to tell the truth and not history? The answer I think lies in a space as liminal as those tidal islands off the coast of Maine—the space between what really happened and what people are willing to reveal about what happened. What gets lost in between are guilty secrets, shameful histories, and marginal figures that no one bothered to look for and record.

My narrator, Tess Levine Henshaw, sees herself as one of those marginal disposables. When she ran away with her English teacher at age seventeen no one went looking for her. Shame keeps her from telling her story, and so it becomes a buried history that warps her and her son Rudy's lives. She is surrounded by stories that echo her own. As are we all. The stories I looked for were ones that Tess, teaching at a boarding school in New England, would be most familiar with—the witches of Salem, Hester Prynne, and a teenage girl who vanished.

Like most American high school students, I came to know the witches of Salem through Arthur Miller's *The Crucible.* In his preface to the play Miller writes of the landscape that surrounded the early settlers: "The American

continent stretched endlessly west,
and it was full of mystery for them.
It stood, dark and threatening, over
their shoulders . . ." Out of this mystery,
out of fear of what lurked in the woods,
the Puritans imagined dark forces—
demons, devils—that colonized their
own wives and daughters (the men,
too, but who do we think of most
when we think of witches if not the
women?). Lurking in this lore of
primeval wilderness, in the envy and
bickering that spawned the accusations,
is another story. Miller gives us
hysterical teenage girls accusing the
townspeople out of jealousy. Abigail
Williams is in love with John Proctor
and when spurned by him accuses
his wife and then him. But as Tess
thinks while she's watching the play,
the historical Abigail was eleven years
old and John Proctor was sixty. The real
Abigail is missing from the story—as she
also went missing in real life. According
to Wikipedia—and where better to
go for contemporary lore—"Some say
she ran off after the trials, becoming a
prostitute, but there is no way to truly
know." The Abigail Williams who
persists in our imagination is a figure
of myth—the deranged girl who falsely
accuses a man and vanishes into a shady,
disreputable fate.

The second missing girl of lore
who haunts Tess is Hester Prynne of
Nathaniel Hawthorne's *The Scarlet
Letter*, a book Tess has read five times
(because it was the only one she had ▶

The Lore of the Lost Girl *(continued)*

on the island) and teaches every year to her students. I imagine Tess returning to this book again and again, with its heroine who bears a child out of wedlock, hiding the identity of its father, as Tess did, and who wears the visible mark of shame on her breast where Tess carries the invisible sequelae of trauma, as a kind of penitence. Hester Prynne herself becomes a figure of legend at the end of *The Scarlet Letter* when "a tall woman, in a gray robe" is seen by "some children" gliding "shadow-like" into the "cottage by the sea-shore where Hester Prynne had dwelt." Hester's very much alive at this point but she's already entered the misty realms of legend— a lost girl returned. For Tess, by the end of my book, Hester has taught her that shame is better worn on the outside than on the inside where it eats away at a person and skews everything he or she does. I've also given Tess a nice cottage by the sea-shore, which to my mind is always the best part of *The Scarlet Letter.*

The third missing girl of lore is Noreen Bagley, the girl who disappeared from the Haywood school. She's based on a very real missing girl—Paula Jean Welden, the Bennington sophomore who vanished from the Vermont Long Trail in 1946. Welden's body was never found and her disappearance, along with others in the area, sparked a local legend renowned in podcast lore as "The Bennington Triangle," and inspired a short story and a book by Shirley Jackson. Noreen doesn't have a book about her, which is why, according to Lucinda Perkins at the Cora Rockwell House, she's not as famous. Tess suspects, though, that the reason Noreen was so easy to miss is that no one really cared about her—just as no one looked for Tess when she stepped out of her life.

So what do these stories tell us about girls who go missing in their own lives? They may be the girls who challenge authority, as Abigail Williams did, or the ones who make the people around them uncomfortably aware of shameful secrets, as Hester Prynne did, or the ones who no one cares about. How many girls like this go missing right in front of our eyes? Maybe they're still here—still in class, living in the house next door, walking next to you on the street—but some piece of them has gone missing. When girls aren't believed, when they express uncomfortable opinions and are silenced, when no one really cares what happens to them, a spark goes out. How many of us—girl or boy, man or woman—lose a bit of ourselves as we make the perilous journey from adolescence to adulthood? And where do we go to find these pieces again?

I go to stories. Myths that tell of girls turned into trees or birds, fairy tales about girls fending off wolves as they make their way through the woods, legends about girls who stand in the sea and light the way for their sisters. I go to the novels about the women these girls become. I hope this is one of them. ᕲ

Reading Group Guide

1. What role does social media play in the novel? How different do you think the story would have been if it had taken place before the advent of the Internet and cell phones?

2. Do you think Tess is a good mother? Why or why not?

3. How does Goodman use isolation—both physical and mental—to build tension?

4. In the first chapter, Tess reflects that the life she has with Rudy is similar to the New England setting: "As with much of coastal Maine the land here is broken up by waterways and pieced together by bridges and causeways like a tattered garment that's been darned." Do you think the metaphor is accurate? How does the setting mirror the other characters' lives?

5. In what ways are Tess and Lila foils for each other?

6. The Haywood students are putting on an "unorthodox" production of *The Crucible* in the novel. Why do you think Goodman chose this play? She also references *The Scarlet Letter* several times. How does the book emphasize the novel's themes?

7. How does Goodman subvert the story of the Ice Virgin?

8. Different missing girls are brought up in *The Sea of Lost Girls*, from Tess to Lila to Noreen to Paula Jean Welden. What effect does the layering of these stories have on the mystery? How do other themes echo?

9. How do power dynamics between the men and women in the story play out? How does shame affect the men and women differently in the novel? How does this relate to the dynamics of the #MeToo and #TimesUp movements?

10. The local myth of the Maiden Stone looms large in the story. How does Luther's death challenge the myth? Have you heard legends local to you?

11. Why do you think Tess survived her time with Luther when so many of the other girls died during their own ordeals? Was it luck or something else?

12. What role does toxic masculinity play in the actions of Luther, Harmon, and Woody?

13. How does Goodman portray female relationships in the novel? What point do you think she is trying to make? ▶

Reading Group Guide *(continued)*

14. Tess is consistently accused of being a "stalker" and breaking Rudy's boundaries. Do you agree with this assessment? What boundaries are broken between other characters?

15. Toward the end of the novel, Rudy says, "People need to tell stories to make sense of all the crazy in the world." How do stories conflict with and reinforce the truth?

16. The line "Tragedy makes for odd bedfellows" is repeated several times. How does it apply to each of the characters? ⟳

An Excerpt from
The Night Visitors

CHAPTER ONE

Alice

OREN FALLS ASLEEP at last on the third bus. He's been fighting it since Newburgh, eyelids heavy as wet laundry, pried up again and again by sheer stubbornness. *Finally,* I think when he nods off. *If I have to answer one more of his questions I might lose it.*

Where are we going? he asked on the first bus.

Someplace safe, I answered.

He stared at me, even in the darkened bus his eyes shining with too much smart for his age, and then looked away as if embarrassed for me. An hour later he'd asked, as if there hadn't been miles of highway in between, *Where's it safe?*

There are places, I'd begun as if telling him a bedtime story, but then I'd had to rack my brain for what came next. All I could picture were candy houses and chicken-legged huts that hid witches. Those weren't the stories he liked best anyway. He preferred the book of myths from the library (it's still in his pack, racking up fines with every mile) about heroes who wrestle lions and behead snake-haired monsters. ▶

An Excerpt from *The Night Visitors*
(continued)

There are places . . . I began again,
trying to remember something from the
book. *Remember when Orestes flees the
Furies and he goes to some temple so the
Furies can't hurt him there?*

It was the temple of Apollo at Delphi,
Oren said, *and it's called a sanctuary.*

No one likes a smarty-pants, I
countered. Since he found that
mythology book he likes to show
off how well he's learned all those
Greek names. He'd liked Orestes right
away because their names were alike.
I'd tried to read around the parts that
weren't really for kids, but he always
knew if I skipped over something and
later I saw him reading the story to
himself, staring at the picture of the
Furies with their snake hair and bat
wings.

At the next bus stop he found the flyer
for the hotline. It was called Sanctuary,
as if Oren's saying the word had made it
appear. I gave him a handful of change
to buy a candy bar while I made the call.
I didn't want him to hear the story I'd
have to tell. But even with him across
the waiting room, standing at the snacks
counter, his shoulders hunched under
the weight of his *Star Wars* backpack,
he looked like he was listening.

The woman who answered the phone
started to ask about my feelings, but I
cut to the chase and told her that I'd left
my husband and taken my son with me.
He hit me, I said, *and he told me he'd*

kill me if I tried to leave. I have no place
to go . . .

My voice had stuttered to a choked
end. Across the waiting room, Oren had
turned to look at me as if he'd heard me.
But that was impossible; he was too far
away.

The woman's voice on the phone was
telling me about a shelter in Kingston.
Oren was walking across the waiting
room. When he reached me he said,
It can't be a place anyone knows about.

I rolled my eyes at him. Like I didn't
know that. But I repeated his words into
the phone anyway, trying to sound firm.
The woman on the other end didn't say
anything for a moment, and looking into
Oren's eyes, I was suddenly more afraid
than I'd been since we left.

I understand, the woman said at
last, slowly, as if she were speaking to
someone who might *not* understand.
I recognized the social worker's
"explaining" voice and felt a prickle
of anger that surprised me. I'd thought
that I was past caring what a bunch of
morally sanctimonious social workers
thought about me. *We can arrange for*
a safe house, one no one will know about.
But you might have to stay tonight in
the shelter.

Oren shook his head as if he could
hear what the woman said. Or as if
he already knew I'd messed up.

It has to be tonight, I said.

Again the woman paused. In the ▶

An Excerpt from *The Night Visitors*
(continued)

background a cat meowed and a
kettle whistled. I pictured a comfortable
warm room—framed pictures on
the walls,throw pillows on a couch,
lamplight—and was suddenly swamped
by so much anger I grew dizzy. Oren
reached out a hand to steady me.
The woman said something but I
missed it. There was a roaring in
my ears.

. . . give me the number there, she was
saying. *I'll make a call and call you right
back.*

I read her the number on the pay
phone and then hung up. Oren handed
me a cup of hot coffee and a doughnut.
How had he gotten all that for a handful
of change? Does he have money of his
own he hasn't told me about? I slumped
against the wall to wait, and Oren leaned
next to me. *It will be all right,* I told him.
These places . . . they have a system.

He nodded, jaw clenched. I touched
his cheek and he flinched. I looked
around to see if anyone had noticed,
but the only other occupants of the
station were a texting college student,
the old woman behind the snacks
counter, and a drunk passed out on
a bench. When the phone rang I nearly
jumped out of my skin.

I picked up the phone before it
rang again. For a second all I heard
was breathing and I had the horrible,
crazy thought that it was *him.* But then
the woman spoke in a breathless rush,

as if she'd run somewhere fast. *Can you get the next bus for Kingston?*

I told you no shel— I began, but the woman cut me off.

At Kingston you'll get a bus to Delphi. Someone will meet you there, someone you can trust. Her name's Mattie— she's in her fifties, has short silvery hair, and she'll probably be wearing something purple. She'll take you to a safe house, a place no one knows about but us.

I looked down at Oren and he nodded.

Okay, I said. *We'll be there on the next bus.*

I hung up and knelt down to tell Oren where we were going, but he was already handing something to me: two tickets for the next bus for Kingston and two for Delphi, New York. *Look,* he said, *the town's got the same name as the place in the book.*

That was two hours and two buses ago. The last bus has taken us through steadily falling snow into mountains that loom on either side of the road. Oren had watched the swirling snow as if it were speaking to him. As if he were the one leading us here.

It's just a coincidence, I tell myself, *about the name. Lots of these little upstate towns have names like that: Athens, Utica, Troy.* Names that make you think of palm trees and marble, not crappy little crossroads with one 7-Eleven and a tattoo parlor.

I was relieved when Oren fell asleep. ▶

15

An Excerpt from *The Night Visitors*
(continued)

Not just because I was tired of his questions, but because I was afraid of what I might ask him—

How did you know where we were going? And how the hell did you get those tickets?

—and what I might do to get the answer out of him. ᵔᵔ